THE BLIND BEAK

Eighteenth-century London. Blind magistrate Sir John Fielding, 'The Blind Beak', had instigated the Bow Street Runners to combat the hordes of criminals so rife throughout the city. Criminals such as Nick Rathburn, who fights his way out of Newgate Gaol. Then, by a twist of fate, Nick becomes a secret agent for 'The Blind Beak'. However, as Sir John, amid the Gordon Riots, is in the hands of the terrorising mob, Nick faces death on the gallows at Tyburn . . .

ERNEST DUDLEY

THE BLIND BEAK

Complete and Unabridged

LINFORD
Leicester

First published in Great Britain

First Linford Edition
published 2008

British Library CIP Data

Dudley, Ernest
    The blind beak.—Large print ed.—
Linford mystery library
    1. Fielding, John, Sir, *1721–1780*—Fiction
    2. Police magistrates—England—London—
History—18th century—Fiction 3. London
(England)—History—18th century—Fiction
    4. Detective and mystery stories
    5. Large type books
    I. Title
    823.9'14 [F]

ISBN 978–1–84782–218–5

Published by
F. A. Thorpe (Publishing)
Anstey, Leicestershire

Set by Words & Graphics Ltd.
Anstey, Leicestershire
Printed and bound in Great Britain by
T. J. International Ltd., Padstow, Cornwall

This book is printed on acid-free paper. . .

'He is one of the figures of his time.'
Chronicles of Bow Street Police Office.

1766 — AGED EIGHTEEN

The Stone Jug

1

It was eight o'clock one night in mid-October, 1766, the clock of St. Sepulchre's Church was striking, the dull heavy notes falling on the misty moon-light air being taken up in varying tones by other clocks in the neighbourhood of Newgate Prison. In his solitary cell on the third floor over the gaol gateway, the manacled figure paused only momentarily from the task absorbing his attention. The past hour he had been twisting and contracting his hands so that they were all bruised and raw in an effort to force them through the gyves clamped about his wrists. He bent his head once more, his teeth gripping the chain linking the irons. From Newgate Street arose the hoarse cry of the night watchman: 'Eight of the clock of a chill October night and all's well.'

Of a sudden the tensed figure in the cell breathed a low hiss of elation as he

3

dragged one hand free. Using his liberated hand to grip the iron clapped around his other wrist he wrenched at it all the harder. Spurred on by his initial triumph, his youthful features contorted as the handcuff's edge bit cruelly into his flesh. He dragged and wrenched until suddenly his other hand drew free. He let the manacles fall to the floor, chafing and massaging his numbed and cramped fingers. They were strong-looking hands, small but sinewy and tapering from broad palms. The long, dark eyes, set deep in his face aglisten with sweat, gleamed beneath their straight somewhat craggy brows, giving his expression a kind of devilish lift so that he appeared aged beyond his mere eighteen summers. 'Small wonder you were so dubbed, Nick,' red-haired and sulky-mouthed Doll Tawdry would tell him, lying in his embrace in the St. Giles's stew. 'For Satan himself looks out of that face of yours, my darling.'

Both hands free at last, Nick Rathburn bent all his efforts to release himself from the fetters encumbering his ankles. He inserted the broken and rusted nail,

4

prised three weeks earlier from the heavy oak floor of his cell against just this very moment, in the huge padlock attaching the chain of his fetters to a heavy iron staple driven deep into the floor.

Nearly an hour later the moonlight which slanted through the barred window high in the cell-wall had swung across the floor to leave him shadowed, an engrossed, graven figure of consummate patience. A rasping click gladdened his heart and the padlock yielded. He was no longer held to the floor but able to move about his cell as much as his leg-irons would permit him. Without a pause to rest himself he crouched upon his haunches and proceeded to twist the chain attaching the iron rings clamping his ankles, so he could obtain some leverage. He could not bite off the groan between his clenched teeth as he tugged with both hands, his biceps bunched, the sweat pouring down his face to drip off his upper lip. Suddenly the chain burst asunder at its weakest link.

With a shuddering sigh he fell backwards to stretch his length on the floor, his heart pounding in his ears. A burst of raucous laughter came from the Condemned Hold beneath, wherein those felons due for the rope's-end at Tyburn were crowded in filth and darkness, the squeak of a fiddle, and then from the women's cell arose the shrieks of a lunatic prisoner in anguish over her new-born child who had died earlier that day. Nick listened to her cries, to be followed inevitably by the shouts and curses of the warders, then more screams of pain from the woman which died away into a low whimpering before the kicks and blows of her captors.

Two years in Newgate had sharpened to a razor-edge keenness his sensibilities, already tempered and toughened by the vicissitudes he had endured before his incarceration: his earliest remembrance was being found, ragged and emaciated nigh unto death in a corner of Rathburn Yard, a noisome Holborn alley, by a chimney-sweep in need of a boy to climb the chimneys. He had at length run away from his brutal employer to make himself despotic ruler of as desperate a band of

6

thieving, rapacious children as ever St. Giles's Rookeries spewed up to haunt London's streets. He vowed to himself even as he had been borne off from Bow Street to Newgate he would not long languish in stench and corruption to wait for gaol-fever to claim him, or rot into premature old age, candidate for the burial-ground or dissecting-table before his time. He would surely find a way to freedom and life, even the uncertain dangerous existence he had led in London's underworld.

To this end he had sought out those of his companions in wretchedness and horror whom he knew might offer him a tid-bit of advice, a low-voiced hint, a fragment of reminiscence of some past prisoner who had escaped from even so formidable a Stone Jug as Newgate. He had speedily learned from cheats and sharpers that deceiving dexterity of the hand which enabled him to throw a loaded dice or marked card, using his winnings to bribe his gaolers in return for food and clothing.

There had also been that drunken

Grub Street hack, long languishing in Newgate for some debt, who had encouraged him to acquire the knowledge of reading and writing. 'You have the face of a sharp fellow, Nick; a little learning would sit neat upon your shoulders.' This individual obtaining for him a battered copy of the Bible and sundry newspapers, together with writing-materials, Nick, realizing the material use to which he could put the teaching he absorbed, allowed himself to be persuaded to equip himself with the rudiments of learning. His progress was so rapid, however, his aptitude so marked, as to arouse the scribbler's wonder. 'You may not know who your parents were, but I vow you were born of no ordinary folk.' Which speculation, while it momentarily amused him, occasioned Nick, engrossed as he was with plans for the future when he should be clear of his present frustrating circumstances, to dwell no time at all upon the past and insoluble riddle of his origin.

When, having noted and stored up all the relevant intelligence and knowledge he could and judging the opportunity to be ripe, he had feigned sickness, and, oiling a turnkey's palm to facilitate the transfer, had been shifted, though still heavily fettered, from the nauseous dungeon wherein he lay to his present, relatively airy cell. The Sessions had begun that day and would continue the next two or three days. Within this time he needs must crack the Stone Jug. Scores of prisoners had to be escorted through to the Justice Hall in the Old Bailey every day and carefully guarded while on their way to and from the prison and the court. Most of them would be awaiting this chance to make some desperate attempt at escape. During this time therefore it would be quite natural for the turnkeys to slacken their vigilance over the young felon, supposedly ailing, in the gateway cell. Early that evening one of the underturnkeys had brought his meal. After the man's customary examination of his fetters and manacles, Nick had begged him to return later in the evening with a jug of beer. To this request the other replied he was too busy to pay another visit to the cell until the following morning, which was in fact precisely what Nick had been counting upon in order to be left the remainder of the night uninterrupted.

Getting to his feet Nick delighted in the new-found freedom of his legs as he stretched them for a few moments. He could move about his cell now, impeded only by the iron bands encircling his ankles. Utilizing the same rusty nail that had secured his freedom from the handcuffs, he probed and prised at the hinges of his leg-irons. Nearly another hour elapsed before first one and then the other ankle was free.

His knowledge of Newgate told Nick it would advantage him little to break open the door of his cell. Accomplishment of this task would not lessen the number of other doors he would have to unfasten before he gained the prison's roof. Only over the roof and thus on to the roofs of the houses adjacent could he hope to get clear away. His way must be up the chimney of his cell into the room above. The explanation for the chimney was that the cell had originally been a kind of office for use of the gaol-staff.

Nick began to climb upwards, soot and filth soon enveloping him. His mind went back to the bitter days when, perpetually begrimed and blackened, he had worked as a sweep's boy in the choking and blinding sooty darkness hour after hour, months on end, until he had escaped into the labyrinth of London's malodorous alleys and crumbling hovels. He was brought up with a jerk by a discovery which momentarily took him aback. The chimney had appeared wide enough for his ascent, but suddenly he was blocked by an iron bar, seemingly making it impossible for him to climb any higher. At the same time as he encountered this check he heard, he thought, someone outside his cell-door. He half fell, half jumped down the chimney back into the cell. Had the sound of his scrambling attracted the attention of a passing warder, or was some official returning to see if he was still captive?

He moved swiftly, placing himself so that should the door open it would give him an opportunity, chancing that the intruder would be alone, to strike him down from behind. He stood there, tensed and waiting, his ears cocked for the scrape of the key in the lock. He could hear nothing but muffled shouting from the debtors' cell across the way. He returned to the chimney and, scrambling inside once again, set about the tedious task of removing the iron bar above his head. Using the nail and pieces of the broken fetters, he scratched and scraped at the brick-work.

St. Sepulchre's, accompanied by the neighbouring clocks, had chimed eleven o'clock some quarter of an hour, when at last he tore the iron bar from its place. He quickly found a use for it as, pushing his way higher up the chimney, he reached the floor-level of the room above the cell, and with the iron length he battered and prised, until at last he had torn an aperture wide enough for him to scramble through the wall.

The fourth-floor room in which he now found himself was directly over his own cell he had just quitted and similar in shape and size. A barred window high in the wall faced Snow Hill and St. Sepulchre's Church. Nick made his way to the door which, as he guessed it would be, was securely locked. Little moonlight filtered into the room through the window, and his strong searching fingers told him the door, strong and heavy, its lock corroded with rust, might not have been opened since its last occupants had departed. He found a nut which helped to hold the plate covering the lockbox. Sharp taps from his iron bar enabled him to force aside the plate. Within several minutes he had shot back the lock with his bare fingers. On his right a few yards farther along the dank passage he came to the cell occupied by a gaudy gamester, whose purse was deep enough to bribe the turnkeys into providing him with every luxury: even wenches found their way into his cell, which was heavily perfumed against the intolerable stench that hung over the prison.

Nick came to the next door he sought, which led into the prison chapel. Running his hands down the door in the blackness enveloping him for a lock or keyhole, to his dismay they encountered nothing and he concluded the door was bolted on the other side. He would have to force a hole through the wall itself to the other side in an attempt to reach the bolt. Once again using the broken nail as he had done in the chimney, together with his iron bar, he set to work to prise loose the first brick, and at length he pushed his arm up to his shoulder through the aperture he had enlarged in the wall. to find the bolt and thrust it back. The chapel was illuminated by the moonlight streaming through the tall, barred windows. It was a familiar enough place to Nick, he had been among the prisoners herded in their pens on many a grim occasion to witness those felons about to kick up their heels at Tyburn, forced to listen, in the condemned pew, to the prison chaplain piously declaiming the death-sermon over them.

Nick crossed to the centre of the chapel and, with one blow, smashing off three spikes surmounting the tall, wooden partition that barred his way, climbed

14

over it. It was at this moment that he heard voices and the sound of a door across the chapel to his left open. He dropped down into the shadows cast by the partition as there appeared in the doorway a tall, ponderous figure outlined by the glare of a lantern held by another man close behind him, whom Nick knew at a glance to be Ackerman, Governor of Newgate. But his gaze was fixed on the black bandage over the first man's eyes, that wide, plump face with its lower pendulous lip above the double chin, and he was back in a rush of remembrance in the dock at Bow Street, those dread words sentencing him to Newgate falling on his ears. For it was John Fielding, the magistrate, who stood there, the Blind Beak himself.

2

The figure in the doorway seemed to tower and swell monstrously, black and menacing, with the lantern behind him swinging a trifle to send his massive shadow reaching out across the floor. Then, his reeling senses steadying, Nick concluded that even as he was about to triumph over the remaining obstacles in his path, the very creature responsible for his cruel incarceration had, by some miraculous intelligence, learned of his attempt at escape and arrived in time to thwart him. He gripped his iron bar, grimly determined to use it to defend himself did the newcomers attempt to apprehend him. Doubtless Ackerman, thinking he heard someone in the chapel as he and Fielding were passing, had been prompted to see who it was. Observing no one he was remarking the noise must be nothing more than rats. Nick recalled it was the custom for the Lord Mayor and

Sheriffs of London to give two dinners, one early and one later each evening, during the Old Bailey sittings, to which the judges, leading members of the Bar and various dignitaries were invited. The renowned magistrate had been one of the guests and was now being conducted by Ackerman from the Court dining hall to the latter's office in the gaol.

The Governor was glancing about him, with Nick hardly breathing as he hunched there. Fortune was with him, the moonlight was suddenly dimmed by clouds, throwing the place into darkness. The pool of light cast by Ackerman's lantern was not wide enough to include the evidence of Nick's handiwork. Came the Governor's suggestion that Mr. Fielding might care to continue to the office where a warming cordial awaiting him to sustain him against the chillsome night air on his way home to his house in Bow Street. Once more Nick experienced the heart-stopping sensation that the blind man was about to step forward and, guided by some antennae-like sense in place of his eyes, drag him forth from where he crouched concealed. Instead, the massive figure slowly turned to follow the other behind him. The door closed on them, the sound of their footsteps died away and Nick was out of the chapel and proceeding along another dark passage until halted by the next stout door.

He heard St. Sepulchre's and its neighbouring clocks striking midnight. It had taken him an hour since he had quitted his cell to arrive thus far on his hazardous journey. Every moment, he knew, added to the risk that some nosy turnkey might glance into his cell, and then he would be swiftly hunted down.

He decided not to attempt to force the lock or the bolt, but instead attack the strip of iron which ran from top to bottom of the door, aiming to prise it clean away from its position, when he calculated the door would fall open. His invincible bar met with tough and lengthy resistance. At last with a tremendous effort he wrenched the door open and then he found himself through a door standing ajar and into the night air. He was on that part of the roof he knew to be the lower leads. Above him rose a wall reaching to the higher leads and which he must gain in order to drop to the roof of one of the houses adjacent to the prison in Newgate Street.

The door through which he had just passed opened outwards on to the leads. Pushing it ajar again, he climbed on to the top of it where he balanced for a few moments on his hands and knees. Clinging to the wall he reached up and drew himself aloft and on to the higher roof. He hurried along the leads until he reached a low wall over which he clambered to the women felons' tile-roofed ward. He was faced with a sheer drop of twenty feet or more on to the roof of the nearest house.

With a sickening shock of despair he realized the drop was much greater than he had foreseen; it would be impossible for him to reach his objective without some means of lowering himself to it. At first he considered leaping down, but rejected the idea. Apart from the risk, the noise of his arrival would awaken the occupants of the house, or he might plunge right through the roof with disastrous consequences.

Suddenly he bethought himself of the clothes he wore. At once he stripped of his stockings, breeches and shirt, all covered with thick sooty filth and sticking to his sweat-drenched body. As he peeled them away he could feel the perspiration drying on his skin before the crisp squalls whipping up from the street. His shoes he slipped on again while he stood naked, knotting the clothes together so he might lower himself by them. One end he tied to his iron bar which he wedged under the coping, to take the strain of his weight as, hand over hand, he descended, feeling each piece of clothing give to his weight. But all held firm and he swung with only six feet below left for him to drop. He released his hold and landed noiselessly on the roof.

For a few moments, gasping and trembling with utter weariness, Nick Rathburn permitted himself the luxury of contemplating his triumphant achievement. The deathly exhaustion his efforts had cost him seemed to vanish from his naked limbs. White and slim in the moonlight he stood and exulted over his success. The manacles which had grappled him to the floor were strewn behind him, as disregarded as the broken handcuffs. Behind him lay broken doors and shattered locks, mutely eloquent witnesses of his prowess. He had broken a way out of his thickly walled cell, chipped the Stone Jug, shattered it. Naught had barred his brave flight until now he stood at last, the free night air of London's streets chill upon his face. He perceived the tower of St. Martin's Church on Ludgate Hill, and, nearer, the spire of Christchurch in Newgate Street, and farther distant stood out the great dome of St. Paul's, black against the sky.

Below, lights shone from several shops still open; he glimpsed people moving about into and out of the beams of the shop-lamps and tallow candles. He began creeping over the roof away from the street, his worn shoes scraping against the tiles. Several minutes later he dropped silently as a cat into a garret, through a window he had chanced upon unlatched, cautiously inching it wide enough to admit him, first reassuring himself the room was unoccupied. He waited, bent under the window, listening for any sound in the room or beyond. He could make out the shape of a bed to one side of the closed door and some furniture. The sight of the empty bed made him long to throw himself upon it and rest his weary limbs. But that luxury he must deny himself. At any moment his escape would be discovered, if it had not been already, the hue-and-cry raised.

He snatched a blanket from the bed and wrapped it round his nakedness, cogitating over the prospects of obtaining some clothing before he risked appearing in the streets and attracting attention. He opened the door and stood on the landing at the head of the stairs, listening. While intuition warned him there were people below, he could hear nobody moving about and he descended, hugging the wall so as to ease his weight on the stairs so they would creak less beneath him. Reaching the next floor he noticed the atmosphere was less chill, while borne up to him from below arose some heavy perfume. A faint glow of candles illumined the darkness and he knew he was approaching that part of the house where he might at any moment encounter someone. Then it happened.

Passing what he took to be a large cupboard he saw a fragment of material projecting from it where the door had been shut upon some garment. Thinking there might be clothes inside, his for the taking, he turned the door-handle. Before he could step back the door swung open, something heavy and yielding toppled out upon him, nearly bearing him down, and sank slowly to the floor, emitting a curious, long drawn-out sigh.

Nick stared at the figure of a man whose head sagged to one side, revealing a terrible gash in his neck, from which a dark trickle oozed slowly. Nick knelt, his hand becoming sticky with blood as he drew back the robe the man wore over his frilled silk shirt and breeches. Blood flowed from half a dozen other stab-wounds about the neck and chest and Nick stood up quickly to move away from the corpse as a sudden movement came from downstairs. Edging his way cautiously to peer through a bend in the banisters he saw a wide door, facing the foot of the staircase, open slowly. A short, thick-set man held unsteadily to the door-post. He had caught up a cloak which dragged behind him, his face incongruously purplish against the whiteness of his body. From the room emanated more powerfully the mingling perfume and smell of wine and then a woman, her voice muffled as if with sleep, spoke.

'It might be him, darling.'

The man's eyes narrowed a trifle and he ran his tongue over his lips. He clung more tightly to the door-post. 'How can it be? You know he will not be back till — till an early hour.' His words were slurred, his speech thick. Then as Nick drew back instinctively he observed those slitted eyes raised towards the landing.

'Do you go and make sure, love.' Nick realized the woman's voice, too, was blurred with wine as well as sleep. 'He is late grown so jealous, I believe he may well be hiding in the house, to catch us together.' She giggled tipsily as if wantonly unconcerned at the risk of being so disclosed, while the expression that flitted across the bloated face told Nick this was precisely the strategem the dead husband or lover, whichever he may have been, had employed. His presence discovered, the tables turned on him, he had been outmatched by his murderous rival and all unbeknown to the woman whose fuddled voice was heard again. 'He may be hiding upstairs, it was thence came the noise we heard before.'

Her voice drifted into a drowsy sigh. The man, with a series of belches, lurched forward to the banister by which he began to haul himself upwards. Nick backed up the stairs until he stood beside the corpse again. Were he caught now, of a certainty the creature ascending towards him, on learning of his victim's dead body having been uncovered, and inevitably constru- ing Nick's identity, would seize the opportunity to shift the blame for the murder on to him. Yet some devilish quixotry impelled him to stand his ground, coupling the simultaneous thought, more practical to his immediate purpose, of the other's clothes in the room below which Nick might easily make his own. A grin playing at the corners of his mouth Nick waited, the corpse between him and the grunting creature whose head was appearing at the top of the stairs. The man stood there swaying, mouth agape at the body, his wine-laden breath sickeningly strong, before he realized Nick's presence. As his eyes rounded owlishly and an exclamation started in his throat, Nick moved and drove a jarring blow against the angle of the other's jaw. The rounded eyes glazed over, he lurched forward, head sagging, and Nick brought his fist down club-like behind the man's ear. Quickly Nick tore his blanket into strips and secured the unconscious figure's ankles and wrists and, appropriating his cloak, bundled him into the cupboard, shut it, and darted downstairs.

At the door he saw reflected in the wide gilded mirror the silk-panelled room within, lit by candles flickering in a five-branched candelabra, the tumbled bed, overturned wine-glasses and flagons and plates of delicacies. Over all, the

26

heavy perfume and fumes from the wine, a pool of which spread like a patch of blood upon the thickly carpeted floor. Moving into the room, Nick's gaze rested on the form among the dishevelled sheets and pillows, one white arm trailing to the floor, pink-tipped fingers curled about a half-eaten sweetmeat. He bent to pick up one of the man's shoes, exquisitely made with diamond buckles. There were stockings of pale lavender silk, a waistcoat richly embroidered and edged with lace, and thrown over the back of a chair a deep crimson coat, very ample in the skirts, and a fine silk ruffled shirt.

The woman's voice caused him to turn so she could not see his reflection in the mirror and he hunched the cloak round his ears. 'Was there no one? Then blow out the candles, love.' In the sudden blackness Nick grabbed the clothes, preparatory to darting out of the room, but her drowsy tones, a rising hint of petulance in them, halted him at the door. 'Love, where are you, love?' Another moment, he guessed, inwardly cursing the woman as he heard her raise herself

27

among the pillows, and she would be wider awake and near to realizing who was in the room. The shock would sober her swiftly enough, dash fuddling sleep from her brain for her to scream thieves and murder to the housetops.

Then suddenly she was snoring. He hurried into the clothes and, carrying the shoes, he slipped noiselessly away, the woman's snores a trifle steadier and louder following him, and was halfway downstairs to the hall when a sudden thought turned him in his tracks and, like a speeding shadow, he ascended to the landing where the corpse lay stiffening. The other man he could hear breathing stertorously in the cupboard, obviously sunk in a heavy, debauched torpor.

Some few minutes later Nick let himself out of the house and set off boldly along the street, answering with nonchalance that was to the manner born the night-watchman's: 'Past one o'clock of a raw October morning and all is well.' He paused at a corner to take a pinch of snuff he had come upon in the waistcoat-pocket, the devilish grin playing across his shadowed aquiline face. The macabre jest he had played on the woman in the bed appealed to his mordant sense of humour.

3

Mr. Fielding's house was a tall, ugly building on the west side of Bow Street, Covent Garden, its ground floor almost entirely taken up with the blind justice's courtroom, the upper floors being his private dwelling, so that he was always conveniently on hand day and night to deal with urgent cases. John Fielding was in his sitting room finishing his breakfast, his massive figure set off by a full-skirted coat of genteel dark blue with gold lace facings, if somewhat faded, over satin waistcoat and breeches of a contrasting shade of blue. The fringe of his shoulder-length wig almost reached the inevitable black bandage that hid his sightless eyes, and his cravat beneath his double chin, above which his full-lipped mouth puffed out as he bent to cool his tea, was plain but of freshly laundered whiteness. His silk stockings were of a dark grey and his buckle shoes of fine

Spanish leather, though a trifle worn, gleamed with polish. It was approaching the hour of eight-thirty by the chiming clock in the corner of the comfortably, if untidily, furnished room when Mr. Bond, his clerk, knocked upon the door.

So agitated was the sharp-featured, bespectacled little man he could hardly pause to accept the dish of tea offered him, but must launch straightway into his news. 'Young Nick Rathburn — the miscreant got clean away, escaped last night and vanished.'

The Blind Beak's tea halted half-way to his lips, then, still without sipping it, he set down the dish, remaining as if graven from stone for several moments before taking up his tea once more with a murmured: 'Say you so, Mr. Bond?' and drinking it slowly. The other's words spilled out upon his listener's ear.

'When the turnkey entered his cell no one was more dumb-founded. It appears a week before young Rathburn had complained of sickness and was removed from the common cell to this other over the gaol gateway. It is obvious, now, the rogue was feigning his distemper.' Allowing the Blind Beak time to nod his appreciation of his clerk's perspicacity, Bond went on to describe the incredulous confusion into which Newgate's watch-dogs were thrown on learning of the escape, together with their open-mouthed wonder as they followed the route Nick Rathburn had taken. 'It is estimated it will cost sixty pounds to repair the damage the scoundrel has caused to the doors and walls through which he broke.'

'Which sum the worthy officers should easily recoup,' was the reply. The Blind Beak suffered no illusions regarding the manner in which, from the Governor himself to the lowest turnkey, Newgate was run. The gaolers robbed the prisoners, the prisoners robbed each other. 'So soon as the news circulates, Newgate will be stormed by the morbidly curious who, by the time they have viewed the empty cell, will have been forced to dip often into their pockets.' He paused to finish his tea. 'I imagine,' he asked slowly, 'there is no suspicion Rathburn was aided in his escape by any one of those in his charge?'

The other blinked and gave a little cough. 'No doubt an inquiry will be held into all the circumstances of this unfortunate affair,' was the non-committal reply. Fielding shook his double chin dubiously from side to side. His mind was cast back to that day some two years before when young Nick Rathburn had stood before him in his court charged with pilfering meat from a shambles. He could hear again the sixteen-year-old boy recounting his dreadful experiences at the hands of his brutal chimney-sweep employer, running away to become a child-desperado of the Rookeries. Here, Fielding had assured himself, was another scrap of human driftwood to be rescued, properly cared for and set upon the path of honesty, instead of being committed to prison where men, women and children all herded together fell victim to the disease and vice rampant about them. Devoted as he was to his work as magistrate and his great obsession, the building up of his detective-force, the Blind Beak found time to be at the forefront of every charity for poor and destitute children.

'It is indeed a melancholy truth,' he had told the youthful offender, 'which I have learned, that there are in London a vast number of wretched boys like you, ragged as colts, abandoned, skulking in dank alleys. As you grow older, encouraged by the loose girls in your keeping, you will undertake such thieving enterprises of the sort of which you are now accused.' The boy had uttered no word, but, Fielding had sensed, stood there rigid and unbending, defiant. 'I will therefore commit you not to Newgate. Instead you will be supplied with food and clothing, then journey to Portsmouth, to serve aboard one of His Majesty's ships . . . ' Whatever concluding words he meant to add were checked by a violent interruption from the prisoner himself.

'I am not for any life at sea. Do you leave me go back to my friends. Let me free, back to St. Giles'. I can take care of myself.' His shouting reverberated more loudly in the crowded, stuffy courtroom. 'Devil take your damned charity, I want none of it. Let me be on my own.'

34

The Blind Beak now knew of a certainty, he was dealing not with some young street-prig, cowed and browbeaten into submission by the cuffings from the police officer who had apprehended him, but instead a bold, resolute spirit determined to give rein to his own will. Even as he reached the end of his brazen outburst he made a sudden dash from the court in a reckless attempt at escape, to be subdued by his two gaolers only after much shouting and blaspheming, kicking and struggling. Stung into impatient anger by such perverse ingratitude in the face of his humane forbearance, Fielding gave way to his choler, there and then reversing his pronouncement and ordering Nick Rathburn to Newgate for the term of three years.

Even as the sentence fell from his lips he regretted what he had done, though the hubbub of general indignation in the court which the boy's behaviour had aroused now reached audible applause at his decision, but he found it impossible to alter his mind. The prisoner had stood his ground for several desperate moments at the door to shout his defiance. 'You shall pay for this; I will revenge myself, never fear. You blind monster, you. May your poxy soul roast in hellfire.' And Fielding recalled how he had warned the gaolers hustling their wildcat-like captive outside:

'Do you keep a close eye on him, it will be his business to make his escape and yours to take care he shall not.'

To which the boy had flung back: 'Then let's mind our own business.' With this snarling retort he was dragged from the court.

And minded his own business he has, the Blind Beak could not resist observing to himself, as he rose from the breakfast table. His clerk paused in his account of the commotion obtaining at Newgate to marvel, as he always did, at the uncanny way the justice avoided any obstacle in his path, so it was often impossible to believe he had not the normal use of his eyes. He had only once heard Mr. Fielding refer to his disability and that a few weeks ago, in a passing mention to a doctor acquaintance that he had been blind twenty-six years. He was now aged forty-five, and had hardly ever noticed it. 'It was an accident everyone but myself deemed a misfortune, but the rational delights of reflection, contemplation and conversation soon made me insensible of any loss I had suffered from the want of sight.'

Brushing the crumbs from his waistcoat, Fielding moved with sure-footed ease to the fire, where he bent to warm his pudgy hands, half hidden by the froth of white lace at his wrists. 'And I a guest at Newgate myself last night,' he mused half aloud, 'enjoying an after-dinner cordial with Mr. Ackerman and he quite puffing up the stoutness of his stronghold, dissuading any attempt to perforate it. Do you have inserted in all the newspapers,' he proceeded, turning from the fire, 'this advertisement and scores of hand-bills bearing it distributed throughout London.' The other procured ink, quill and paper from a debris of documents cluttering the nearby desk, and began to write to Fielding's dictation. 'Nick Rathburn did break out of Newgate Gaol, where he was imprisoned for thieving, in the night between the fifteenth and sixteenth of October. He is eighteen years of age, of slender height of about five foot ten inches, pale-complexioned with dark hair and eyes and of a character bold and cunning. Whoever will discover or apprehend him so that he may be brought to justice shall have twenty guineas reward to be paid by Mr. Fielding at his house in Bow Street, Covent Garden.'

The clerk's quill had barely finished scratching when a murmuring was heard in the street below. At once Bond crossed to the window. 'The mob heading already for Newgate,' he said, peering over his spectacles at the people streaming in the direction of the prison. 'The story of the escape is fast spreading over the town.'

'Very soon,' the Blind Beak, who stood at the window listening attentively, said, 'the ballad-mongers and broad-sheet vendors will be busy crying their wares.'

There came a rap at the door and Bond admitted Mr. Ackerman, tall and pompous of bearing in his high-collared greatcoat of heavy cinnamon-hued stuff.

Refusing an offer of refreshment with grateful thanks none the less, though he admitted to having partaken of no bite of breakfast that morning, he said: 'Why I have been so neglectful of my stomach, you will know by the startling intelligence which has reached you from Newgate.' The Blind Beak indicated the advertise-ment his clerk scrawled which Ackerman read. 'I followed the route the young blackguard took,' he said, looking up from the paper, 'and with the aid of ladders, for indeed his was a perilous progress from the upper leads of the prison-roof to the roof of a house adjoining, I myself, by noting a cracked and broken tile or two, eventually found a garret-window opened, through which he had entered.' He paused and handed the advertisement back to Bond. 'The woman of the house, hearing our approach, appeared at her bedroom door — she was in night attire — and hysterically begged me to see her husband whom she declared she had just woken to find beside her in bed.' Ackerman grimaced. 'You may think that news of itself, that in

London nowadays a wife should wake and find her *husband* abed with her.' The clerk smirked, Fielding offered no comment, and the prison governor resumed his serious aspect. 'He was dead, which perhaps explains the phenomenon,' he said, 'murdered.'

And while the Blind Beak remained silent, abstractedly warming his hands at the fire, the other described how he had interrogated the woman. 'But,' he concluded, 'you will have surmised who is responsible for this foul crime.'

'You mean,' the clerk said slowly, 'the escaped felon, Rathburn?'

Ackerman nodded grimly. 'He must have awakened the husband, who attempted to intercept him, whereupon the dastardly villain stabbed him to death. And so,' pointing to the advertisement Bond held, 'you may alter the amount offered for his apprehension; one hundred pounds being the price set upon a murderer's head.'

'With whose dagger?' Fielding interposed quietly, speaking for the first time since the other had begun his graphic account. Ackerman and Bond stared in faint perplexity at the massive, quiescent figure by the fire.

'Doubtless he carried a knife on him,' Ackerman said somewhat impatiently.

Fielding's full lower lip protruded. 'He was naked. He had, you say, used his clothing as a means of descent from the prison roof. Is it likely he would be carrying a dagger? And then to incur the risk of discovery by returning the corpse — most unfashionably attired for bed, do you not agree, in shirt and breeches — beside his wife, who incidentally was not awakened by her husband or his struggle with his assailant?'

'No doubt she was drowsy with wine,' Ackerman argued, the note of impatience rising more rapidly in his tone. 'There were empty bottles and two glasses in the bedroom, and winestains on the carpet.'

'She allowed both she and her husband had been drinking before retiring?'

'Oh, yes,' was the prompt reply. 'They were a little merry.'

'So the surgeon,' the Blind Beak murmured softly, 'should have an opportunity of exhibiting his skill.' Ackerman

41

and Bond regarding him uncomprehend-ing, he expounded: 'Examination of the contents of her husband's stomach will reveal if the woman is speaking the truth.'

'Damn it, Mr. Fielding,' the other snorted, 'to waste the sawbone's time with such tomfoolery. For what reason should she lie?'

'And we know that she did,' the justice answered, 'our next step will be to discover the reason. You are at a loss,' he went on while Ackerman scrowled with vexation and the clerk's mouth fell a trifle agape, 'that I doubt young Rathburn is your murderer? He had, you say, entered the house in his desperate flight and would have let no one bar his way. You described with excellent clarity the scene, so it stays in my mind's eye, the dark staircase down which he must have descended to the bedroom. Circum-stances, with unerring aim, point to young Rathburn as the obvious culprit. And my experience in investigating crime is never misled by the obvious; more often that which is ambiguous draws us nearer the truth. Wherefore while we wonder how the suspect came by the dagger, and what occasioned him to dispose of the corpse in so rash a manner, let us follow the example of the ancient prognosticators and divine the message in the victim's entrails.'

Meeting Mr. Bond's glance Ackerman rolled his eyes upwards significantly and crossed to the window. Above the clamour of the coaches and carts, the rattle of carriages and hackneys, shouts could be heard, louder and more frenzied. 'Young thief broke out of Newgate,' someone yelled up at several people leaning excitedly out of a window. And other cries rose. 'Gaol-breaker, called Nick Rathburn . . . cracked his way out of the Stone Jug . . . A thief named Rathburn . . . Broke out of gaol.' Nick Rathburn's name was borne up and down like leaves on the autumn wind which set the shop signboards and tavern signs acreaking down Bow Street, round about Covent Garden and Long Acre and beyond. Ackerman turned to the Blind Beak and made as if to argue with him, but instead he shook his head, realizing he would never fathom what deep speculation and immutable ponderings were working behind that black-bandaged, enigmatic countenance. As for John Fielding, he was lost in an attempted analysis of what considerations, what inner promptings, had impelled him to reject the other's out-of-hand view that Nick Rathburn was guilty of murder. While it went against his principles to condemn without proof, while his instincts, sharpened by practice, had fastened upon the flaw in the evidence: the significance of the dagger, the corpse's return beside his wife, yet some other underlying compulsion had motivated his opposition to the prison governor's conclusion.

Exasperated by the Blind Beak's mountainous taciturnity, Ackerman could only wave a hand ill-temperedly in the direction of the noisy street. 'Do you say what you will, Mr. Fielding,' he declared vehemently, 'I do wager you any sum that the howling mob will soon be changing their tune, yelling themselves hoarse not over his escape but sending him on his way to Tyburn.'

1770 — AGED TWENTY-TWO

Bartholomew Fair

4

Nick Rathburn moved through the press of people crowding close as a barrel of figs about him, one hand engaged in banging the large drum strapped in front of him, while the other held the tiny ankles of Queen Mab, the diminutive figure perched upon his shoulder and holding aloft a gaudy, ribbon-decked banner bearing the garish legend: 'DR. ZODIAC'S WAXWORKS AND MUSEUM OF WONDERS'. The air was filled with the squeaking of penny trumpets, the beating of other drums, large and small, competing with Nick, the raucous shouts of stall-holders and booth proprietors, the shrill screeches of lottery pickpockets, while the atmosphere of the sultry August evening was heavy with the unwholesome odours of the sweaty multitude mingling with the varied aromas of roast pig, beer and wines wafted from the eating-stalls and taverns and grogshops of Bartholomew Fair.

It was some four years since Nick's escape from Newgate and he felt confident no turnkey nor informing fellow convict would recognize him now as the thin, prison-pale youth who had so astonishingly chipped his way out of the Stone Jug. In his out-landish jester's costume of varicoloured silks, sleeves jangling with bells which caught the admiring eye and ear of all beholders, he stood, two inches added to his height, his frame filled out. His saturnine features were set off by a white streak which had suddenly appeared, no doubt caused by the stamina-sapping rigours of his imprisonment and his exhausting flight to liberty, cutting the centre of his dark hair.

Immediately after gaining his freedom he had been thankful to lie low as he had planned among the cellars and hovels of St. Giles' until the hue-and-cry had died down. Reaching his familiar haunts he had met his first blow of disappointment, for, seeking Doll Tawdry, with whom he had anticipated joining forces again, he had been unable to discover her. At last he had received news she had paid the price of so many of her sisters in the same profession and had died in the Lock Hospital, to which she had been conveyed some several weeks before. The shock of Doll's death caused him completely to change his outlook for the future. He gained no pleasure or excitement from the adulation of the criminal fraternity among whom he moved and who knew him for his sensational escape. In fact, he quickly realized to continue his stay in the Rookeries would be courting disaster. Even if the Blind Beak's police force failed to seek him out, inevitably some informer skulking in the cellars and flash-haunts would find an opportunity to play the Judas and earn his twenty pounds reward. Amused at reading Fielding's advertisement, Nick was unaware he had the justice to thank for the fact the price on his head had not been increased to the sinister sum of a hundred pounds, nor had he heard any more concerning the corpse he had left for a crude jest in the woman's bed. Accordingly he had decided to vanish from the neighbourhood of his past exploits, shifting his ground over the river to Southwark. There he lost his identity in a world of tinkers and fair-folk. A year ago he had obtained his present occupation with Dr. Zodiac.

Convinced of his security in this life of fake and charlatanism, Nick had decided to stay put until opportunity would present itself when he might venture forth once more, if only to strike in revenge against his accursed enemy, the Blind Beak. Thus with characteristic boldness he had long shut the door of his memory upon Newgate, together with the possibility that he might be dragged back behind its grim walls.

He was adding his voice to the clamour of his drum, to drown those others about him. 'This way to the most marvellous waxworks of the age,' he bawled. 'See your notorious criminals depicted in lifelike fashion. Feast your eyes on Jamie McFee, the Edinburgh poisoner and his six brides, all most faithfully portrayed in their death agonies. See Captain Hind, notorious highwayman, hung in chains from the gibbet. See the lifelike effigies of

Charles the First on the scaffold, Mary Queen of Scots and Lady Jane Grey, their heads on the block, and other historical celebrities.'

'Do not forget me,' Queen Mab cried, her tiny foot kicking his ear, whereupon Nick shouted the louder:

'See the beauteous Queen Mab,' inviting the sweating swarm around him ankle-deep in the filth and dust of Smithfield to gaze their fill upon the fairy-attired creature of only three foot six inches in height poised upon his shoulder. 'Real-life fairy in her daring dance on the tight-rope of death.' Then giving Mab time in which to bow and smirk at the mob, Nick continued extolling Dr. Zodiac's more lurid attractions. 'Death and horror, ghoulish and gruesome — that is what the addle-pates want, my boy,' the old man always assured him. 'See the horrid laughing dwarf, who eats fire and swallows flames. See the dog-faced boy. Feast your eyes on Pharaoh's mummified daughter, all beautifully embalmed and as she was in life in ancient Egypt.'

He received ample competition from the owners of the booths and stalls, barrows and baskets on his either side, the motley array of ballad-mongers, and costermongers, bullies and bawds, cutpurses and corncutters, tinderbox men and petty chapmen, hoarsely roaring their wares.

'Buy a mouse trap, a mouse trap or a tormentor for a flea,' a fellow there cried. 'Buy any pears, very fine pears, pears fine,' a costermonger called. 'Have you any corns in your feet or toes?' another begged to know. Here a tinderbox man with an assortment of trinkets and toys for sale: 'What do you lack? Rattles, drums, halberts, horses, dolls of the best: A fine hobby-horse to make your son a tilter? A drum to make him a soldier? A fiddle to make him a reveller?' A puppet-show owner described the entertainment he had to offer. Next to him a little twisted woman with baskets of gingerbread and all ignorant that her husband, a thin, grasshopper-thighed man quietly let out the inner room of her booth to passing strumpets and their amorous gulls. Beside her an enormous woman, a mound of fat, offering bottled ale and roast pig. And Nick grinned to hear Nell Nightingale serenading song-lovers with the Delicate Old Ballad of the Ferret and the Coney, while her pick-pocket partner, young Tim Coke, busied himself among her audience. There went a madman who haunted the fair, ragged, long-bearded and wild-eyed with a rabble of laughing, mocking followers on his out-of-leather heels.

Nick and Queen Mab had now gathered quite a satisfactory press of people to follow them to Dr. Zodiac's booth. Beating his drum and shouting as loudly as ever, Queen Mab smiling and waving invitingly, Nick passed a conjurer's booth where the conjurer had just begun his performance by blowing his nose upon the people, who laughed heartily at his jest.

A group of rural sots were elevated to a high pitch of merriment by a female fiddler who, her carcass loaded with more liquor than her legs could carry, behaved herself with much impudence in singing ribald songs in a hiccupping voice. Now came a couple of seamen, just stepped from aboard ship to give themselves a taste of the fair's delights. Here was a woman very well dressed and masked, wearing a demure appearance in an attempt to belie she was as ready at the beck of any libertine as a porter plying at a street corner. Another strumpet wore blue aprons and a straw hat and raised her voice with much loud bawling of oysters. And all about at the back of the booths, roundabouts turned, swings flew in the air and acrobats and stilt-walkers balanced precariously above a sea of upturned faces.

Then Nick spied a tall figure, head held high, accompanied by a woman who hung on his arm and was dressed most extra-vagantly, the pair of them the object of all eyes. Nick drawing level, the man glanced in his direction. He appeared to be about forty years of age. His eyes in his dark, handsome face were startlingly bright, their expression bold and disdainful, and Nick saw him glance at Queen Mab, a little smile playing at the corners of his full-lipped mouth.

'Who is that handsome beau?' he heard an overpainted wench whisper to her escort, a rakish-looking gallant.

'Do you not know? Then had you better watch your skirts. It is none other than Casanova, visiting London for the first time.'

Nick eyed the more sharply the adventurer whose amours and exploits had excited the interest of all Europe, enviously taking in the magnificence of his apparel. His gaze moved to the woman and he would have paused but that the tiny feet in his ear urged him forward. 'Why do you stop?' Mab called down in her high, childish voice. 'We have a goodly crowd eager for our show.'

'Do you not see,' Nick muttered to her, 'it is Casanova with that pretty woman on his arm. What a handsome figure he makes!'

'Never mind who he is or her,' and Nick caught the jealous rasp in her tone. 'Beat the drum and tell the crowd about me, the beauteous Queen Mab,' and she kicked him in the ears again.

'I shouted all about you but a moment since,' Nick grumbled. 'You know it is the gruesomeness and the horrors pull them in.'

'It is not so,' she cried back, her artistic pride and vanity outraged. 'They come to see me, Queen Mab, and do you not shout about me and loudly, pox on it, I will break the banner over your stupid head.'

'See the lovely and beauteous Queen Mab, real-life fairy, and her most marvellous daring dance on the tight-rope of death . . . '

Presently Nick and Mab were returned to Dr. Zodiac's booth, the throng about them of most varied persons — gallants elbowing yokels, women of the *bon ton* cheek-by-jowl with wide-eyed serving-wenches, lured on by Nick's exhortations and Queen Mab's winsome smiles. Outside the gaily festooned booth, Dr. Zodiac stood upon his platform beside a brazier ornamented to represent a fearsome dragon, from whose mouth the flames spurted. He was an old man, toothless and cadaverous, with a booming voice and long, filthy, lice-matted grey locks beneath a conical wizard's hat inclined to fall askew. He wore flowing robes of Oriental design, decorated with the signs of the Zodiac, one hand holding a serpent-entwined rod of gilded wood while waving his other in eloquent appeal and persuasiveness, experiencing no qualm at all if, for instance, some freshly perpetrated and particularly atrocious murder was all the talk, in changing Charles into the criminal concerned, with the gallows-rope round his neck.

Both the dog-faced boy, a pathetic half-witted, disfigured creature and the laughing, monstrously crook-backed dwarf, bought from the gypsies who had permanently carved the clown-like grin upon the child's face at birth, helped Nick. As for Pharaoh's daughter, she was the corpse of a young girl obtained from a body-snatcher and whom Dr. Zodiac had succeeded in embalming by injecting the veins with oil of turpentine and camphorated spirit of wine, packing camphor into the abdomen, giving the deceased a life-like tint with carmine injections and the addition of glass-eyes of which there was a plentiful supply. Nick had assisted at this gruesome operation and it had been an experience which had rattled even his iron nerve.

Of nights Dr. Zodiac slept at the back of the booth, as did Mab. The other two members of the troupe slept where they could, Nick, however, having the important task of keeping one eye open while he slept, watching over the waxworks and the mummy in case of thieves. At first he had found the mute company of wax and corpse hardly conducive to sleep. The figures in the gloom it sometimes seemed to him would move and come to life; he would start and sweat until reassured it was merely his imagination playing him tricks. He was not to be allowed to suffer such awesome moments alone for long, however. After having joined Dr. Zodiac but a few days, Mab, whom he realized had from the first been subjecting him to appraising sidelong glances, appeared on the scene one night to satisfy herself, she explained, the new employee was not enduring an excess of nervous strain as the result of his eerie vigil.

Mab, a fascinating miniature of a beautiful woman, and sweetly tender face belying her experienced green eyes and vixenish disposition, and who might have been any age to judge by the variety of amorous knowledge she had acquired, was marvellously successful in taking his mind off the still and silent images about him in the dark, so he did not think to discourage her from keeping him company every night following. Underneath her viciousness and colossal vanity he discovered a lonely, innately unhappy creature, so he could not but help respond to her advances, which might have merely amused, then repelled him, with a compassion that went curiously with his nature, and which he took great care to conceal.

Bearing a basket of mysterious-looking packets before him, Nick went to peddle his wares to the press milling outside the booth. Dr. Zodiac was already launched upon his audience in his familiar exhortation.

5

'My lords, ladies and gentlemen,' intoned Dr. Zodiac, startlingly blue, green and orange flames leaping from the brazier as he dexterously slipped a pinch or two of chemicals into the coals, 'you that have a mind to serve a sound mind in a sound body may here at the expense of sixpence furnish yourself with a packet,' pausing to wave his serpent in Nick's direction, 'which, though it is but small, yet contains mighty things of great use and wonderful operation in the bodies of mankind against all distempers whether homogenial or complicated, whether derived from your parents, got by infection or proceeding from an ill habit of your own body. My assistant,' Dr. Zodiac continued, with another wave of serpent wand, 'will move among you so you may avail yourself of this life-time opportunity. Upon opening your secret package, which I beg you not to do until you reach home lest the foul night air destroy its health-giving properties, you will find it contains a number of pills, not much bigger than a garden pea. Yet is this diminutive panpharmica so powerful in its effect and of such excellent virtues that if you have twenty distempers lurking in you, boils, carbuncles, biliousness or eruptive sores, too much wind or too little water, it shall carry them off. At the same time, my lords, ladies and gentlemen, do you wish to use them so, these pills make an excellent application when melted down by the aid of a little heat into a plaster, good against all green wounds, old fistulas and ulcers, pains and aches, in either head, limbs or stomach, sprains, fractures or dislocations or any hurts whatsoever received either by sword, walking-stick or pistol shot, knives or hatchet, hammer, nail or tenterhook, fire, blast or gunpowder, or any calamitous encounter.'

Of a sudden Nick saw pushing their way towards him the tall, handsome figure of Casanova and his companion. At once he edged his way in their direction, until he stood boldly before them and held one of Dr. Zodiac's packets invitingly towards the girl.

'To be sure, one so handsome and genteel as Signor Casanova or so beautiful and charming as you, madame, will have no use for its contents, yet I would be honoured were you to accept it, without payment.'

Casanova's dark eyes glittered with amusement. 'I had no notion my fame had reached so far as Batholomew Fair.' His voice, soft and musical, was marked by a Venetian accent. 'We are overwhelmed by such frank generosity, especially as you will be sixpence the loser' — glancing round him — 'and with so many eager to buy this miraculous cure-all.'

'Do you not worry overmuch about that. I fancy these oafs are so anxious to obtain it they will easily pay twice over.' Nick turned to the girl, still keeping his voice low, 'You may find these pills useful as polish for your shoe-leather. They are made of best wax and water.'

He could hear Dr. Zodiac's peroration

reaching its climax and he would have to make ready to admit the mob into the booth. So pressing the package into her hand with a wink at the Venetian, he moved off, reimbursing himself with the extra sixpence as he had reassured Casanova he would do, by neatly charging a fat merchant twice over, his basket fast emptied. He went into the booth where he was pounced upon by Mab.

'Why must you spend so long with that strumpet?' she demanded, her pretty little face twisted up at him.

'It was not she who interested me, but Casanova — he whom I pointed out to you earlier.'

'I saw the way you could not take your eyes off her before,' she snapped, 'and now you had to fondle her hand under pretext of giving her a pill-package.'

Nick gave a shrug and sighed inwardly, mopping his face, moist with perspiration, with his sleeve. Mab's possessive rages were becoming increasingly intolerable. Intrigued as he had been by the ardour of her passion for him and touched by its fundamental pathos, he

63

had come to feel, light and fragile as she was physically, the weight of her vain and overbearing ego bearing him down so that he soon must break away. Involuntarily his thoughts flew enviously to that dark, handsome figure outside and he knew the hour was speedily approaching when he must free himself from this environment of cheap chicanery, spread his wings to reach upwards, emulating an adventurer on the grand scale such as Casanova.

'Do you not stand day-dreaming of her now?' Mab's childishly petulant voice brought him out of his reverie. 'The pack of fools will be crowding in.'

Nick moved rapidly about the booth, lighting the lanterns and thick tallow candles to illuminate to their best advantage the effigies before the onlookers gawking at them. He was at great pains to sprinkle a powerful citronella perfume over Pharaoh's Daughter, the corpse exuding an unpleasant odour; then as Dr. Zodiac appeared, jostled by his eager audience, he vanished beyond the curtains of the stage at the other end of the booth.

Presently, when all interest in the wax-works and Pharaoh's Daughter was exhausted, would follow the laughing monster's fire-eating and flame-swallowing exhibition assisted by the dog-faced boy, who would first whimper as if with fear at the fearsome fire, then lead the applause by barking. Nick would meanwhile be making certain Queen Mab's tight-rope, which was some eight feet high from the stage, was held secure at either end and that the tiny, gaily coloured parasol and skipping-rope with its prettily jingling bells on the handles were ready.

While in front of the drop-curtain Dr. Zodiac discoursed glibly upon the fabulous characteristics of his two monstrous protégés, Nick was testing the tight-rope at one side of the stage, in readiness for when Mab would arrive, painted and powdered, her hair shimmering in gold-dust and her slim, tiny figure revealingly attired in spangled tights and low-bodiced costume, when through a crack in the curtain he observed Casanova and the girl faintly amused by the spectacle. At the same moment he perceived a young woman, whose trade he instantly recognized, stumble, as if jostled by those around her, against Casanova who gallantly gave her his hand to restore her balance. She smiled her thanks and moved away. With a glance to see Mab was not spying on him, Nick was through a gap in the canvas proscenium and into the audience. Edging his way speedily round the side of the booth, he was just in time to sight the girl disappearing outside. He went after her.

By now the August sky had darkened, and hissing flares, lanterns and spattering tallow candles threw their unsteadily dancing light over the boisterous scene. He caught up with her as his quarry made to turn the corner of the booth and vanish into the darkness beyond. His hand closed over her wrist and she gasped and turned to face him.

'I will thank you for that handkerchief,' he said.

Her eyes darted from side to side before they returned to meet his in a bold stare. 'I know not of what you speak,' she tried to brazen it out.

For answer Nick jerked her towards him and tore open her bodice, whipping the handkerchief from her, she spitting at him with the fury of a cornered cat, her free hand clawing at his face so he had to draw back. She yelped with pain as he spun her round, throwing her violently to the ground.

A few moments later he was in the booth searching among the audience for Casanova and the girl. He was discomfited to find them gone, and after making certain they had slipped out during his brief absence he decided to attempt to catch up with them. Sighting the Venetian's tall figure and the top of the other's fashionably feathered hat some thirty yards ahead, he sped after them, the handkerchief thrust deep into his pocket.

His progress was impeded by the roistering mob and he would lose track of his quarry in the dark patches round the booths where the strident lights failed to reach. When next he saw them he involuntarily quickened his pace. Casanova and the girl were unsuspectingly being hedged in by a gang of unprepossessing-looking individuals whom Nick instantly recognized as footpads marking down their victim.

Nick saw Casanova glance sharply about him to realize he and his companion were quickly being surrounded and pushed out towards a dark backwater between a big confectioner's stall and a theatrical booth. Nick saw the impossibility of reaching the rogue's prospective prey in time by staying in the flow of the crowd. Turning aside he sped behind the stalls and barrows to the booth ahead whose position he had marked.

As he hurried unimpeded through the shadows, he stumbled over a young gallant lying in a drunken stupor. Picking himself up without apologies his hand encountered the hilt of the other's sword. Grateful for this usefully opportune reinforcement he withdrew the sword from its sheath and hurried onwards.

6

He came up between the stall and the booth just as the ring of desperadoes were about to close round Casanova and the girl. His sword already drawn and with one arm protectively about the latter, white-faced with terror, Casanova had backed towards the wooden side of the big confectionery stand as some protection against attack from behind. Uttering a bloodcurdling yell Nick plunged between two of the bullies to the other side of the girl and jabbed his sword at the nearest thieving cove.

'Do you stay tight between us,' he shouted to the girl, who had turned to him in bewilderment, followed by a grateful gasp, while Casanova, his eyes gleaming, threw him a word of thanks. '*Merci, mon brave.*'

'Have no fear,' Nick answered with jaunty encouragement and the air of an expert fencer, though he had never held a sword in anger in his life before, and proceeded to cut and thrust with the wildest enthusiasm. The gang of cut-purses had drawn back momentarily in face of this unexpected show of resistance. But Nick caught the glint of a dagger and waving his sword windmill fashion, was about to leap forward to dispose of this threat.

'*Non, non. Ne l'ondoyer pas. Lounge — lounge,*' Casanova, translating for Nick's benefit: 'Do you not wave your sword. Thrust — thrust.' Illustrating the action, Casanova lunged to the attack, his skilful blade spitting forth like a snake's tongue. There were yelps of pain, and, Nick, following his mentor's instructions, the ruffians were now bunched together to be forced across into a crude canvas shelter over the entrance to the stage at the back of the booth.

'*Sacré Nom,*' exclaimed Casanova, as Nick's sword neatly transfixed one rascal in the fleshy part of his shoulder, bringing forth an agonized yell and a spurt of blood, 'he has a flair for the game.'

With a devilish grin on his face Nick

leapt forward. 'Do you watch this swordplay, Signor Casanova,' he yelled. He slashed at the ropes holding up the canvas structure which, with cracks and tearing sounds, suddenly collapsed. There were muffled shouts and curses as the trapped bullies fought each other to extricate themselves from the canvas, then more up-roar and curses from within the booth itself as the actors and some of the audience rounded upon the interrupters of the play.

A little while later Nick had guided Casanova and the girl, both recognizing him from Dr. Zodiac's booth and deeply grateful for his brave intervention, to a nearby tavern against St. Bartholomew's Hospital. Sitting at the windows of the first-floor room, crowded and the air thick from many tobacco-pipes, fumes of beer and wines, they overlooked the fair. Returning the stolen handkerchief, Nick explained how it had sent him after them. Casanova had presented his alluring pink and white, blue-eyed companion as Marianne Charpillon. They drank their small beer spiced with bitter cucumber, and Casanova's attention was diverted by a trio of young men seated nearby, ridiculously attired in absurdly small cocked hats, large pigtails and very tight-fitting clothes of striped colours, each carrying tall walking-sticks ornamented with tassels. 'Why, they are wearing two watches from their fobs. How can they indulge in that absurdity?'

'They are dubbed macaronis,' Nick explained. 'And they wear two watches to show what o'clock it is and what o'clock it is not.'

Then a fellow with a great scar across his forehead picked out a pair of pocket-pistols and laid them beside him on the table. 'And who would he be?' Casanova asked Nick in a low voice.

'Do you hear the waiter call him 'Captain'? He is a man of considerable reputation amongst birds of the same feather and resolute as any who cocked a pistol upon the road. He fears no man in the world but the hangman and dreads no death but choking.' Nick's gaze shifted to another customer before whom was a glass of champagne and a platter of oysters. 'That man,' he said, 'handles false dice and cards with much dexterity and will drain the pockets of a large company in but a few minutes. You see him wearing his country cloth coat, all over dust, as if he had come a fifty-mile journey, though he has only travelled from St. Giles's. Being a rare talker he could outflatter a poet, outhuff a bully, outwrangle a lawyer and out-face truth.'

Nick took a drink of his beer and Casanova placed a hand upon his sleeve. 'What has been your employment in the world that you are so well acquainted with its scandalous society?' The question was casual enough, but Nick intercepted a look between Casanova and the girl which, though it occasioned little surprise, set his wits more atingle.

'Let us say,' he answered easily, 'there is no sharper nor cut-throat but I am wary of him. For that matter,' after an imperceptible pause, 'no Bow Street Runner's disguise could fox me, nor any police informant either.' He broke off with an indrawn hissing breath and Casanova saw in the crowd immediately below them who it was had attracted his attention. The huge towering figure with the black bandage beneath the shadow of his three-cornered hat. Accompanied by a short, lean man close beside him he moved slowly, before his dominating approach the milling throng falling back. 'Speak of the devil,' Nick muttered.

'Who is it?' The strange, enormous creature and his companion, whose spectacles glinted in the flaring lights, becoming lost to view, Casanova turned to Nick.

'Mr. Fielding, the Bow Street magistrate,' Nick grated. 'The Blind Beak himself.'

'He is blind? And yet he is a magistrate?'

At the other's puzzled expression the girl vouchsafed an answer. 'He is well known in London, people crowd his police court; they say that, stone-blind though he is, when a crime is committed he will visit the scene himself to question those concerned at first-hand.'

As if she felt Nick's gaze upon her she fell silent abruptly, while Casanova's eyes over the rim of his glass studied Nick with an odd intensity. He might be any age twixt twenty and thirty, the Venetian conjectured, idly speculating upon what vicissitudes and quirks of destiny had contributed to the sardonic humour of his look. He glanced at Marianne Charpillon, but her face was turned away, idly bent apparently upon the crowd.

It was with an elaborately casual air that Casanova took three playing cards from his pocket, placing them face downwards on the table. Nick's gaze flicked to the cards and back to Casanova, who leaned forward murmuring quietly: 'Your hands, however much you have used them, you have taken pains to keep well cared for. It is said a card-sharp may make his fingers more delicate by treating them with chemicals, but that seems a dubious practice. A Venetian sharper will rub his finger-tips with ointment or creams to add to their sensitivity.'

Now Nick glanced at his hands and then grinned frankly, picked up the cards from the table, looked at them and threw them down so they fell face upwards; queen of diamonds, ace of hearts, ten of clubs. Casanova turned to the girl, who eyed the cards disinterestedly. '*Cherchez la femme*,' he urged.

Nick took up the three cards with his left hand, holding them so their faces were hidden. He transferred a card to the right hand, leaving the other two where they were, a finger separating them. He showed Marianne Charpillon the bottom card, the queen. 'Remember well where it is.' He turned the cards again, passed the right hand holding the card to the left, which he placed on the table, passed the left hand to the right where apparently he placed the bottom card, then returning to the left appeared to put the top card down beside that on the table. The girl found herself fascinated by the dexterity with which Nick handled the cards. She fixed her eyes upon the first one he had put down while he slowly shifted all three cards round. 'Find the lady.' Unhesitatingly she pointed to the card she had kept under the unwavering gaze. Nick turned the card up and she gave a cry of surprised dismay. It was not the queen of diamonds.

'Fortunate you had not wagered on it,' Casanova commented. 'Very neatly done,' he complimented Nick at whom the girl was staring. Casanova then took the cards, his hands flashing with magnificent rings, and went through the same manœuvres Nick had performed. 'Mark well where she is,' showing the girl the queen of diamonds as Nick had done. Again she concentrated her attention upon the cards, and closely as Nick watched did not perceive the exact split second when Casanova placed the top, not the lower card, the queen on the table. '*Cherchez la femme*,' and Marianne Charpillon picked up the card, looked at it and threw it down in disgust. 'Foolish and simple game,' Casanova laughed, 'but thousands of dupes lose money by it and will ever continue so to do, so long as these exist.'

He slipped the cards back into his pocket, considered his highly polished nails for a moment, turned to the girl, whose attention appeared again abstractedly bent upon the crowd, and leaned forward to Nick. 'By a curious coincidence, it so happens I am in need of someone in my service such as yourself.' Nick remained silent, but behind his half-veiled gaze his brain seethed at the prospect of this sudden opportunity of gratifying his hopes but a little while since as far off realization as a distant star, together with a shrewd speculation touching what lay behind this implied invitation. He waited for the other to put his offer into words. 'And you care to attend my house in Spring Gardens, Pall Mall, later this evening you may secure a change from your present employment. Come at nine o'clock.'

With a nod to him, Casanova, together with the girl, who gave Nick a faint smile, rose. Nick watched them make their way out of the room. From the window he saw them mingle with the crowd so swiftly, never glancing back either of them, they became lost to his sight.

7

The house in Spring Gardens which Casanova had rented for his stay in London comprised a ground floor and three upper storeys. It was well furnished, everything was scrupulously clean, the linen and carpets, the silver and china of best quality. The housekeeper, an old crone named Mrs. Rancour, kept her kitchen with its rows of shining pots and pans in first-rate order. Marianne Charpillon occupied the entire floor of the second storey, though she often came down to join Casanova and Nick at meal-times. Without acquainting Dr. Zodiac or Mab of the sudden change in his fortune, Nick had quietly taken his departure and removed himself from Batholomew Fair, returning to the booth merely to doff his motley for his ordinary clothes and then steal away. It was not Dr. Zodiac so much as Mab he had shrunk from bidding adieu. Anticipating only too vividly the jealously passionate storm into which she would fly on learning he was leaving her, he had hardened his heart, dispensing with any fond farewells, but disappearing there and then while the going was good. Thuswise had he drawn the curtain on this stage in his story.

Settling smoothly into his new employment, Nick attempted to fathom the secret of Marianne Charpillon's association with Casanova. It was obviously not entirely of the nature usually connected with the notorious adventurer. He began to draw his own conclusions and speculated when proof positive would be forthcoming. That the pair were, as he had surmised at the Bartholomew Fair tavern, engaged in some dubious enterprise became more and more evident to him. Casanova expended his guineas freely enough — visiting the theatre, coffee-houses and attending the most elegant *salons* of the *bon ton*, though, Nick noted, he rarely entertained at home, and then never of an evening. He was amply supplied with introductions to the leaders of London's *beau monde*, he led the life of a man of fashion and appeared altogether the most genteel personage.

Nevertheless Nick had not the faintest doubt in his mind but that the engagingly handsome Venetian, with his fascinating foreign accent and deliciously eyebrow-raising reputation, was a creature of little substance, his appearance of wealth and prodigality a façade behind which he moved about some dark purpose. From the first Casanova had treated him less as a servant than as a companion. A junior partner, Nick thought to himself, in some venture. There were times when it seemed his new employer's attitude was almost ingratiating, as if aimed at securing his co-operation against some future possible jeopardy.

'I am attending Madame Corneleys' assembly in Soho Square,' Casanova told him one evening shortly after Nick had been installed. 'Do you accompany me, remaining discreetly in the background to convey the impression you are my factotum, the while you observe and hear what goes on about me, what gamesters, rakes and their trulls press their attentions upon me.'

That night, while Casanova decked himself out for the occasion in splendid magnificence and the house reeked of a dozen perfumes and pomades, Nick attired himself for the first time in his new black velvet coat and breeches Casanova had recently ordered his own tailor to make for him. As they entered Madame Corneleys' house, all eyes turned on the Venetian. The women, quizzing one another through lorgnettes, or eating jellies, sipping lemonade and sherbets, fixed their admiring gaze on the newcomer, resplendent in his coat of dove-grey velvet falling in rich folds over a brocade waistcoat of costly lace, with more gold-edged lace frilling about his throat, down his shirt and spilling from his sleeves over beringed fingers. From his neck hung a diamond-spangled order by a scarlet ribbon. Like a shadow against this dazzling display, Nick hung back a pace or two, while Casanova, one hand resting on his jewelled sword-hilt, sauntered through the guests to pay his respects to Madame Corneleys, a delectable vision of elegance in the highest fashion. 'We met in Holland,' he confided to Nick on their way to Soho Square. 'She is still mad for love of me.' Leaning back in the carriage with a sigh, Nick pondered idly how Marianne Charpillon fitted into the picture.

Presently the dancing began, then the guzzling and drinking, the guests proceeding in troupes to partake of the vast extravagance of foods and wines. Nick and Casanova standing aloof from the press of people, Nick quietly pointed out to the other a thin fellow in a very elegant frieze coat whom he recognized as a member of the light-fingered fraternity. Then Madame Corneleys returned from dancing, all very excited. Earl Percy of Northumberland had arrived, and was asking for Casanova, whom he had met in Turin. Casanova winked at Nick. 'You see,' in an undertone, 'all sorts of persons come here,' adding: 'He once tried to buy a dancer love of mine from me. In the end

I had to give her to him.'

Now were the faces of the beaux becoming warm with dancing and wine, the women bright-eyed, some with their clothes somewhat disarrayed but in most inviting fashion, so a man could scarce be forgiven if his hand strayed, to the accompaniment of little shrieks and much pouting. Presently Casanova and Nick took their leave and returned to Spring Gardens. Never did the fair Marianne accompany Casanova, always it was Nick went out with his employer each night. It was as if his meeting them together at Bartholomew Fair had set in train some course of action already predetermined by the pair and which required the girl to occupy herself several hours in the evening. To Nick's sharpened senses and razor-edged perception the house in Spring Gardens fairly reeked of intrigue but, he reminded himself, it was not to seek its solution for which he had been hired by Casanova. Every instinct warned him he was enmeshed in a web of dubious enterprise, even though he had no exact knowledge of what it was, but at least, he felt, he was leading a life which was a cut above what he had known before. He was swift to profit by his acquaintance with Casanova, absorbing from him the benefit of his worldly wise experience and something of a philosophy which on occasion went a trifle deeper than the cynical superficialities he was fond of uttering.

'Be not misled by a woman's smile and flattery. Tear aside her simpering and endearments as you might strip her face of its painted complexion, and a more calculating being never appeared in view. You are fortunate that in my company you will have opportunities to advance your knowledge of the world and society,' adding warningly: 'never flatter yourself you know more than but a fraction. I have seen a great deal of life, but I have a great deal yet to see.'

In the following weeks, Nick, listening and learning all he could, playing the shadow to Casanova's larger-than-life magnificence, began to acquire quite the air of a beau himself. The lace at wrists and throat was always meticulously white against the inevitable black of his full-skirted jacket, his shoes speckless and his dark unpowdered hair always freshly combed and brushed.

Casanova would take Nick to Henry Angelo's famous fencing establishment at the Opera House, Covent Garden, where Nick, aided by his natural boldness and agility, proved himself to be an apt pupil at the *lounge* and *passade*. They would drive together in Rotten Row on a Sunday morning, Casanova pointing out this famous dandy and that notoriety, while Nick would show him some prigging cove. Casanova would point to a surgeon, Nick to a resurrection-man, Casanova indicate a young blood in search of adventure, Nick a procuress sporting a new selection of jilts, smiling and ogling at every passing blade from their carriage. Nick would conduct Casanova to a flash tavern where highwaymen, fresh from Hounslow Heath, Bagshot and the Windsor Road, gathered, together with footpads from the by-lanes about Bloomsbury Fields, Edgeware Road and the new route from Islington to London, and daring marauders from Birdcage Walk. Nick enjoyed Casanova's admiration for the confident manner with which he would saunter into a tobacco-smoky parlour, heavy with the stench of liquor and the sweat of its crowded occupants. While the company might stare at him sharply, and though he might recognize here and there a face from St. Giles's, he himself was never recognized and challenged.

From scraps of overheard conversation and fragments of intelligence he contrived to come by, Nick learned of the discouraging effect his hated enemy, the Blind Beak, was having upon the underworld. Fielding's Bow Street Runners were making themselves felt by enforcing law and order upon the metropolis. Once Nick and Casanova were passing a half-hour in a notorious cellar in Charing Cross when a creature with the gallows-look upon him came in excitedly waving a newspaper. 'Does anybody here read?' he shouted. 'There is news for all of us in this.' Espying Nick, he thrust the newspaper into his hand. Amused, Nick read where the man's filthy finger indicated.

'WHEREAS many thieves and robbers daily escape justice for want of immediate pursuit' — the crew around Nick grown of a sudden quiet — 'it is therefore recommended to all persons who shall henceforth be robbed on the highway or in the streets, or whose shops or houses shall be broken open, that they give immediate notice thereof, together with as accurate description of the offenders as possible, to John Fielding, Esq., at his house in Bow Street, Covent Garden. Immediately, a set of brave fellows will I despatch in pursuit, who have been long engaged for such purposes. It is to be hoped that all persons for the future will give the earliest notice possible of all robberies and robbers whatever, whom I am sworn to defeat.'

As they drove away in their hackney from the thieves' kitchen, to return to Spring Gardens, Casanova declared grimly: 'Such a person as this Blind Beak would quickly end up another corpse for the canal.' Nick merely shrugged his approval of these sentiments. He was coming to know Casanova better and he could not but help recognize the Venetian was a mere husk of his former self. Even his powerful physique and iron constitution had been weakened by his excesses: he was still suffering from syphilis, though boasting of a cure by a course of manna pills prescribed by an Augsberg doctor, whom privately Nick thought as big a quack as Dr. Zodiac; and there were many occasions when that bright eye would dim, the vigorous frame sag, the keen brain nod.

This contrast between the prematurely aged adventurer and Marianne Charpillon, sharp-witted and alert as could be, gave Nick considerable food for reflection. Casanova's manifest infatuation for her, despite his characteristically feverish liaison with Madame Corneleys and other promiscuous dalliances with bordello strumpets, was obvious. She treated him with indifference, not to say scorn, and forced Nick to fear that whatever the outcome of the enterprise the pair were engaged upon, Casanova might emerge from it with less profit than Marianne

Charpillon. Since he himself was bound to be involved, he felt he had every reason for a certain uneasiness about future prospects.

That night Nick and Casanova were at Drury Lane. Casanova's main interest lay not in seeing the great David Garrick, but in spending an amusing hour or two behind the scenes in the green room. Standing for a moment in the auditorium by one of the boxes, Nick was gazing down at the stage lit by hundreds of tallow candles, when Casanova, gorgeously apparelled as usual, and talking loudly, distracting most of the audience's attention from the play, lowered his voice a trifle to tell Nick: 'There is that extraordinary creature we saw at Bartholomew Fair.'

Nick's head came round with a jerk. For a few moments he was unable to speak. A genteel-looking fellow nearby, noting the direction of Casanova's gaze, leaned forward. 'That is our famous magistrate, the Blind Beak. You may attend his court in Bow Street at any time, where he dispenses justice with fine impartiality. Being a great friend of Davy Garrick, he is here tonight to enjoy his acting, which he follows marvellously well.'

Casanova nodded thanks for the information and, with a glance at the massive figure who seemed to fill the box opposite, followed Nick, already edging towards the nearest way out. Casanova took him by the arm. 'Shall we shift our ground?' giving Nick a quizzical look. 'Let us see what entertainment the green room at Covent Garden can offer.'

Presently they were pushing their way through the crowd of beaux and rakes, women of the town and Covent Garden's actors and actresses who were hobnobbing with their friends during the interval before they appeared on the stage. Casanova's arrival brought the entire green room, it seemed to Nick, swarming about them. Among the various jilts was a young creature who affected an elegant muff and plume of feathers. 'Fanny Brilliant,' Nick told Casanova, explaining how the story went that the girl refused cash for her favours, accepting only diamonds. The Venetian observed her with some amusement ogling him outrageously, positively dazzling in her necklace and ear-rings, bracelets and rings — all of diamonds. Neither Fanny Brilliant nor any other strumpet taking Casanova's fancy, he was murmuring presently to Nick they should seek elsewhere for entertainment.

They left the shrill chatter of the women and the laughter and raucous jokes of the men-about-town behind them for the rattle and rumble of Covent Garden's night traffic. In the glare of the torches held aloft by the link-boys, sedan-chairs took up and set down their fares, richly dressed women and elegant blades contrasting vividly with the decrepit and ragged wretches skulking in the shadows to slouch forward whining for alms. Casanova hailed a link-boy, directing him to conduct them down Long Acre. They halted before a house standing slightly back from the street, several steps ascending to its front door, ornamented on either side by a brightly burning red lamp.

Entering, they were greeted in the

dimly lit hall by a gross creature whom Casanova addressed as Mother Sulphur. Her face, sunk between mountainous shoulders, was wrinkled and begrimed with powder and paint beneath a pink-ribboned mob cap. 'Welcome, my handsome bucks,' she leered, 'and are you all arut for my pretty little dears?' Behind her, Nick noticed a Tyburn-visaged fellow hovered watchfully. There was some whispered haggling between Casanova and the bawd, the jingle of guineas, and the waddling monster led the way, calling for a bowl of arrack punch, through rich curtains into an anteroom, its walls decorated with pictures of nymphs and satyrs depicted in various obscene contortions. Having partaken of some of the liquor, served by a negro boy, with many winks and knowing looks, Mother Sulphur chattered the while in innuendoes: 'All my goods are excellent peaches, fresh and ripe, yet not a rotten fruit among them, that I do vow.'

Nick followed Casanova into the Mirror Room. The walls, ceiling and even the floor were covered with mirrors.

Several large divans, draped in various colours and spread with cushions were placed about the room, lit by candelabras, reflected over and over again, so it appeared to Nick at one moment the room expanded vastly and the next it contracted again. From somewhere music began to play, part of one of the mirrored walls swung back and some half a dozen simpering girls cavorted into the room. Nick was nauseated by their archness, their painted smiles, their ill-simulated passion. The negro boy was snuffing out the candelabra, until the room was suitably dim.

As if experiencing some terrifying nightmare, Nick felt trapped in some mirrored hell, the shrieks and laughter in his ears, the guffawing Casanova and his companions filled him with horror. Unmindful of the vixenish cries which swiftly gave place to the giggles and simpering, the pointed nails that reached for him, he sprang to the door of the Mirror Room and slammed it behind him. As he headed for the front door, the sinister-looking individual he had seen earlier appeared. 'You are departing this early?' The crafty face darkened with suspicion. 'Why so hasty?' Nick observed his hand unobtrusively shift to inside his jacket as if reaching for a dagger concealed there as he said: 'It is usual to leave some token with the keeper of this cage of love.'

'Then here is my token,' and Nick caught the other a terrific blow in the mouth so that he was knocked half-way across the hall. At the same moment the dagger he had drawn flew from his grasp and skidded along the floor. The creature let out a yell of pain and alarm, blood pouring from his mouth, and two men appeared as if from nowhere and advanced upon Nick. Already, long knives gleamed in the pair of bullies' hands and murder from out of their eyes. Nick, wearing no sword or dagger, would have been powerless against them. He had gained the door and, wrenching it open just as the two men threw themselves at him, he leaped down the steps into the dark street.

8

Behind him, Nick heard the door open again, shouts and rushing footsteps. He darted across the road in front of an oncoming post-chaise. As it swept past between him and his pursuers he jumped for the step, found it with one foot and, grabbing the door-handle, hung on grimly. The vehicle gave a lurch, but the post-boy apparently decided they had merely encountered a deep puddle in the road. Glancing back Nick saw two shadowy forms dashing wildly about the street, vainly seeking him. He was awaiting an opportunity to slip quickly off the post-chaise, which now turned into a quiet street off Piccadilly, when it pulled up outside a house, the post-boy jumping down to attend to one of the horse's harnesses.

A footman appeared from the house carrying a flambeau, behind him a feminine figure, a hooded cloak about her. Nick was about to vanish into the darkness when the hood fell back and he saw the girl's face. He stopped, staring. She could be aged no more than seventeen years. As he stood there transfixed by her extraordinarily appealing loveliness she called out to him:

'I did not expect anyone to escort me such a short distance and since I am so late.' She spoke haltingly, with a French accent he found enchanting. For a moment he did not answer, then, realizing she was mistaking him for someone who had arrived in the post-chaise for her, he stepped forward with a little bow. The footman, with a 'Good evening, sir,' opened the carriage door, then turned to the girl. 'Good night, Comtesse,' whereupon Nick's eyes glinted, and as he put out his hand to help the girl into the carriage, he found his voice:

'Permit me, Comtesse.'

The footman paused with an expectant glance at Nick, who grinned to himself, climbed in and took his place beside the girl. As the footman closed the door he heard him instruct the post-boy: 'Back the way you came to Lady Harrington's,' and they set off.

Nick recalled Casanova had said something earlier to him about a ball Lady Harrington was giving at her house that night. Obviously this was a carriage sent for the Comtesse, who had mistaken him for one of the guests. He thought for something to say which would prompt her to tell him more about herself. 'I regret I did not catch your first name when Lady Harrington sent me along. Any more than when she described you,' he added, his gaze holding hers. 'I did not realize you were so fascinating as you are.'

'I am called Chagrin.' The way she spoke the name, it sounded as if it were a sigh, so that his heart seemed to constrict with a rush of tenderness he had never before known. 'I am sorry,' she continued, 'to be late. But the boat from Calais was delayed. I arrived in London but two hours ago.'

Nick inquired after her journey. Had the crossing been rough, the coach journey from Dover interrupted by any accident? She replied the Channel had been stormy, but she was a good sailor and was not much alarmed. The coach journey had been uneventful. Chagrin who? Beyond having learned she was some French Comtesse, who was she? 'Unfortunately,' he hesitated, showing a disarming frankness, 'I do not speak French and I was puzzling how you would spell your name.'

'De l'Isle,' she responded, smiling and carefully spelling it for him, as now he had no doubt about her identity. The Comtesse Chagrin de l'Isle. The chaise gave a lurch as a wheel dipped in the pitted road and she was thrown against him, and at her nearness he was irresistibly impelled to take her hand which had clung to him and press it to his cheek, and she, making no attempt to take it away, he kissed her fingers gently, lingeringly. 'You are a trifle bold for so complete a stranger,' she whispered in his ear, but there was no anger in her voice and he turned, kissing her cheek and still finding no resistance, only a yielding soft smile and her eyes shining up at him.

'Tell me,' he begged her, 'when I might

hope to see you again?'

Her smile became enigmatic. 'We shall meet again, but, for tonight' — she hesitated as if finding difficulty in choosing the right phrase not in her own tongue — 'be discreet.'

For answer he took her hands in his and covered them with kisses, searching desperately for some means by which he could stay with her, not let her out of his sight, but knowing all the time there was no way, that he must leave her soon or he would have to face her scorn when she learned of his deception. They had reached Lady Harrington's house, the windows ablaze with light, from within which could be heard the sounds of music. Now Nick and Chagrin stood in the big hall, the girl quite dazzled by the light from the huge chandelier and the whirlpool of guests in all their finery and splendour. This was the moment, Nick knew with a heavy sadness, when he must beat a hasty retreat, or his deception be discovered and he unmasked before the girl. Suddenly he gave an exclamation. She turned to him questioningly. 'My gloves, I must have left them in the chaise. And if I hurry I may recover them.' A footman moved towards him as if to offer to go, but Nick interrupted him. 'No,' then to Chagrin: 'Do you join Lady Harrington and I will find you.' She was regarding him curiously and he realized she must think he was acting strangely, but with a quick smile he turned and hurried off.

Never looking back he walked through the dark streets, his mind a turmoil, only the faint, subtle, elusive whisper of her perfume which haunted him to reassure she was not a figure of some strangely wonderful hallucination, so he hardly knew how he found himself returned to Spring Gardens. So preoccupied was he that his pace had slowed, thoughtfully, or he must have been in time to observe, as he drew near Casanova's house, a form, accompanied by another, both muffled to the ears and whose appearance might have been not unfamiliar to him, hurry forth, step into a waiting hackney and drive away.

He was in his shirt and breeches, idly

brushing his hair and seeing in the mirror not his, but another's face. Even had it not followed, as indeed it had, hard upon his flight from Mother Sulphur's brothel, his encounter with Chagrin must have made an impact upon him of such transcending power unique in his experience. He could scarcely credit it had happened, that even for those all-too-brief moments he had actually enjoyed the company of someone so delicate and sublime. Every nerve and fibre of his being quickened with excitement, his blood ran afire with wonder. It was as if he had encountered a vision from some celestial realm, an angel of goodness and sweetness, of tenderness and enchantment.

He turned away from the mirror and paced his room on the third floor, his brain spinning, the palms of his hands moist with perspiration, his heart full, as if it would burst with the tumult of emotions that racked it. He kept telling her name over to himself like a votary telling a rosary, losing himself in the magic of it. Chagrin . . . Chagrin

. . . Comtesse Chagrin de l'Isle . . . This was something he had never before known; this was honour and truth; this was no cheap and fast-ebbing passion, no lust of the flesh. This was something of ineffable beauty and delight to be cherished and adored. And yet, which was the marvellousness of it, she was no cold, marble figure without heart or sensibilities, or ardour. For she had responded to his half-bold, half-shy advances with a delicate charm; aloof, yet warm; her eyes reserved, yet her soft mouth provocative, curving with tender humour.

He turned back to the mirror, still seeing her face in its candlelit depths, but now his thoughts ran seared with bitterness. She had responded to his caresses upon her perfumed hand, white like flower petals in the darkness of the coach, and her soft cheek, and had not turned away. For she had not known him for the upstart vagabond he was, riffraff from the foul stews of St. Giles's, a one-time charlatan's assistant, lately promoted to strut in the reflected glory of a handsome adventurer, who, for all his

103

extravagant attire and fine manners, was himself no more than a charlatan. Else would he have felt impelled to slink off upon some feeble pretext, like any thief or knave, to quit her presence when he ached to stay? Had he been what she had mistaken him for, and not a mere impostor, he would be with her even now, holding her in his arms in the dance, drinking in her beauty amongst the gay throng, the lilting music, attending upon her every word, proud and basking in her smiles.

He grated his teeth as he realized how worthless he would appear in her estimation, how utterly beneath her contempt she must hold him should she become aware of the truth concerning him, and there surged within him a tremendous yearning to become the individual of substance and status she had mistaken him for. So close had he been to her and yet so far; and harrowed by a terrible longing for the unattainable that mocked him he offered up a silent prayer that in spite of the helplessness of his situation somehow, by some miraculous stroke, he would find a way to meet her upon her own ground, her own terms. And then his reflection derided him in the mirror as he realized the cruel impossibility of his dreams. The door opening noiselessly brought his thoughts back to the here and now.

'You both must have come home most quietly,' Marianne Charpillon was saying. 'I did not hear you.'

'I returned alone.'

Closing the door behind her she advanced towards him, her loose robe of filmy lace, clinging to every curve of her slim form. Her eyes were very wide, catching in their blue depths the flames of the candles on his dressing-table.

'Why, what happened? Where did you leave him?'

'With friends,' he answered her cryptically. 'Myself I felt a trifle indisposed, so came away.'

'His friends,' she sneered. 'You mean the Corneleys bitch.'

'In fact, we were not at Soho Square. They were other acquaintances we called upon.'

'It is a matter of indifference where he is,' she said, taking the hairbrush from him. 'That white streak,' she murmured softly. 'Bend your head so I may brush it into place.' He remained perfectly still, a whimsical quirk lifting the corners of his jutting brows.

'I have already brushed my hair.'

He did not move and she pouted. 'You are so tall, you would have me on tiptoe.' The wide sleeves of her robe slipped back over her slender arms, gleaming with dazzling whiteness. She laughed softly. 'Do you please bend your head.' He could not resist lowering his gaze past her moist, painted mouth and the curve of her throat.

'You asked me to bend my head,' he mocked, 'not lose it.'

Her arms twined round his neck, she writhed against him, her teeth gleamed, her perfume heady, like wine in his nostrils. 'Why are you so cold, so unyielding?' she queried. 'Never once have you looked my way as do other men.'

'My employer, for example?'

Her eyelids veiled her melting look for a moment, but she made no answer. 'I could come to you when all are gone to bed. No matter how late I would wait for *your* return.'

'I should have imagined you too wearied after your evening's work,' he insinuated. But she only squirmed closer, forcing his arms around her to hold her to him. Suddenly she tensed and stared over her shoulder. Casanova's voice came up to them.

'Marianne, where are you? Nick, are you returned?'

The girl drew away, making as if to cross to the door, then paused indecisively. 'Marianne,' came the voice again and footsteps hurried up the stairs.

'You had best answer him,' Nick said, enjoying the situation.

She flashed a glance at him, then reached for the door-handle. 'He must not know I am with you,' she whispered.

'Surely you are not at a loss for some lie,' he mocked her, and her eyes snapped back at him viciously. 'Tell him you were frightened by the dark.'

But she remained speechless, utterly disconcerted by Casanova's approach. Nick crossed to her and pulled upon the door, just as there came another shout for Marianne. 'We are here,' he called down, then in an undertone to the girl: 'Best think quick of something to tell him, unless you prefer to make it the truth.'

'I hate you,' she grated, and there was suddenly a malevolence in her look that made him realize with a shock the deep undercurrent of hatred running beneath her alluring prettiness. She hurried past him, calling with forced brightness to Casanova as she went downstairs. Not bothering to try and overhear what took place between them, Nick closed his door.

Presently he put on his quilted dressing-gown and made his way downstairs. He found Casanova in the sitting room, leaning back in an easy chair, his cloak, hat and jacket strewn about while he sipped abstractedly at a glass of cognac. Nick kicked a log in the grate so that sparks flew from it and a flame began to lick round it anew. Casanova did not open his eyes — it was as if he had been expecting Nick, but after a few moments he said through a yawn:

'I regret this evening's entertainment amused you so little you had to leave before I did.'

'You are, no doubt, accustomed to such a surfeit, but it was too much for my inexperienced stomach.'

'I fancy,' Casanova continued drowsily, 'you will scarcely be a welcome guest there for the future.'

'I regret,' Nick said, 'if the manner of my departure caused you embarrassment.'

'Not a bit. I was amused and reminded of those brothels I have had to fight my way out of.' There was a silence. The log crackled as the flame got a firmer hold about it, then: 'I also wondered if you had better entertainment in mind elsewhere.'

'I did not think,' Nick said, with a movement of the hand in an upstairs direction, 'she could give you a very convincing story.'

'Indeed, she made no excuses at all; merely flounced into her bedroom, leaving me to think what I might. Since you are not entirely unattractive, I concluded the worst.' He sighed heavily. 'The little girl is more than a match for me, though I have fed myself on the wisdom of the ancients. She has only to look at me with those glorious eyes of hers and I take in the poison of her glance at every pore. Well she knows it,' he added, sipping at his cognac.

'Because she cheats, should I also?'

Casanova opened his eyes and now they were glittering with their familiar brilliance. 'Do you give me to understand she made advances which you rejected?' Nick shrugged. 'Pox on it' — the other banged his glass down on the table so that some of the liquor slopped over — 'if you do not wear the air of a man who had repulsed such an assault.'

There followed another silence while Casanova drained his glass and said casually: 'We have, however, Marianne and I, between us concocted a kind of charade.' Casanova filled up his glass and replaced the decanter on the table. 'It includes for its performance a certain merchant of high repute and a deeper purse who, unlike you, reciprocates the alluring Marianne's advances.' A further pause, and then slowly: 'I wonder if you may also have guessed the role in our mummery for which you are cast?'

'I await your advice on that score with consuming interest.'

'This,' Casanova said, 'might be as appropriate a time as any to impart it to you. Then must we rehearse together, all three of us.'

'With mentors of such experience I cannot fail to prove an apt pupil.' Casanova caught Nick's tone and glanced at him sharply, observing the faint flicker of amusement that etched the corners of his mouth.

'You speak almost as if you are already aware what direction your lessons will take.'

'This,' Nick murmured, 'might be as an appropriate time as any for me to impart to you I was not altogether frank with you when I first entered your employ.'

'Few of us have nothing in our past we would prefer hid,' and Casanova sighed heavily, 'if you mean that. But what is it concerning which you are minded to undeceive me now?'

'I recognized Marianne at Bartholomew Fair as a girl from the Rookeries,' Nick replied, 'whose cunning in her own particular way was much admired. For myself I was considerably satisfied that, though I recognized her, my own appearance had so changed she in turn knew me not.'

Casanova stared at him unbelievingly for several moments and then gave a roar of laughter. Presently his mirth subsided and, growing serious, he fell to outlining details of the deep-laid design he fervently anticipated was to yield them, Nick to receive his fair share, so rich a haul, and that soon.

* * *

At breakfast next morning any romantic reverie concerning Chagrin was edged from Nick's mind by Casanova's casual reference to a cock-fight they would attend together that evening. Something in the other's tone convinced Nick that Casanova had brought forward the timing of his scheme's climax. Was it because he was anxious to secure its success and then rid himself of Marianne Charpillon's company? The Venetian, however, chose to remain reticent concerning what was in his thoughts, turning the conversation to a discussion of cock-fighting.

It was Nick's first visit to the royal cockpit in St. James's Park, which was a small arena with rows of matting-covered seats rising from the pit itself, brightly illuminated with lanterns and tallow candles. Nick and Casanova took their places and watched for a couple of hours while the cocks, some of which were valued as high as a hundred guineas, all armoured alike in silver helmets and spurs, were set down in pairs to fight each other with amazing bloodthirstiness, the air splitting to the uproar of the spectators crowded round. The betting was prodigious, Nick noting considerable sums of money passing from hand to hand. He could not help a twinge of pity for the losers of the savage contests as they were mangled and torn to the encouraging shouts of the hard-faced audience. Casanova appeared to exhibit similar sentiments, for presently he turned to Nick with an expression of repugnance, suggesting they had seen enough and that they left the cockpit.

Outside, Nick realized Casanova's reason for leaving the place so early was the more important rendezvous he had in mind. It was now just after seven o'clock and the early December evening was chilly with a drizzling rain. Casanova led the way to a waiting hackney carriage and, to Nick's surprise, who had anticipated they would go to some tavern, the driver was directed to convey them forthwith to Spring Gardens.

'Now is the moment approaching,' Casanova spoke quickly and in low tones, 'for you to enact your role.' He then took Nick through the line of action which they, with the girl, had rehearsed together. 'At first you will be distraught and I shall have to struggle to restrain you from satisfying your honour by the sword, and do you calm down most reluctantly.'

They went over each step in the approaching drama, whose final curtain was to yield such a handsome sum from their gull. Casanova rolled the amount round his tongue so Nick could almost hear him smacking his lips. 'We cannot know our parts word for word beforehand, since one of the characters must remain unaware of the part he is to play until our entrance.' He chuckled a little, yet Nick could detect the nervous quiver in his tone. 'So we must extemporize accordingly.'

Casanova lapsed into silence, and each remained busy with their thoughts, until they were outside the house. Swiftly they went up the stairs to the first floor, Nick leading the way and catching a glimpse of Mrs. Rancour's startled face as she appeared at the bottom of the stairs. They approached Marianne's bedroom and Nick suddenly raised his voice.

'Where are you, darling wife? Where are you, love? My friend and I have returned sooner than we thought to.' He opened the door and went in. The scene that met his eyes appeared to be posed precisely as had been anticipated. Marianne loosed an expert scream and caught a robe about her with an expression of excellently simulated surprise combined with mortification. The tubby, middle-aged man, with mouth agape, was reacting in a manner expected of someone caught in such somewhat compromising circumstances. But something deep down inside Nick's very core warned him all was not what it seemed. Despite the artistry with which the picture was composed it hung awry.

Nick thrust aside his inner conviction that the performance was foredoomed to disaster, and uttered that anguished cry to Casanova, who promptly appeared in the doorway to lend his presence as witness of the discovery of an outraged, unsuspecting husband of his wife's infidelity. Casanova risked a knowing wink, so obviously satisfied was he with the way the plot was going. Nick drew his sword and adopted the conventional threatening attitude, advanced towards the bed: 'Pox on you both, I know not which of you should be first.' This producing the desired effect upon the girl, who, screaming, grovelled herself sobbing in his path.

'No, husband, no.'

Casanova begged him put down his sword, which Nick, with most convincing show of controlling his racked emotions, slowly did. Next he allowed himself to be dissuaded even from obtaining satisfaction through the process of the law. Then, his magnanimity taking a practical turn, the matter of some monetary reward was mentioned. It was when the sum of ten thousand pounds, no more no less, was mentioned as the price for silence, and their man had agreed to fork out, that the long, richly embroidered curtains drawn across the window-recess were suddenly pulled apart.

An individual moved into the room and snapped an order, and from behind the curtains over the other window-recess a man, whose red waistcoat of a Bow Street Runner showed beneath his jacket, stepped purposely forward. Casanova stood there utterly dumbfounded, then, with a gabble of Italian, grabbed his sword. As its point sped towards the first figure Nick brought the flat of his own blade across the other's wrist so hard it drew forth a gasp of pain, forcing the sword from Casanova's grasp.

'Do you not see the black bandage?' Nick grated. 'He is blind.' Nick twisted round as if to make a dash for it, only to snarl a curse at two other Bow Street Runners who appeared in the doorway, their pistols raised to his heart. From behind him came those dreadful soft tones.

'Quite a useful catch on one hook. Casanova together with a felon escaped from Newgate, Nick Rathburn. I remember his voice.'

9

Imitating Casanova, standing beside him, Nick Rathburn held his perfumed handkerchief to his nose in an attempt to mitigate the fetid atmosphere of Bow Street police court, packed with as motley a crowd of spectators as had ever collected there. It was two hours after their arrest at Spring Gardens, and elegant beaux and women of fashion, jostling jilts from Covent Garden and footpads, journalists and players who had hurried along after the theatre, to view the notorious Venetian in his misfortune, the sensational news of whose arrest was circulating London like wildfire.

Casanova had soon perceived Madame Corneleys together with Lord Pembroke in the small gallery at one side of the courtroom. Nick followed his gaze, not failing to notice how the fickle jade's expression, when directed towards her lover of but a night or two since, was now bereft of sympathy. For all the elegance of his apparel, Casanova wore a bedraggled appearance, like some eagle of magnificent plumage dashed from the sky to earth, chin sunk forward as if he would never more raise his head. For his part Nick had accepted the situation with characteristic fatalism. His intuition all the time warning him disaster lay ahead, the Charpillon whore's perfidious betrayal was less of a shock to him than it had been to Casanova.

The girl was in her place at the side of the court reserved for witnesses, sitting with a cloak around her, eyes fixed demurely on her folded hands, never raising her face until addressed by the clerk of the court or the justice. 'You are accused, Signor Casanova, of conspiring with your companion to extort money with menaces from a certain Luke Edgworth Esquire.' So the massive figure, the inevitable black bandage round his eyes, had begun the proceedings. 'The accusation will be supported by several witnesses, including your proposed victim himself, together with the third accomplice in your nefarious scheme,

Marianne Charpillon.'

'I deny all that she may utter against me. I have given her nothing but marks of affection and she has answered with the basest ingratitude. I am placed in this wretched position through her and her alone. I am a foreigner in a strange country' — Casanova had produced a sob in his throat palpably aimed at gaining sympathy — 'what small omission, what trifling illegality I may have committed in error — '

'I am fully aware you may be strange to our customs and laws, though not so strange, it seems, to maladroit practices. Nevertheless, this court condemns no one out of hand. You will have every chance to defend yourself.'

Casanova had inclined his head in a little bow and the Blind Beak briefly outlined how, acting in his dual capacity of law-officer and justice, he had, on information received, secretly vouchsafed him by one Marianne Charpillon, set out to unmask the conspiracy directed at lightening the beguiled Mr. Edgworth's pocket by a considerable sum. Describing the girl in the case, who was artfully to seduce the dupe, as a typical product of London's criminal environment, he went on to explain how, undergoing a sudden change of heart, she had approached one of his officers laying information against Casanova. 'You may say she is no better than those she has betrayed, but I choose to regard her action as an honest effort to reform herself from following further the path of crime — '

Marianne Charpillon raised her gaze sufficiently to display the tears trickling down each cheek, which was too much for Casanova who yelled: 'False tears, you traitorous bitch.'

'You have forgot the money the gull paid her,' Nick shouted above the uproar which broke out following Casanova's violent outburst.

'If you knew her as I did' — the Venetian was exerting himself at the top of his lungs — 'you would know she must have been rewarded by a goodly sum.'

Whereupon Marianne Charpillon promptly dropped her demure attitude, jumping up to scream, 'You foreign filth. Try to blacken me because I would not give in to your lust, you depraved old goat.' She turned to John Fielding, and, remembering to adopt her other pose of remorseful humility, begged him not to listen to her traducers. While Nick, realizing their accusation had struck shrewdly home, shouted in Casanova's ear to restrain himself.

'Do you stay still. Violence towards her will make it not any easier for us.'

Casanova relaxed his belligerent posture; his chin sank on his cravat again. The clerk of the court, Mr. Bond, leapt to his feet in an attempt to quieten the commotion, only the Blind Beak still grim and silent, and the hubbub subsided. Casanova raised his head in time to see Madame Corneleys and her companion quit their places in the gallery, their expressions supercilious and full of disgust. Order restored, Mr. Fielding, sternly warning Nick and Casanova that a repetition of such atrocious behaviour would result in their being flung forthwith into Newgate until their tempers were cooled, proceeded, 'As you censure me for dealing with this witness and conniving with her against her former accomplices, I do answer you frankly. So determined am I to root out crime that flourishes so foully in our city I will make use of whatever means, provided they be in themselves not illegal, which do come to my hand; informers, ex-felons, whoever will side with me against evildoers.'

Marianne Charpillon gave evidence with her resumed humility, which many of her listeners could not but find affecting. She told how, receiving her instructions from Mr. Fielding accordingly and, with Mr. Edgworth's collaboration, the snare of these she was to betray had been laid. It was when, coincidentally enough, she recounted how, the night before the trap was sprung so gratifyingly, the justice, during Casanova's and Nick's absence, had personally conferred with her upon last-minute details at Spring Gardens, her words sent Nick's thoughts winging back to Chagrin so that every nerve of his being chilled to ice and his air of cynical self-possession dropped from him like a discarded cloak.

Chagrin was staring straight at him.

No sign of recognition showed in the glance bent upon him from the gallery; only the merest flicker of her eyes, which had not long since smiled tenderly into his, told him she knew him. He strove to will her to offer a sign she was not without sympathy for him in his extremity, but her features remained cold and expressionless. Then, as if she found the sordid tale too much for her sensibilities, she turned to her escort, a genteel-looking man at her side, and with a nod he followed her out of the court. Sick to the stomach Nick turned away, his eyes closed in abysmal misery. In that instant when he seemed to reach his nadir of wretchedness a flash of revelation pictured to him the past as it was in all its squalid bitterness. The birds of presentiment whose dark wings he had heard about his head when he had first joined the Spring Garden *ménage* had come home to roost. That night, when his spirit had been so elevated that he had glimpsed, during his brief moments of enchantment with the girl who had just turned from him in aversion, a prospect of what might have been, he should have apprehended what must be his fate.

Now it was too late, long as he might with a longing from his innermost heart to be granted an opportunity of starting his life afresh. That fatalism and stoic cynicism ingrained in his very nature were undermined by a torrent of bitter regrets which swept through him, engrossing all his mind and emotions so that he had been half listening only to what was going on about him. A nudge in the ribs jolted him back to his immediate surroundings.

'Do you hear that?' Casanova's whisper tingled with exulting excitement. 'He is not here. Edgworth has failed them.' Nick shot a look at where the clerk of the court bent beside the Blind Beak, his spectacles raised now and then in Marianne Charpillon's direction. There was, indeed, no sign of Edgworth, and from the faces of the law-officers and the murmurs running round the courtroom Nick gauged his case had taken an unexpected turn. Once again Casanova's feverish mutter was in his ear. 'Pox on the gull if he is not too shy to show his face. That must be it, and without his evidence that blind hulk cannot proceed against us.'

Mr. Fielding asked quietly: 'Is Mr. Edgworth not yet present?' A hush fell on the courtroom, necks craned and every eye was directed towards where the girl and the law-officers waited. 'Mr. Edgworth, is he here?' The clerk glanced round over his spectacles, gave a shrug and a sniff of disapprobation.

'The witness has not put in an appearance, Mr. Fielding.' The magistrate sat impassively for a few moments while Mr. Bond returned to his place to scratch away with his quill pen at the document before him. Now the hubbub among the onlookers rose excitedly, until Mr. Bond flung down his quill, irritably bobbing up to cry: 'Silence in court. Do you be silent.' John Fielding pursed his lips, waiting for the whispering and murmuring to die down.

'Signor Casanova, do you stand forward. I am desirous you should give me your close attention.' Casanova moved from his place, advanced, his step jaunty as of old, his fine feathers no longer wearing a bedraggled look, until he stood but a pace or two from the magistrate. 'Despite the seeming blackness of the case against you, it appears it must break down for want of one person's evidence, namely Mr. Edgworth, who, for reasons best known to himself, has failed to present himself here to prosecute his case.'

'Perhaps, your honour,' Casanova insinuated, 'it is because the witness is as worthy as his accusation. Being no less a liar than she' — flinging an accusing finger at Marianne Charpillon — 'he is afraid to face me in public.'

'You choose to forget,' the Blind Beak pointed out chillingly, 'I myself overheard what transpired at your house tonight.'

'True,' Casanova retorted brazenly, 'you and your officers were trespassing on my premises, though that, of course, is by the way.' A gasp ran round the court at the Venetian's insolence. Nick, still in his place before the bar, raised his eyes upwards in an expression of dismay.

'And you,' Mr. Fielding lashed out witheringly, 'trespass any further upon my patience, Signor Casanova, you will experience something of the less pleasant side of this court's justice. Rest content with your good fortune tonight that your prospective victim, no doubt feeling reluctant to suffer the publicity involved, has decided to offer no evidence in this case. The charge against you is dismissed. You are bound over to keep the peace for the remainder of your stay in London.'

Casanova gathered his wits together sufficiently to answer with an assumed humility: 'I thank your honour, and express my appreciation of the uprightness of justice as dispensed in your court.' Reaching Nick, he paused as if to learn what was to be his companion's fate.

'As for the other accused, arrested as an accomplice of the person against whom the charge has been dismissed, the case is different.' Now the Blind Beak was addressing Nick directly. 'You are the same Nick Rathburn I did send to Newgate from this court six years since upon a charge of stealing. Four years ago you escaped from that prison, to which you must now return.' Nick felt Casanova's hand upon his shoulder. 'Alas, disaster has overtaken our partnership and so here it ends. Adieu. Good fortune will still come out of this sorry business, never fear. As for me, I shall have to go back to Paris and the three-card trick again.'

Nick could not forbear a crooked grin as he took the other's hand in good-bye and watched Casanova go out of the court and his life.

Nick was hustled out into a small bare room at the back, there to await conveyance to Newgate. Dejectedly he sat on a bench, guarded by an officer, until presently another returned, accompanied by the clerk of the court. Nick, imagining the carriage which would bear him to Newgate was awaiting, stood up slowly and was surprised to hear the clerk's: 'Mr. Fielding will see you in his room.'

Nick, cogitating furiously upon what could have prompted this unexpected interview, found himself on the first floor over the courtroom. The clerk rapped on the heavy door and Nick and his two guards followed him into the sitting room. A bright fire burned cheerfully in the grate and the massive oak table, reflecting the light from a heavy silver branch of candles, was cluttered with a decanter and glasses, books and parchment documents.

'The prisoner,' Mr. Bond announced unnecessarily, with hesitant glances between Mr. Fielding and Nick, whose handcuffs clinked incongruously against such warm, peaceful surroundings.

'Remove his irons!' And in a few moments Nick was massaging the blood back into his cramped wrists. 'Sit at the table,' next came that familiarly sibilant voice. 'A glass of port wine? Mr. Bond will pour you some.' The latter registered disapproval, while he proceeded to fill a glass from the decanter. 'Now, would you, Mr. Bond, retire with the officers, for I have business to discuss with Mr. Rathburn,' and the clerk's eyes bulged behind his spectacles. 'Station yourselves so that in the unlikely event should I need your assistance you will be within earshot.'

There was a long silence after the door had closed. Nick, his brow creased speculatively, sat, his drink untouched before him, a score of questions chasing round his head, and waited for what the Blind Beak had to say. 'You have not tasted your glass,' Mr. Fielding remarked, so that Nick gave a slight start, for it seemed impossible the blind man should have known whether or no he had touched his glass. They made a curiously contrasting picture, the one towering and enormously stout, beside the other equally tall but lean, his thin saturnine face alertly watchful, as opposed to the other's plump, impassively quiescent. 'I required you to know,' slowly, soft protruding lower lip at the rim of his wine-glass, 'I am not unmindful of your action which stayed that Venetian rogue's sword. I am sensible you may have saved my life.'

'Any other man, except perhaps Casanova,' Nick replied, 'would have done the same for a — ' He broke off a trifle awkwardly and the other took him up.

'For a blind man, you were going to

say . . . ?' Nick murmured something and the other sipped his port unconcernedly. 'Possibly you thought I should have commented upon your concern for my welfare tonight in mitigation of your offence, for I am reckoned a just man.' He paused, a thumb and forefinger pinching his double chin reminiscently. 'Some six years ago, however, I permitted myself to be provoked into committing a young offender to Newgate, when I should have been more patient. No doubt you recall the occasion in question?'

In passing he mentioned casually how he had argued the governor of Newgate out of putting a murderer's price on Nick's head, and how investigating that strange murder at the house near the prison he had exposed the wife's lover as her husband's slayer, the man presently arrested swallowing a fatal phial of poison. Mr. Fielding had moved beside the fireplace to warm a hand against the blazing logs. Nick took a sip of the port wine, smooth and rich to his palate, and leaned back. He had been unable to resist an inward, ironical smile at the thought now that it was Chagrin, not he, the other should have thanked that Casanova's sword had not speeded to its deadly work. It was only Chagrin's tender memory had stepped between him and his hatred of the Blind Beak.

He brushed away the recollection of her face as she had last looked upon him in his agony of degradation and forced himself to concentrate his attention on attempting to determine what ulterior motive lay behind the Blind Beak's present demeanour towards him. He found it difficult to believe this was the same individual he had feared and hated, against whom he had wildly vowed vengeance, now seemingly so benign and warm-voiced, having little in common with the acid-toned justice of the probing mind able to penetrate the heart's innermost secrets.

John Fielding drew to the crux of the business uppermost in his mind, yet conveying the impression he was concerned with nothing more important than holding his half-empty glass beneath his nose to savour the bouquet of the wine. 'I am going to offer you a chance to carve for yourself a more commendable niche in the scheme of things than you have in the past had opportunity of securing. I must tell you,' his lower lip twitching ever so slightly, 'my motives are not entirely altruistic.' A shadow passed across his face. 'It occurs to me,' he continued, 'it is I you may have sought to hold blameworthy for the death of a certain poor Doll Tawdry.' At Nick's hiss of indrawn breath, the Blind Beak turned to the fire, murmuring over his shoulder: 'I recognized you by your voice, though it has grown a trifle less loud, as the champion of that wretched child. That her unhappy fate cannot in truth be laid at my door, who meant to save her from just such an end, you must know. She paid the price so many of her sisters in the same profession pay.' His words fell slowly, like pebbles cast by a wilful child into a still pool, upon the heavy silence of the room.

'What do you want of me?' The lines of Nick's saturnine features were inflexible and his eyes narrowed. The Blind Beak turned back to him and now he appeared to tower and expand in the light of the candles. Nick experienced the sensation that the other, despite his lack of sight, was watching him closely, exploring deep into the recesses of his mind.

'Remember my word earlier tonight? I am so resolved to root out this rank weed of crime battening upon London I will welcome any ally: felons, informers, whosoever will join me in my fight.' Nick stirred, leaned forward in his chair. The other hesitated, then went on. 'A cardinal rule of mine,' he said, 'is quick notice and sudden pursuit. But,' his voice rising slightly, 'I grow daily more convinced prevention is better than cure; the only way I can so fashion my Bow Street Runners into an overpowering force is to possess foreknowledge of what depredation thief or sharper plans. Forewarned I shall be forearmed indeed.'

'You have in mind for me,' Nick grated of a sudden, 'I should turn my coat, become your private spy?'

'My train of thought has not altogether eluded your grasp,' the other complimented him. 'That is my offer to you,' he nodded. 'In exchange for freedom, my complete trust and confidence in your ability to serve me to the utmost, and, naturally, not ungenerous payment.'

'It would be dirty money.'

Nick watched Mr. Fielding cross to the table and put down his glass, noting with what assurance the bulky figure moved, and remain impassive for several moments without answering. Then: 'What do you suppose is my interest in living almost every hour of the twenty-four in the most foully nauseous air and unwholesome atmosphere of all London? If the payment I receive were ten times the sum it would still be the dirtiest money in the world. My interest, nay, my deepest obsession, is,' the words forcing themselves through his teeth, 'the annihilation of the underworld. Of all who come to my mind who can help me in this purpose you are he.' Nick suddenly saw a vision of Chagrin, her face bent on him in pride, and his pulses stirred, his blood began to race. 'You choose to dub the employment with harsh names,' the Blind Beak continued. 'Police spy. Dirty money. Very well, but what debt of gratitude owe you your erst-while wretched acquaintances in sordid shame? Can I not strike a spark of obligation in you towards me when I urge you to follow a path which can lead you upwards from the depths?'

Nick stood up, his hands clenched and dark eyes aglint beneath their straight, black-jutting brows, a hope and a dream, whose bones and fibre had nigh disintegrated into skeleton-dust, uplifting him. 'I exhort you, who scrupled little when on the side of evil, to change your allegiance, and own as few scruples on the side of good. It is I, or them. Mine could be the voice of Destiny, speaking to you, offering you a fateful choice. It is for you, Nick Rathburn,' and a deep fervour he had never before known shook Nick from head to toe as the soft, dominant voice drummed a summons in his ear to which he could give but one response, 'it is for you to choose.'

1777 — AGED TWENTY-NINE

The Spy

10

The tall lean man in the black velvet suit
and riding-boots, of elegant cut and most
highly polished, pushed back his gilt chair
from the faro-table and stood up, giving
his place to another punter eager to bet
on the cards. With a nonchalantly graceful
air, his spurs chinking, he sauntered away
from the corner of the gaming room and,
as the click of chips on the table and the
silky shuffle of cards receded, sang softly
to himself:

‘’Twas midnight in the faro-bank,
Faces pale and eyes aglow,
A score of beaux were gathered there
Watching Fortune’s ebb and flow.’

He took a pinch of snuff from a gold
and diamond snuff-box then fastidiously
touched his aquiline nose with a snowy
handkerchief. Pausing at a tall window,
opened so the cool air of the late autumn

night of 1777 might freshen the atmosphere heavy with varied perfumes, pomades and tobacco-smoke, he looked on to St. James's Square. A hackney clattered past and a link-boy held his torch aloft for a passenger alighting outside the house from a sedan-chair. The sky was starless and appressive-looking and he caught the growl of thunder in the distance.

'Good God,' a somewhat tipsy voice in his ear brought him round slowly to meet the swivel-eye of a fop, the enamel on his face cracked by his vapid grin, 'but you are dressed, Mr. Rathburn, as though about to hold up a coach on some lonely heath.'

Nick Rathburn raised a sardonic eyebrow. 'You flatter me since I am, in fact, on my way to the masquerade at the Pantheon as none other than the notorious Captain Lash.'

The beau eyed him owlishly, his fuddled wits seeking to weigh whether or no he was being mocked. Talk that ran round the gambling-hells and the bordellos, coffee-houses and green rooms of Covent

Garden and Drury Lane invariably dropped to an undertone when it concerned itself, as often it did, with the raffishly mysterious Nick Rathburn. Deciding, for he also recollected Nick Rathburn's reputation with the sword or pistol, the other refrained from commenting, as was on the tip of his tongue to suggest, that the attire was not inappropriate for one of his notoriety. Instead, giggling tipsily, he continued unsteadily on his way to the faro-table.

A footman appeared in the doorway, whereupon Nick casually sauntered over. The man uttered behind his hand: 'He has just left the tavern, and headed for Blackheath.' Out in the hall the footman helped Nick on with his riding-cloak, handed him his riding-whip, giving a sidelong glance at the two pistols which Nick transferred to his coat pocket.

'I also have a black mask,' he vouchsafed, catching the other's look, 'to complete my guise.'

The man's hollow laugh mingled disbelief with understanding that the remark was intended for the benefit of any eavesdropping informer who might be listening on the stairs or behind a door. 'A masquerade at the Pantheon, Mr. Rathburn?'

'A masquerade,' and, pulling his cocked hat over his eyes, slapping his whip against his boot, Nick swaggered out. Presently riding at a steady pace, he had left Westminster Bridge behind and was making his way through the labyrinth of lanes and alleys of East London. Gaining the Elephant and Castle, the coaches, wagons and shadowy figures of people on the streets began to give way to open fields and stretches of commonland. Behind him receded the striking of a church clock, the cries of the mob milling outside a noisy tavern and a twisting row of wretched hovels, while the familiar stench which hung perpetually over London grew less oppressive as the road opened out beneath his horse's thudding hooves, and trees and hedgerows flew past him on either side.

For the past five years Nick Rathburn, serving the Blind Beak as undercover agent in London's underworld, had diligently fostered the dark suspicion he was a rake-hell ne'er-do-well, shady gambler and sharper favoured by incredible good fortune which saved his neck, as yet, from the hempen collar. His lean, angular figure, inevitably attired in black velvet relieved by the snow-white cravat and lace at his wrists, was to be seen at every disreputable tavern round about Covent Garden, Moll King's Coffee House, the White Lion in Drury Lane, the Rose in Russell Court; never a bagnio from Curzon Street to Pall Mall but did not know his custom. Vauxhall and Ranelagh and the Pantheon in Oxford Street, the gaming-houses of Jermyn Street, Cleveland Row, King's Street and St. James's — at all these Nick Rathburn was certain to put in his appearance at some time or another.

He had developed his technique to a high degree, relying not only on the chance word of a *habitué* in this brothel and confirmed by a whisper let fall in that gaming-hell, but using employees of the various establishments who were only too ready to keep their own ears and eyes open on his behalf, for the appropriate fee. Such a source of information, for instance, was the ostler from the Rose Tavern. He had brought him news he had been awaiting that evening concerning Captain Lash, to the effect that the notorious hightobyman had just set off to hold up the Dover to London coach, the Flying Hope. The desperate Captain was one of the few remaining highwaymen John Fielding's Bow Street Runners had so far not succeeded in clearing off the roads about London.

Earlier that week Nick had received an impression from Captain Lash's latest light o' love which suggested he had in mind a daring enterprise in the near future. Then yesterday one of the desperado's drinking companions had in a drunken moment confirmed the hint with news the *coup* was for the very next night. This time, however, the spot on Blackheath, deserted and unfrequented, selected by the Captain on previous successful occasions, although apparently still as desolate as ever, would in fact be somewhat less lonely.

Ordinarily Nick, having passed on to

Bow Street the intelligence he had acquired, would have taken little further interest in what subsequently transpired. He had, however, come by an extra item of information that the passengers in the Flying Hope would include a certain Paris jeweller, called Boehemer. At the name, when Nick mentioned it to him, the Blind Beak evinced intense interest. He informed Nick he had grounds for believing Boehemer was travelling to London upon business of a nature different from that he purported would engage his interest.

'Secret business,' Mr. Fielding, his soft, pudgy fingers thoughtfully twisting his badge of office hung by a ribbon around his neck, murmured. 'In fact the business of spy, no less, for Madame Du Barry herself.'

The first shots fired that April in the American War of Independence had been hailed as a signal by the war party in Paris political circles for increasing their pressure upon Louis XVI to reopen hostilities with the hated enemy across the Channel and avenge France's humiliating defeat at the hands of the British twelve years before. Foremost among those urging war with England, now being harassed on the other side of the Atlantic, was the notorious Madame Du Barry. As Nick was aware, the Blind Beak had for the past several weeks been in receipt of reports from English secret agents in Paris. Mr. Fielding imparted to Nick that he had knowledge Boehemer would carry evidence of the sinister object of his visit in the form of a document introducing him to one Morande, French so-called journalist, who, giving writings against various notabilities there, had arrived in London several months since. In fact, a dossier, part of whose contents Nick had supplied, at Bow Street revealed Morande as using his *emigré* scribbler pose to mask his real purpose for being in London; he had been entrusted by the Du Barry to set up there her espionage organization.

It being essential to his ultimate aim that Morande in London and his fair employer in Paris should continue, until such time as he chose forcibly to unmask them, to remain unaware their evil designs were known to him, Mr. Fielding's concern was how to obtain proof of the ulterior motive behind Boehemer's journey without arousing any suspicion. Nick, reporting Captain Lash's nefarious Blackheath project, came up with a stratagem which would fulfil these respective requirements. An appreciative smile darted across the Blind Beak's rotund features as he listened to the plan outlined. 'An excellent device,' he had declared with enthusiasm, 'by which we should kill two birds with one stone.'

Behind Nick, the dim glow of London's street-lamps, the lights from houses, taverns and shops reflected against the lowering sky receded as his horse's hooves beat out their steady tattoo along the Dover Road. A squall whipping across from Deptford on his left brought a salt hint of ships nosing their way up the River Thames from the sea. The night was still starless, though somewhere behind the swollen clouds the moon hid and Nick had all he could do to discern the pale road ahead, crumbled by parched summer and worn by rainstorms of winter, and to avoid the deep puddles of mire and the wheel-ruts churned up by coaches and wagons. He handled his mount superbly: his service for Bow Street calling for him not only to improve his dash and skill with the sword, attain singular proficiency with the pistol, but to excel in horsemanship. The strange double life he led had, while keying him up to never-failing watchfulness, case-hardened vigour and sense of power, achieved for him something he had never before experienced: a purpose in existence. And all the time Nick held in his heart the burning belief that one day his Destiny would lead him back to the one being whose exquisite loveliness and fascinating charm of voice would never be effaced from his dreams. And when he found her again he would have wiped out the past, proved himself worthy so that he might somehow persuade her to stay with him evermore.

Presently Nick was making out a scattered glimmer of lights lying to his left to be Greenwich and discerned the dark shape of Greenwich Hospital low against the skyline. For a few moments the moon showed itself in a rift in the storm-clouds and by its pale light he saw the gibbet at the side of the road. A carrion bird suddenly screeched off the figure hanging upon it. Riding on, he was now some quarter of the distance across Blackheath, opening out before him on either side, desolate and deserted, with here and there a tree — dark skeletons against the black sky. Ahead of him the road began to incline for the next half-mile and he approached a small copse extending some thirty yards back from the road. Slowing his pace, he turned aside, cantering over the heath, his horse's hooves noiseless on the rough grass. He gained the edge of the copse which lay between him and the road, halted, listening for a few moments, the wind soughing in the branches above, then gave a low whistle. An answering whistle came at once from within the darkness of the trees and Nick identified the burly figure who quickly rode out on the big bay as Langrid, in charge of the horse-patrol of whom half a dozen more remained hidden in the copse. 'He passed some quarter of an hour ago,' Langrid muttered, 'to the exact minute we expected him.'

'So soon as we hear the Flying Hope, gain we the top of the hill in readiness to pounce.'

Langrid turned back into the copse with a low-voiced order. Led by Nick, he and six horsemen, their mounts' harness muffled against any jingling, approached the hill's brow. Not a hundred yards away Captain Lash would be astride his horse in the shadow of a clump of trees beside the road he had for the past several years made his hunting-ground, ears cocked for the first sound of the coach.

Picturing the notorious highwayman, who all unsuspecting waited not far distant, in his mind, Nick waited, tensed as were his companions. The faint crack of harness-leather and muffled pawing of a hoof, then a night-bird crying, to be answered by its mate some way off, and silence heavy and sinister over all. Nick was about to loosen his cravat against his throat, taut with suspense, when Langrid suddenly grunted and Nick's head jerked up. Faintly came the echo of the distant clop-clop of horses' hooves approaching.

'Do we move?' Langrid muttered hoarsely.

'Give him a moment,' Nick whispered, 'and we will nab him with his pistols cocked.' The crack of the coachman's whip rang out from the oncoming Flying Hope and Nick touched his horse's flanks: 'Now,' and the others raced him over the top of the hill. They descended upon Captain Lash even as Nick had hoped, masked and with pistols cocked. So quiet and sudden was their approach he had barely time to wheel his animal round to meet them with a string of curses before they closed in, forcing him from his saddle, to drag him back into the trees, there to be swiftly handcuffed, bound and led secure Londonwards.

Nick Rathburn himself had taken no part in the arrest, but set his horse in the clump of trees where lately Captain Lash had waited. The patrol with their prisoner kept to the heath until they disappeared over the brow of the hill as Nick adjusted the mask which he had previously slipped over his face, and himself cocking a pistol in either hand, gave his horse a touch of spur. The coach was but a few yards off as he barred its way. 'Stand and deliver,' he roared, his eyes glittering behind his mask, his voice brutally harsh. 'It is Captain Lash, so will you fork over quietly enough. Your money or your life.'

As Nick brandished his pistols there came nearer now a long roll of thunder; the coachman dragged at the ribbons of his four-in-hand, slowing the Flying Hope to a stop. A man's head pushed through the coach window to inquire what was amiss, saw Nick's masked and threatening figure, gulped: 'Highwayman — it is a highwayman,' and ducked back inside again.

'Small haul you will make this night, I tell you,' the coachman said in surly tones, quietening his horses. 'Be only six passengers inside. So wild the weather not a soul would ride on top.'

'Quality, not quantity, is always Captain Lash's maxim. Keep your place and your nags quiet.' So saying, he urged his horse alongside and, pushing his pistol through the window, commanded fiercely: 'Outside every one and quickly.' There was a girlish gasp of fright, muttering voices, then first alighted a middle-aged woman, large and indignant, closely followed by a young girl clutching tightly at the other's hand. Next into the circle of light cast by the flickering coach-lamps a round-shouldered individual wearing clerical attire who was running his tongue over his lips in evident terror. Then a tall man of about sixty, elegantly behatted and wearing a high-collared coat of rich dark cloth, who snapped: 'You shall choke at Tyburn for this and I will be there to see you.'

'You have too much regard for my welfare,' Nick retorted. The choleric old dandy was none other than Lord Tregarth, a most talked-of sportsman of the town who raced his own thoroughbreds and plunged heavily on the prize-ring. Nick was not surprised to see stepping out of the coach after him a heavy-shouldered fellow of battered features and sporting a cauliflower ear; Jem Morgan, middle-weight champion of England. No doubt they had returned from France, where the pugilist had been engaged in a prize-fight.

'And he had not his pistols,' Morgan growled, 'I would soon settle one in his guts.'

'Best not incense him,' the man dressed as a clergyman quavered, clasping his hands together in a prayerful attitude.

'And the sixth passenger?' Nick wanted to know. There appeared to be no one among these before him who could be Monsieur Boehemer, and he anticipated the appearance of the last remaining passenger upon whom he intended concentrating his attention with interest. Obviously the jeweller would carry proof of the ulterior motive for his journey not in his baggage, fearing it might be lost or stolen, as all too frequently happened, but in a valise or package he would never relinquish out of his sight, perhaps secreted somewhere about his person.

Nick's procedure would be to grab the valise or package to which the man clung, informing him bluntly he was also known to have jewels hidden in his clothing, then hustle him into the trees. There he would strip him of all he stood up in: coat, breeches, waistcoat, hat and even shoes, leaving him to reclothe himself as best he might from apparel in his baggage or by borrowing from his companions. 'He will suspect no more than that he has an unlucky mischance,' Mr. Fielding had opined. 'As for any valuables of his you may procure, they will be confiscated and,' with a droll smile, 'the proceeds devoted to my charity for poor, deserted children. Thus, out of evil a trifling good may spring.' Leaning forward in his saddle, Nick thrust a pistol menacingly inside the coach. 'Have I to blast you to perdition?'

'Must you subject her to such indignity?' he heard Lord Tregarth protest bitterly.

'Her?' Nick's glance raked the man of clerical appearance, obviously seemingly petrified and mouthing prayers under his breath, the young girl and her large, buxom aunt, Lord Tregarth and the bruiser. It seemed impossible to believe any of them could be the Paris jeweller. He turned back to the coach with a jerk of his pistol, whereupon the young girl squealed: 'Aunt, will he murder her?'

There came another rumble of thunder. Suddenly tense in his saddle, borne upon a rain-filled squall came the faint oncoming drumming of horse's hooves. Even as he made sure of the sound, Lord Tregarth uttered a gratified exclamation. 'Sounds like a chaise, or someone on horseback.'

'You in there,' Nick snarled. 'Out quickly or death to you.'

The remaining occupant of the coach appeared at the door, her face shadowed by the hood of the long cloak she had drawn about her as if to hide herself from scrutiny. Nick had to admit she appeared unlikely to be the creature he sought, disguised, but was determined not to allow the coach to proceed on its way without being completely satisfied the French spy was not in it. Peremptorily ordering the woman in the cloak to stand beside his horse he turned his pistols upon the others, watching anxiously. 'Get back into the coach, the rest of you. You coachman, if whoever it is approaching stops to ask do you require help, fob him off with some excuse.'

'What excuse?'

'A stone in one of your team's hooves — use your wits or lose your life.' And swinging his pistols at the group by the coach-door: 'You play up to him.'

'And what,' his lordship inquired, 'will you be doing?'

'Waiting' — jerking his head in the direction of the trees — 'with my prisoner. Should any try to play me false I will shoot her without compunction.'

The hooded figure beside his horse remained still, giving no sign she was affected by his threat, though the man in parson's attire wrung his hands, murmuring nervously: 'Of course we will do as you say.'

'Or,' Nick jeered, 'your prayers will be needed for a departed soul this night.'

Before the compulsion of his dangerous-looking pistols, the others got quickly back into the coach, and Nick escorted his hostage, who kept close to his saddle into the trees. Now the hooves were nearer and, together with their steady beat, could be heard the rattle of carriage-wheels. Nick, leaning down, observed in low tones: 'Most silent you are for a woman, and I think not because fright has lost you the use of your tongue.'

The other made no reply, but stood there quiet and cloaked and somehow strangely mysterious. Impossible she could be Boehemer, who, according to the description of him, was a middle-aged, prosperous-looking individual. Overhead, rainy gusts stirred the trees starkly black against the threatening sky. Now Nick made out a post-chaise against the dim road spinning along at a fast lick. At the appearance of the coach standing there, the chaise pulled up, the post-boy calling out if ought were amiss. Nick turned, heard the hooded creature at his stirrup utter a faint gasp as the coachman coughed and mumbled before he found his voice. 'One of my horses slipped and I thought a trace had snapped,' he extemporized, 'but it will hold.'

The post-boy urged his pair of horses onwards again, with a 'good night' and a 'God speed'. In a few moments the chaise had disappeared into the stormy darkness, to be revealed brightly by a flash of lightning, the echo of rattling wheels and hooves dying away.

Nick prodded the figure at his saddle in the back with his pistol and bent forward. 'Now for a closer view of one so silent,' and, with a quick movement, jerked back the hood obscuring her face. As it fell away she turned, her eyes blazing up at him.

'Do you keep your hands from me.' Her voice was low and her French accent did not disguise the contemptuous hatred charging it, and as another lightning flash clawed the darkness from the sky Nick found himself staring into the face of the Comtesse Chagrin de l'Isle.

11

At the same time the lightning flash was illuminating the darkness of Blackheath and Nick Rathburn found himself gazing at the Comtesse Chagrin de l'Isle, the bronze ormulu clock on the mantelpiece of Madame Du Barry's boudoir at the Hôtel de Brissac, Rue de Crenelle in the Faubourg St. Germain, that most fashionable quarter of Paris, struck the quarter past the hour of ten. The sweet chimes reached the pretty ears of the gloriously fair woman lying in her bath in the gilt and mirrored bathroom, and she called to her *femme de chambre*, who at once appeared with the loose wrap in which to envelop the beautiful body.

A few minutes later the Du Barry, clothed in silken petticoats and over them a *négligé* of rich Brussels lace, faced the great mirror of her muslin-draped dressing-table and, aided by her woman, deftly applied the cosmetics from the delicate jars of porcelain and jewelled bottles before her; dark brown colouring for her wonderful eyebrows which contrasting so vividly with her magnificent fair hair, black for her thick eyelashes, enhancing her marvellous eyes shining like sapphires, carmine for the small, perfectly shaped mouth. Then blue to emphasize the veins in her white slender hands, and rose tinting for her fingernails. From the richly cut crystal bottles the sweet and heavy perfumes of carnation, rose, musk and amber spilled upon the warm air.

Here at the Hôtel Brissac, home of Louis-Hercule, Duc de Brissac, where she had permanent apartments, she was in her thirty-ninth year seeking to regain a semblance of the position she had known before the death of Louis *le Bien-Aime* two years before. The fifty-year-old Brissac, himself involved in machinations behind the scenes of Louis XVI's and Marie Antoinette's court, found her an apt pupil. Quickly she grasped that if France was to avenge her defeat a dozen years earlier by her traditional foe,

England, she must support America, now desperately engaged in her War of Independence against Britain.

If only, went her lover's argument, which she echoed, Louis could be persuaded to recognize America's independence now. Now, while Burgoyne's apparently over-whelming forces of redcoats were on all sides encountering unexpectedly determined onslaughts from the Americans bent on retaking Philadelphia. France would not only turn the balance in America's favour, but bring Spain and Holland into the alliance. With such a powerful array against her England must be forced to admit defeat, and France would regain her former pres-tige and glory.

These thoughts were circling the Du Barry's mind as presently, preceded by her youthful negro servant, Zamor, she made her way through the large house to Brissac's private study, passing below the picture gallery crowded with Italian and Dutch masters and where hung that painting of herself her lover so much admired which, however, superstitious-minded as she was, she had never really cared for since that time Diderot, the author, swore he perceived a line round the neck separating the head from the body.

Across the library she followed the scuff of Zamor's shoes echoing among the books all around stamped with the Duc's arms, Brissac being a great reader and very well informed on the novel ideas the new philosophers were expounding. Zamor opened the heavy study door and Brissac, tall and quietly elegant in a coat of pale lavender, a sapphire brooch gleaming among the folds of his cravat, came towards her at once. But it was the other figure in the tapestry-panelled room who tonight took the Du Barry's immediate attention. The shortish, bald man with a fringe of white hair over the collar of his brown coat. 'Monsieur Franklin,' and she hurried to take his hands in hers, 'you do Monsieur le Duc and myself a great honour.'

'On the contrary, Madame la Comtesse,' was the response in French with a schoolboy's accent, 'it is I who am honoured, not to say charmed, to meet you.'

She kept her white, pretty fingers over his gnarled, gouty old hands. 'To us you are the greatest American, if not the greatest man of the age.' She glimpsed his long cloak and the fur hat cast upon a gilt and cream chair. 'It is all the more to be deprecated we should have to receive you secretly like this at the back door.'

Across Benjamin Franklin's features, which had relaxed into their familiar reposeful, Quakerish air, flickered a tiny smile. 'It is as flattering to me as any other door.'

'But since France must as yet appear neutral,' Brissac said, 'and we know you are surrounded by the English Ambassador's spies, it required us to employ the greatest discretion.'

'True, Lord Stormont appears to regard me with some suspicion,' was the wry reply, 'though as to the matter of his spies, their attentions persuade me, and doubtless Paris also, that my business in France is upon not unimportant grounds.'

'We did not drop that mysterious message over your garden wall at Passy,' the Du Barry said, 'merely for you to hear

166

us express our approval of your defiance of Britain. While Paris rings with the glorious news of your heroic attack against Burgoyne at Philadelphia, we seek to strike a blow on your behalf.'

Franklin, whose face had become shadowed at the mention of the battle raging, perhaps already won and lost, for the city he knew and loved so well, was regarding her now with a quizzical expression. 'But, Madame la Comtesse, as Monsieur le Duc has just reminded me, all the world knows France remains neutral.'

'As yet,' Brissac interposed significantly.

'What all the world does not know' — Madame Du Barry's eyes flashed — 'is that July the fourth was the signal for some of us to declare secret war against the British. We spoke just now of their spies in Paris. I also have my spies in London,' and the American's eyes widened, 'whom I have entrusted with the task of acquiring information such as what British troops are *en route* for America, what equipment and military supplies are being shipped for use against American soldiers.'

'You may regard our contribution to your cause as of relatively trivial consequence,' Brissac remarked, 'but it is the utmost we can offer against the day when we shall openly stand shoulder to shoulder with you.'

'On the contrary,' Benjamin Franklin answered warmly, 'I am sorely in need of every scrap of intelligence as you may furnish me. I cannot sufficiently express my gratitude to you for all your energies to that end. As to the moment when we join forces, every day do I urge your foreign minister to conclude a speedy alliance with us, but still he hesitates to advise his monarch accordingly.'

'Rest assured,' Brissac told him, 'France needs only the appropriate trumpet-call and she must be convinced it is her hour also to strike.'

'Meanwhile,' the Du Barry went on enthusiastically, 'we carry the war surreptitiously to the enemy's camp.' She included Franklin and Brissac in a conspiratorial look. '*Par exemple*, a certain jeweller had agreed to journey to London, ostensibly upon business matters, to meet my agent already installed and bring back his despatches. At the last minute, however, Monsieur le Duc himself chanced to observe a creature in the shadows across the street watching this house at the time of the jeweller's visit for instructions.' Brissac gave a confirmatory nod. 'Caution dictated me to substitute in his place someone else less likely even than a respectable jeweller to be suspect.' She was interrupted by a hurried knock on the door. A manservant, looking somewhat flustered, appeared.

'A messenger for your guest, Monsieur le Duc,' he announced, low-voiced.

'For Monsieur Franklin?' Madame Du Barry glanced at Brissac questioningly, then at the American.

'He describes himself as having just landed at Nantes and bearing important despatches from America,' the manservant said. 'He has driven here post-haste.'

A minute later a young man hurried into the room, overcoat thrown loosely about his shoulders, his hair awry, and travelweary in appearance. 'I am come direct from your home at Passy, sir,' he told Franklin. 'I was informed you were not there, but after much insistence on my part and stressing the urgency of my business, your confidential servant conveyed to me where I should find you.'

Benjamin Franklin's voice trembled as he asked: 'What report bring you that is so pressing? Have our fortunes at Philadelphia failed?'

'No, sir. Philadelphia is ours again,' and as Franklin and the others uttered a great glad sigh and tension in the room slackened: 'But I bear even greater news. General Burgoyne is defeated. He and his whole army are our prisoners.'

They stared at him, dumbfounded with disbelief — even the old sage was momentarily bereft of speech. Then, with a ringing cry: 'America is saved,' he fell upon the young man's shoulders with joy.

Madame Du Barry turned to Brissac, her blue eyes ablaze with excitement: 'And the hour has sounded for France.'

12

Chagrin de l'Isle watched the chair-men make off towards Piccadilly before she turned into the alley, gloomy and chill as if the sun never reached down into its cramped confines, and knocked at the door of a narrow, low-built house, mean and dingy-looking. She heard the scuff-scuff of footsteps approaching and a man keeping well back in the doorway stood silent and immobile waiting for her to speak. She could barely distinguish his features hidden as they were in the darkness of the hall.

'Monsieur Morande?' She spoke to him in French.

'And if I am?' he asked in the same tongue. She sensed his entire form tautening with suspicion.

'I have a message for you.'

Coming closer, slanting a look along the alley towards Half Moon Street, his expression still distrustful, he muttered:

171

'Who are you?' She gave him her name and his eyelids flickered. 'To what,' with a thin sneer, 'do I owe the honour of your visit?'

She was somewhat nonplussed by the evident hostility in his manner. 'To the instructions of someone,' she answered, 'it is an honour for both of us to serve.'

Still making no move to admit her into the house he held the door only half open as if in readiness to slam it in her face, eyeing her silently up and down. 'You are from Paris?' he asked at last.

'I arrived in London last night.'

He fixed her with another long appraising glance, then held the door wide for her. As it closed she was in a musty blackness but for the glimmer of light from a room at the end of a passage. He brushed against her and she experienced chill fingers running down from the nape of her neck, so for a moment she almost panicked and would have turned blindly back and fled the house. Bracing herself resolutely, she followed him, the aroma of stale cooking, a damp and frowsty atmosphere, closing about her like a fog.

The room was shabby and ill-lit by a candle in a tallow-encrusted candlestick on the table, with tattered curtains half drawn across the tall window looking out upon a small area from which any daylight was obscured by the wall of a house opposite. A fire burned fitfully in the grate. Morande indicated an old, wing-backed chair, while he lounged by a low table scattered with books, newspapers and journals, writing-paper, quills and ink, some of the papers spattered with tallow drippings. Pushed against one wall was a sagging couch used as a bed, its bedclothes strewn in disorder, beside it a small table with the remains of a meal. Glasses and wine bottles littered the mantelpiece and a low shelf. His long dressing-robe, faded and begrimed with the stains of food and wine, was pulled carelessly over a greasy shirt and threadbare breeches.

She produced from an inside pocket of her rich sable cape a parchment envelope. Taking it from her, he tore it open with greedy anticipation and, extracting the bill of exchange, which he glanced at sharply and was apparently satisfied, next unfolded the brief, guardedly worded despatch bearing the myrtle and roses device and the Du Barry's seal, introducing the Comtesse Chagrin de l'Isle.

'What happened to Boehemer?' he asked, tapping the paper. 'This is the first advice I have received you would be taking his place.'

'A last-minute notion of Madame Du Barry's that his prospective journey had come under suspicion of Lord Stormont's spies.' As she was speaking his gaze roamed over her, appraising the curves of her slender form and every detail of the French riding-habit of elegant cut she wore.

'But as the well-known Paris jeweller travelling to London on business,' he objected, 'how should he be suspect?'

'As to that,' she answered, 'did not your last despatch advise Madame Du Barry of increasing vigilance in London as the result of reports from Lord Stormont?'

A trace of amusement showed on his unhealthy, pale, cadaverous features. 'It is true,' he conceded, 'there is a heightening

174

wave of opinion in London that most any French visitor is a potential spy. Mr. Fielding, for instance, of Bow Street, reputedly has instructed his Bow Street Runners, for whose activities he is responsible, to keep a sharp watch for secret agents from Paris.'

She was back in the crowded, stuffy courtroom that night five years ago, and then forced her attention to bear upon the business concerned with her visit to this wretched, shabby house and its unprepossessing, sinister occupant. 'We in Paris,' she told him, leaning forward earnestly, 'are aware the political climate in England has altered radically since July the fourth.'

'Thanks to my despatches,' he interposed.

'Political circles here,' she continued, 'appreciate the possibility of France seeking an opportunity to attack a Britain pre-occupied with America. London must realize even as we do the obvious disadvantage of her position should Louis recognize America's claim for independence and ally himself with her.'

'You have quite the political jargon for one so young and attractive,' he told her. He went on insinuatingly: 'I should have imagined you would prefer to employ your time less dangerously.' Regarding themselves, as he knew, second only to kings and princes, the De l'Isles traced their lineal descent from mighty Charlemagne himself, distinguishing themselves in the cause of France over the centuries. The father of the young woman facing him had been the late Louis XV's most devoted counsellor. With the king's death, De l'Isle's continued implacable hatred of France's erstwhile enemy had consequently lost him the new monarch's favour and his place at a Court which was in accord with the more cautious and placatory policy of Louis and Marie-Antoinette.

'Now,' she was saying in a businesslike voice, 'since the method of communication between Madame Du Barry and you has for the immediate future been decided, I would be glad for your advice as to the safest means of conveying information to and from Paris.'

'Do not tell me you must return so quickly!' he exclaimed in exaggerated dismay.

'I shall be here several days yet, but that we should not meet more often than is absolutely necessary must appear obvious to you.'

He was standing close to her now, bending his fixed stare upon her, a sickeningly musty odour emanating from him, so that she was conscious of the increased beat of her heart and she had to clench her gloved hands tightly to save herself from rushing out of the room. 'We may meet here as often as we choose. I live alone except for a drab who comes in to clean for me. When she remembers.' His gaze shifted from her, briefly to survey their surroundings, his face twitching with disgust. 'We may frame our schemes over supper and a bottle of wine and be in no danger at all. No danger, that is,' his face drawing closer to hers, 'except to me.'

'To you?'

'The danger,' he answered, showing his blackened teeth in a lascivious grin, 'that lies in your own fascinating person.'

She pushed back her chair to face him, quivering with furious indignation. 'You do forget yourself, *Monsieur* Morande,' and he could not mistake the underlining of the prefix.

'So *Comtesse*?' he snapped with a retaliatory sneer, 'I remember only that you and I are no longer designated by rank, save that of spy, each compelled by our trade to cheat and deceive, each, if caught, liable to the same penalty.' He drew a dirty finger significantly across his neck. 'So why not enjoy life — and love — while we may? Who knows what fatal dawn a night of pleasure may precede?'

'*Cochon!*'

She twisted away from his grasp only to find he now stood between her and the door. She turned swiftly, placing herself on the other side of the table, backing before his watchful approach, calculating how she might dash for the door and wrench it open before he caught her. With a sudden snarl of fury, he hurled the table aside, sending the papers, books and candlestick to the floor. The candle-flame sputtered a second and then went out. In the sudden darkness Morande's harsh breathing, as he came at her, seemed to fill the room.

13

Midday following his dramatic Blackheath meeting with Chagrin, Nick Rathburn sat before the sitting room fire of his St. Martin's Lane lodgings over a pipe of tobacco. His first fear as he had stared at Chagrin in the lightning flash was she would recognize him, and he by virtue of the secret nature of his employment not free to offer her the true interpretation of his circumstances. But she gave no sign she had penetrated his disguise, her face merely showing fearless scorn. 'Do you keep your hands from me.'

Then the thunder had crashed and the black swollen sky split repeatedly in ragged flashes of lightning, and the cloud-burst descended upon them. Impulsively leaning from his saddle, he pulled the head of her cloak over Chagrin's head, and, shielding her as best he could from the storm's onslaught, urged her back to the coach. Coupled with the shock of his encounter with Chagrin was the puzzling absence of Boehemer among the passengers. There being no further object in detaining them, the storm served as an admirable excuse to disentangle himself from the situation. Ordering the coachman, striving to calm his four-in-hand plunging and whinnying with terror, to drive on, he watched the Flying Hope disappear into darkness. Then seeking a short cut which would fetch him out upon the Dover Road ahead of the coach he headed his horse across the heath.

Some time later, mud-bespattered and drenched to the skin, he was back at Bow Street facing the Blind Beak, a warming glass before him. Mr. Fielding listened to what had transpired at Blackheath. With a philosophic shrug he expressed the view that Boehemer had, for reasons best known to himself or the Du Barry, delayed his journey, or decided against it altogether. The only other alternative was that the information received concerning the jeweller had been incorrect. 'Though,' the justice observed, 'the item reached me direct from a source in Paris close to Lord Stormont himself.'

Now Nick picked up and folded the newspaper he had let slide to the floor, wherein was reported the hold-up of the Flying Hope. No mention of Captain Lash's apprehension. It had been the Blind Beak's intention to give out the news of the arrest with the object of preserving the fiction it was the notorious hightobyman and not his secret agent who had waylaid the coach. Nick, however, had persuaded Mr. Fielding that the news be withheld for the time being. 'What may withholding the news of the rascal's capture gain you?' the Blind Beak had asked him.

'I knew her before,' Nick had admitted, having described the Comtesse de l'Isle's presence in the coach. 'I want to see her again.'

'You fancy you may be able to ascertain from her some indication of the reason for Boehemer's absence?'

Nick, seizing upon this excuse, readily agreed they should wait upon the result of his next meeting with Chagrin before deciding when the newspapers might publish that Captain Lash was already languishing in his cell. Nick expelled the curl of tobacco smoke and watched it obscure the sky-blue patch of window and then disappear. His mind still revolving round Chagrin's image he rose to his feet, his expression suddenly expectant, as a strange-sounding footstep halted outside.

His visitor, smirking, and shifty-eyed, stumped into the room to perch, grunting and wheezing, on the edge of the table, his wooden leg sticking out before him and which served as a peg for a foul, lice-infested old hat. Ex-blackmailer, sneak-thief and thoroughly reprehensible rascal, Ted Shadow had formed an attachment for Nick, convinced he was an elegant criminal preying upon the *beau monde*, from which fond belief it was suitable not to dissuade him. 'She is staying at Beaumont's in Jermyn Street,' Shadow was saying. 'I kept an eye peeled for when she should take the morning's air and follow her. That way I might learn what her business was in the town.' Ted Shadow's shrivelled gums showed in a grimace of mortification. 'Presently I saw her come out to get into a sedan-chair, then just as I was off after it, pox me if a passing carriage did not splash into a stinking puddle to fill me peepers with muck. When I gets them open again she had disappeared.' Nick, realizing his informant's clothes were indeed filthier-looking than usual, relit his pipe in an effort to combat the street-puddle stench permeating the warm room. 'A servant at the hotel,' Shadow continued, 'give me the news Lord Tregarth had called earlier and she is going with him and a party of friends to the Pantheon this evening.'

Nick wondered idly if the party would include a certain Sir Guy Somersham, whose wife had lived in France as a child and knew the De l'Isle family. Chagrin's companion at Bow Street on that nightmare occasion had been, as he had subsequently discovered, Somersham. It seemed apparent her visit to London would be concerned with meeting her old friends again as he queried: 'And no one else other than Lord Tregarth inquired for her, so you might have discovered if they were the object of her venturing forth?'

'I began my watch when the clocks were striking the hour of seven. Between that hour and when she went out no sight did I get of any caller for her, except him I mentioned. No messages nor nothing I would not have had a way of knowing about, for a certainty. But,' winking and smirking, 'I chanced it as how them chair-men had took her Piccadilly way. I were not far out neither, for if I did not run into the very chairmen, what I recognized as carried her, coming back empty.' His next words brought Nick's teeth clenching hard on his pipe-stem, almost snapping it in two. 'They tells me she orders them to set her down at Half Moon Alley in Half Moon Street.'

Pocketing his remuneration for the intelligence he had so perseveringly acquired, Ted Shadow took himself off several minutes later, leaving Nick in his chair staring at the fire.

Presently Nick was holding a perfumed handkerchief to his nose against the stench from a vast puddle resulting from last night's storm and fouling half the length of St. Martin's Lane. He engaged a hackney and leaned back in a corner, taking a pinch of snuff, to ponder deeply Ted Shadow's news as the carriage sped across Leicester Fields towards Piccadilly. He was in Piccadilly now, busy with traffic: great lumbering mail-coaches signalled by the sound of their post-horns, around which darted flying chaises; horse-riders making their way to and from Rotten Row; the dawdling throngs of beggars and beaux, country wenches and women of fashion enjoying the sights of the town in the crisp autumn morning. Now the hackney turned into Half Moon Street and halted. Waiting until the driver was headed back the way he had come, Nick, casually taking a pinch of snuff, gazed round him the while to note if he was under any particular surveillance. He proceeded up the street, the sounds of Piccadilly receding. As he neared Half Moon Alley, what seemed to be an animated bundle of filth and rags lunged out from the shadow of a doorway to screech at him for alms. Whether a man or a woman it was difficult to tell, as moving out of the creature's path he threw it a coin.

'God bless you, sir,' the croaking voice followed him. 'This will bring you a day of good fortune.'

At the entrance to the alley, Nick paused and, once again masking his watchfulness with a casual air, glanced about him to make sure he was not being observed. He turned into the alley and, contriving to tread quietly, neared Morande's house. The air was cold and musty with damp, and from the walls and doors of the houses around him the plaster had fallen away, the paint peeled. The windows were dark and lifeless, giving him the blank stare of sightless eyes. The door at which he stopped sagged heavily on its hinges. He swung round at a sudden movement behind him. The curtain of a window on the first floor of the house directly opposite was still moving, as if someone had been watching him and quickly dodged out of sight. His attention on the window, he waited. Several moments passed before he saw the ragged curtain move again and then suddenly the bright, darting eyes of a tiny monkey fixed on him with human-like concentration. A woman's hand appeared and grasped the animal, then the woman herself was gazing sleepily across at him, her other hand holding a robe casually about her naked shoulders. Her lazy coquettish smile changed into a pout as he turned away towards the street. He came back in a few minutes, noting that now the curtains opposite were closed. He tried Morande's door. The handle turned and he went in.

He grimaced to himself at the pungent, sour smell of the house. Becoming accustomed to the dark he moved cautiously towards the edge of light round a closed door at the end of the passage. Drawing nearer, he made out a man's voice and a woman's — Chagrin's, both speaking in French. He cursed himself for having such little knowledge of the language. All he could gather as he stood listening was the sneer in the voice he took to be Morande's and Chagrin's cool, imperious tones. A sudden movement, the scraping of a chair followed by the man's thick, rising tones and the crash of falling furniture, then the glimmer of light round the door-edge went out. At Chagrin's cry of horror, a desperate growl in the man's throat, and the girl's cry again, Nick flung the door open.

In the dim light from the curtained window and the dying embers of the fire the two faces turned to him were pale and ghostly. The man still held the girl to him, one arm round her waist, and Nick took in her disarranged clothes and terrified expression. The girl's look changed to one of amazed thankfulness, the man's eyes greeted him with implacable hatred. Nick recognized the cadaverous features and lank hair: Morande had been pointed out to him on several occasions. Suddenly the Frenchman became galvanized into action and he bent swiftly and a wine bottle smashed against the door-post a few inches from Nick's head.

In a flash Nick's hat was skimming across the room and he was out of his encumbering overcoat. The other, who had flung the girl aside, dived for another wine bottle. Nick sprang at him and they grappled, Morande uttering a flow of curses, then tearing himself out of his dressing-gown he eluded Nick's grasp and twisted across the room to where a knife gleamed beside the dirty plate on the bedside table. Chagrin gasped with horror; then Nick, catching Morande's wrist, wrenched it round so the other gave an agonized scream, pushed the knife up and away from him, his other arm clasped round the small of Morande's back. With a sudden movement Nick brought his head with terrific force under the Frenchman's chin. Morande groaned, and Nick applied more pressure on his wrist, and he heard the knife clatter to the floor. They sprawled together across the bed, and out of the corner of his eye Nick saw Chagrin dash forward and pick up the knife.

'Do you leave him to me.' Chagrin relaxed and watched wide-eyed. Morande brought his knee up into Nick's stomach, forcing him to release his grip and stagger back. Grunting with triumph, Morande swept up the small table, hurling it at Nick, who dodged aside so it merely grazed his shoulder. The Frenchman flung himself at him, but Nick managed to push off his adversary, who was kicking and struggling, with his left hand round his throat. He brought over his right fist with a terrific blow upon Morande's nose, and there was a crunch of breaking bone. In a last desperate effort Morande, blood streaming down his face, leapt towards the fireplace and grasped a heavy poker. Nick side-stepped the murderous rush, caught Morande by the waist, lifted him bodily off his feet and, with a tremendous effort, flung him against the curtained windows. The rotted window-frame gave way and with a ghastly shriek Morande disappeared, dragging a curtain after him amidst the crash and splinter of broken glass and woodwork.

Chest heaving and his face streaming with perspiration, Nick stared down from the shattered window at the crumpled figure some dozen feet below. The distorted shape made no stir but lay there, head twisted at an angle so that Nick knew Morande's neck was broken.

14

The struggle apparently attracted no attention from the neighbours, and Nick, reassuring himself Chagrin was recovered, hurried her away from the squalor of Half Moon Alley. A short distance down Half Moon Street they got into a passing hackney. As they drove off he observed: 'We seem destined briefly to meet, drive together, then bid one another adieu.'

She did not answer his bleak smile and he saw she was white faced and trembling. Gently he slipped an arm round her slim shoulders, experiencing that same leap of the blood reminiscent of the night of their first encounter.

'What will happen about him? I mean the — the body?'

Did he detect an undercurrent, not so much of horror in her question, but as if something she had recalled was arousing her fear? Fear of what? He speculated while he answered her: 'He may lie there till someone finds him or he rots. What is it to you or me?'

The shadow in her eyes faded, he thought, though answering him she gave a shiver. '*Rien, rien*. It was only the thought of him lying there.'

'He will not catch his death of cold,' he answered her grimly.

She met his sardonic expression squarely enough and covered his hand with hers. 'And he could have done the same to you, he would,' she said.

'It is a point of view towards which the vagaries of my profession incline me,' was his response as he adjusted the set of his overcoat.

As they turned into Piccadilly, Nick was considering the results of his visit to the house in Half Moon Alley. He had gone there with the object of confirming Ted Shadow's news Chagrin was keeping a rendezvous with Morande. Beyond this his purpose had been half formed: as he could not be sure what her meeting with the individual, who was the Du Barry's spy, implied. That she was acting as a courier between Paris and London appeared evident enough, though the possibility remained she might be an innocent dupe. Yet it seemed to him even if the Du Barry herself had not let fall some hint of the nature of the mission upon which Chagrin was being sent, her first glimpse of Morande, the circumstances in which he lived, would have awakened her suspicion that her errand was concerned with some business not altogether innocent.

It was unfortunate that in order to save her from Morande's attentions he had been forced to reveal himself. It behoved him to endeavour to give her a convincing explanation for his presence upon the scene if he was to have any hope of success in discovering exactly the truth about her visit to London. He congratulated himself she had not penetrated his Captain Lash disguise. Under the circumstances his appearance in Half Moon Alley might now strike her as a suspicious coincidence, and then she turned to him, her manner somewhat more animated.

'No doubt you are pondering,' she said

lightly, 'why, when I could be more comfortable with my friends, I choose to stay at an hotel.'

'Sir Guy and Lady Somersham?' She nodded and he went on. 'It was from their house I took you to Lady Harrington's,' and while her eyes widened, he explained: 'You see I discovered quite a little about you.'

An enigmatic expression flickered across her face. 'I can well believe you to be quite expert in such matters. How else could you have learned so quickly I was staying at Beaumont's?'

It occurred to him that, intuitively realizing she had come under his suspicions, she was boldly taking the initiative, to satisfy his speculations. 'How come you to be aware I acquired that information?'

'Else,' she replied, 'how came you to have sent me your message?' He frowned at her questioningly. 'That you required to meet me,' she told him, 'at the house we have but lately left?' He raised a craggy eyebrow at her. 'Your messenger very discreetly omitted to mention who had sent him, but after last night . . . '

'And you elaborate upon what chanced last night,' he said, 'that concerned either you or I. My mind is a trifle hazy.'

'Doubtless you are suffering from the effects of the drenching you received, together with your disappointment at the absence from the coach of the Paris jeweller.'

He met her mocking smile with the realization she was no longer the young girl beside whom he had sat in such enchantment five years before. He found himself wondering what had accounted for this strengthening of her personality. 'I compliment you,' he said softly, 'on having pierced my disguise.' Her look took in that sardonic lift at the corners of his dark jutting brows, the glint in his long black eyes, now veiled by sleepily drooping lids. 'I set one of my cronies at once to discover where you were residing,' he explained to her.

'I would have known your hands anywhere,' glancing down at the strong, broad palm with the tapering fingers. She did not add how, discovering it was none other than he, had filled her with tumultuous excitement, mingled with dismay at finding him pursuing still his criminal career. Since that night five years ago when, as she had ever since reproached herself, she had failed to help him in his hour of need, she had striven vainly to banish him from her faintest remembrance. The memory of him had returned to her again and again. 'That you knew me,' she said to him, 'your expression made plain.'

'At what hour did he call at Beaumont's — the fellow who brought you my message?'

'Ten o'clock this morning, or thereabouts.'

Ted Shadow had been emphatic no one else but Lord Tregarth had asked for her at the hotel. When it came to keeping watch upon the unsuspecting object of his attention his lynx-like eye could not be questioned, and his having no reason to be other than honest in his report, Nick knew Chagrin was lying.

'What did he look like? A desperate-seeming rogue stumping upon a wooden leg?' His casual tone gave her no indication of the trap he was baiting for her. It was obvious she was seizing upon her recognition of him last night to explain away her visit to Morande. Did not this anxiety to forearm herself against any doubt he might hold regarding her rendezvous at Half Moon Alley imply her sense of guilt? None the less, she was too shrewd to be caught by his question.

'Just an ordinary man,' she answered, adding she had been so puzzled at the time to receive the message she could not remember rightly how he looked.

Nick must be careful not to let her suspect he was aware she was lying. 'All this is most interesting,' he said, 'since I sent you no message.'

She looked at him in excellently simulated surprise. 'Then who did? Who else could have known you and I were already acquainted?'

'The messenger omitted to mention my name,' he reminded her. 'You merely assumed he came from me.'

She gave him a perplexed frown. 'But no one except my friends knew I was in London.'

'One person there is who does not occur to you,' he answered, experiencing a curious sensation as if he were a cat playing with a mouse. Her look was innocently blank. 'Morande, receiving intelligence from France of your journey, planned to entangle you in some nefarious scheme he had in mind. He would have his own means of learning where you were to be found in London.'

'And I believing it was you had sent me the message,' she said, as if in acceptance of his theory. His hopes gave a sudden leap at the slender chance that what he had been saying for her benefit might, in fact, have a basis of truth. He tried to pretend Ted Shadow had either by some mischance failed to discover there had been another caller for her that morning at Beaumont's, or had forgotten to mention it to him. She shuddered. 'Thank *le bon Dieu* you arrived when you did.' Then she queried: 'How did you know I should be there?'

'My livelihood depends no less upon my obtaining information regarding persons in whom I am interested,' he replied glibly.

Appearing satisfied with his explanation, she said lightly: 'I had no notion my visit would be the object of so much concern. Since you know so much about me, it seems superfluous I should have to confess my motive for journeying to London.' At the pressure of her fingers in his, the hard lines of his face softened, a tenderness flickered at the corners of his mouth. Was he about to come by so easily the truth behind her meeting with Morande? 'You do not appear over-curious.'

'You mistake me,' he replied. 'I am speechless with curiosity.'

'Though I have tried not to admit it to myself,' she began slowly, as if uncertain how he would take what she had to say, 'I would not come to London again for fear of meeting someone whom these past five years I sought to banish from my heart.' He was remembering her as he saw her when he had stood accused beside Casanova. As if reading his thoughts, she said: 'Forgive me for that night, when I might have shown my faith in you.'

She was buoying him up with the

promise of the fulfilment of his innermost longing, the realization of a dream he scarcely dared to dream. And yet, with her so near to him, with the allure of her voice in his ears and the haunting fragrance of her intoxicating his senses, he wanted only to believe every syllable she was uttering. The hackney was slowing down, for they were approaching Beaumont's and he felt a sinking of the heart.

'May I hope,' she was pleading softly, 'for your continued interest in me during the remainder of my visit?'

'You do forget,' he smiled at her thinly, 'the nature of my profession. It may be you will see me again at Bow Street. Or' — nonchalantly flicking a speck of dust from an immaculate knee of his black velvet breeches — 'perchance you may witness me perform my little jig at Tyburn.'

Her face paled and her finger-tips dug into his hand. 'At least let me thank you for saving me from that dreadful creature.' She passed a hand across her face in the manner of one collecting her thoughts. 'I shall be at the Pantheon tonight.'

201

'I had a mind to attend there myself,' he interrupted her. She hesitated and he continued reassuringly. 'Do you not concern yourself Lord Tregarth will recognize me as Captain Lash.'

The carriage-door was opened. 'Tonight then,' she nodded, and crossed to the hotel entrance, there to glance over her shoulder at him, glimpsing the white streak in his hair as he raised his hat.

Presently he stood again outside the house in Half Moon Alley. The curtains across the window at which he had seen the woman and the monkey were still closed, no sign of anyone watching. No sound as he made his way along the gloomy passage to the room. The door was open as he had left it, hurrying Chagrin away; the draught through the smashed window bellied one tattered curtain into the room — the other had been dragged down with Morande. He took a cursory look through the window, saw the inert form still lying, the head twisted. Satisfied no one was approaching, he crossed to the fire and kicked an ember into a flickering flame. From it he lit a taper and found the candle which had been precipitated to the floor. By its light he searched among the scattered books and papers on the floor.

He found what he was looking for in a pocket of Morande's discarded dressing-gown, a folded piece of paper, which, as he held it up to the light, exuded that faint elusive perfume he had come to know so well. Written in French, it bore no address, only the embossed myrtle and roses and dated four days before. The few sentences were addressed to Monsieur Morande and appeared, so far as he could decipher them, to introduce the Comtesse Chagrin de l'Isle. No signature, just a seal inscribed 'D.B.'.

He caught the faint but distinct echo of footsteps in the alley. Returning the paper to the dressing-gown pocket, he snuffed the candle, and slipped like a shadow out of the room. Making out a short flight of stairs ahead of him, he ascended them as the front door opened. He waited there in the darkness, glimpsed a glow of candle-flame, then sounds of someone moving round the room he had just left as if searching. There was a sudden silence. The candle went out, footsteps receded slightly along the passage, the front door opened and closed once more.

The echo of the footsteps in the alley died away and he returned to the room where that intriguing perfume lingered and looked for the folded paper in the dressing-gown pocket. It was no longer there.

15

As the Somershams' carriage drove off from Drury Lane she leaned back in the corner exchanging conversation with Sir Guy and his pretty young wife, and all the time the image of that tall, rakish form in black engrossed her mind to the exclusion of aught else. She had sat in the box at the theatre apparently intent upon David Garrick storming his way through *Richard II*, never hearing a word of the play nor seeing the actors in their splendid costumes, her ears and eyes filled only with that other voice, that other figure. Just as when before the performance she had accompanied the Somershams into the green room to gossip with friends and acquaintances, she had been keyed up in the hope that across the chattering throngs of elegant beaux and women of fashion Nick Rathburn's dark, sardonic gaze would suddenly meet hers.

'Do you not concern yourself Lord

Tregarth will recognize me as Captain Lash,' he had reassured her, but she could not help feeling fearful for his safety, which conflicted with her longing to see him again. Since he had left her at Beaumont's she had been the victim of a turmoil of emotions at war with one another. Her heart raced with excitement at the memory of Nick bursting in to save her. The sense of elation with which his presence had uplifted her then mounted in intensity as the hour approached for her visit to the Pantheon. Dawdling luxuriously in her bath, fragrant with perfume, the serving-maid had several times been obliged to disturb her from her reverie, and never could she remember having taken so long before her mirror, over the elaborate mode in which she arranged her hair and her apparel. Sir Guy and his wife and others at the theatre had remarked upon her loveliness and the heightened brilliance in her eyes.

'La, Chagrin darling,' Lady Somersham was remarking now as she leant across to her, 'and I did not know your heart were made of ice, I could believe you to be at last in love.'

She gave a little start and then smiled enigmatically. 'It is the excitement of seeing you both,' she explained, 'and London again.'

The glare of light from a street-booth they were passing as they drove into Oxford Street illuminated the interior of the carriage, their gleaming jewellery and magnificent apparel only half cloaked by the dominoes they wore, and she perceived a look pass between the Somershams. 'Fine cooked eels for sale,' the booth proprietor was shouting, 'fine cooked eels, all piping hot.' Suddenly a louder commotion arose from the crowd pressing round the booth and another cry was taken up by a score of voices: 'The Bow Street Runners . . . A thief has been taken.' With dread clutching at her heart, Chagrin glimpsed a bedraggled wretch struggling in the grip of two burly men, whose red waistcoats showed distinctly in the harsh light of the flares.

'Some rogue taken by the Blind Beak's men,' Somersham said, and Chagrin caught a glint in his eye. 'Soon every footpad and rascal will be cleared from the roads.'

'Did the sight upset you?' Lady Somersham asked her, and she forced herself to give a casual shake of her head. She must learn to mask her thoughts. She reassured herself that, even if she cried out the truth behind her presence in London, the Somershams would merely conclude she was joking or had taken leave of her senses. How would they comprehend the complex pattern of motives which had impelled her to play her sinister role? Fruitless to explain to them how her father, faithfully serving his beloved Louis, *le Bien-Aime*, had, upon France's defeat by the English twelve years before, suffered unendurably. On his death-bed he had wrung from his young daughter the vow she would help restore France's glory and pride. The new king with his Austrian queen sought friendship with Britain in an effort to forget past bitterness. The De l'Isles, remaining implacably opposed to such a policy, had banded themselves with others in France, equally devoted to the dead Louis XV's memory. This faction, advocating war with Britain, were to find their leaders in Brissac and the Du Barry.

Tutored and encouraged by the rest of the De l'Isles she had bent her mind and energy to one end. Such, for instance, was her inner motive for engaging herself in friendship with the Somershams. Concealing her true feelings was something she came to regard as a stratagem which, her mentors argued, the English themselves never shrank from adopting. She would hear Sir Guy boast how, an officer on Wolfe's staff during the last war, he had deliberately used his wife's acquaintanceship with certain people in France who had links with French-Canadians in order to obtain items of information required. 'All is fair in love and war,' he had laughed complacently. 'If we have to fight the French again I would do the same.' The English capacity good-humouredly to fraternize with a defeated enemy encouraged Chagrin to imagine spying against them was a game, a kind of charade with nothing sinister about it, only a hint of danger that made it exciting. Her encounter with Morande had for the first time forced upon her the realization she had set her feet along a darker path.

Was it because, she wondered now, she herself pursued this subtle way of duplicity that Nick Rathburn had aroused in her an overpowering attraction? Had she found in him, professional criminal treading a tight-rope of danger, one slip from which would precipitate him to ignominious destruction, her affinity?

'We are here!' Somersham exclaimed as the carriage came to a halt. Sir Guy escorted his wife and Chagrin towards the entrance of the Pantheon, the ugly exterior only partly revealed in the torch-light and lantern glow.

'La, but we must mask ourselves,' Lady Somersham cried, and Chagrin and her husband followed her example, producing their black masks. A dense crowd, laughing and chattering, joking and ogling, milled about them in the entrance vestibule, everyone's elegant attire hidden by dominoes of all colours and every face masked. Chagrin and the Somershams drifted with the stream of revellers into the large ballroom which was embellished with every luxury. Overhead, suspended from the beautiful stuccoed ceiling, represented as the heavens filled with gods and goddesses, hung a magnificent chandelier of enormous dimensions throwing its light upon the galleries supported by gilded pillars and the surrounding walls panelled to represent Raphael's loggia in the Vatican, while the friezes and niches were edged with alternate lamps of green and purple glass.

Already the floor was overflowing with dancers. Somersham had just sighted the loggia occupied by Lord Tregarth and his party when a sudden stentorian voice caused Chagrin to turn round.

'Watch your pockets. This is Townsend, the Bow Street Runner, warning you all. Watch your pockets, I say.' Regally making his way through the crowd, Chagrin saw a tub-like figure masked and wearing a domino which fell away to reveal the robin-red waistcoat indicating his profession.

'It is the famous Mr. Townsend,' Lady

Somersham exclaimed, and again Chagrin experienced that feeling of dread, though quickly forcing herself to show a smile of interest.

'One of Mr. Fielding's crack thief-takers,' Somersham put in. 'Always to be seen at these sort of assemblies and a great favourite with the sprigs of fashion.' By now the police officer was becoming obscured from view as, followed by admirers, he continued on his way round the ballroom uttering his familiar cry: 'Watch your pockets. It is Townsend warning you all. Watch your pockets, I tell you.'

The panic fluttering Chagrin's heart subsided, and so as not to arouse the others' notice she would cast a glance about her hopefully for a sight of that tall, dark form. Lord Tregarth's loggia was decorated with little coloured lanterns and she and the Somershams edged their way through those crowded round Lord Tregarth, making himself heard above the music and chatter extolling Jem Morgan's prowess in the prize-ring.

Those who were not interested in

prize-fighting were giving their attention to the huge platters of oysters and bottles of champagne. Pausing in his account of how his stalwart protégé had finally overcome his opponent, the Orleans Butcher, Lord Tregarth greeted Chagrin effusively. She was at once the object of admiring glances from the men and envious looks from their fair companions. Chagrin sipped absently at her champagne and pretended to evince interest as for the benefit of his listeners her host launched himself into a graphic account of how the Flying Hope had been waylaid on Blackheath. He had toasted Chagrin in praise of her intrepid demeanour in the face of danger, when there was a sudden disturbance outside the loggia, the raucous voice of a broadsheet-seller was heard above the laughing chatter and lively music. 'Captain Lash, the highwayman, taken. Read the story of his life and wicked crimes.' The stem of Chagrin's glass snapped in her fingers, and at her evident distress several glanced at her so that she was thankful for her mask which partly concealed her terror-stricken

213

expression. 'What is it, darling?' Lady Somersham wanted to know as Lord Tregarth gallantly applied his fine lace handkerchief to the champagne which had splashed her domino.

'*Ce n'est rien*,' she gasped. '*Ce n'est rien*. I felt a little faint,' and she murmured apologetically to Lord Tregarth, who called for another glass of champagne. The broadsheet-seller had gathered a morbidly curious throng about him as he repeated his cry, and she could see him waving the broad-sheets he was offering for sale. Lord Tregarth turned to her triumphantly. 'Do you hear the news, Mademoiselle la Comtesse? They have nabbed the scoundrel who waylaid us last night. I told him I would see him jig at Tyburn, and by God I will.' Someone passed a broadsheet to him and Chagrin saw the crude black lettering blazoning forth the notorious highwayman's arrest. Lord Tregarth handed her the broad-sheet to read. 'You have not been to Tyburn, Mademoiselle la Comtesse? This is a unique opportunity to spend an amusing hour. We will make a party.' His enthusiastic smile included the Somershams and others around him. 'It will be a memory of London to take back to Paris with which you may regale your friends.' And then cutting the hubbub of music which mocked her and the babble spinning about her came a voice smooth as silk in her ear.

'And I cannot offer you a more intriguing memory than that of a stretched neck to take back to Paris, Mademoiselle la Comtesse, I will hang at Tyburn myself.' She swung round to stare up into Nick Rathburn's black mask, his eyes gleaming sardonically, his saturnine smile bent upon her.

16

She continued to stare at him without being able to speak. Some fop behind her called out: 'I would know those lean chops despite any mask. Nick Rathburn, upon my life.'

'Monsieur Rathburn,' she struggled to say, 'I little expected to meet you — '

She was interrupted by an exclamation from Lord Tregarth. 'By God,' he said to Somersham, 'and I did not know Captain Lash was in the Bow Street Runners' hands I would have mistaken him for the villain.'

Chagrin noted but the tiniest flicker in the expression behind the mask. She had recovered herself sufficiently to turn to Lady Somersham. 'I met Monsieur Rathburn the last time I was in London.' She saw Sir Guy's eyebrows shoot up as she continued. 'Quite by chance we met again this morning.'

'A most fortunate coincidence,' Nick drawled.

Lord Tregarth's features seemed to have become suddenly withdrawn, and Chagrin observed a significant look exchanged between the Somershams, and interpreting it she could not but smile to herself. It was obvious Sir Guy and his wife now imagined themselves in possession of the reason for Chagrin choosing to stay, instead of with them during this visit to London, at an hotel. But how, she puzzled, had he contrived to be at one and the same time a notorious highwayman languishing in gaol and here debonair and nonchalant as ever at her side? Lady Somersham and her husband manœuvred themselves besides Chagrin, the former not being able to wait to know all about him. 'Guy declares he is none other than the *notorious* Mr. Rathburn,' she whispered behind her fan. 'He is decidedly attractive. But his reputation . . . ' rolling her pretty eyes expressively upwards. 'La, darling, Guy says all the talk is he has the murkiest past, he is nothing but an adventurer.'

'Not at all the most suitable person, if I may say so' — her husband shook his head — 'with whom one should become too friendly.'

Chagrin laughed lightly. 'Truly I am grateful to you for your warning, but be assured I shall not behave rashly. Anyway,' turning to Lady Somersham, 'it seems I am not the only one who finds his company amusing.'

They followed her look to where Lord Tregarth and several of his cronies, their women companions hanging on their arms, were encircling Nick Rathburn, listening to him as, in his quiet, sardonic voice, he recounted some gaming-house anecdote. 'It is his air of mystery,' Lady Somersham murmured, 'that makes him so fascinating. I am consumed with impatience to see his face when the masks are off.'

'He is quite agreeable-looking,' Chagrin smiled, 'in a somewhat bizarre way.'

The other shook her head at her in affected despair. 'Whatever may be said of his past, it is certain, darling, he has, in your estimation, quite a future.'

Her husband gave a shrug. 'You women are all alike; a man can be a thorough-paced rogue, but that his person meets your favour is all you care for.'

The orchestra had begun a minuet and Nick was approaching Chagrin with a bow. In a few moments they had joined the other dancers and she complimented him upon his buoyancy of step. 'To be light-footed,' he replied, 'is as useful an accomplishment in my profession as it is to be light-fingered with the dice, or adept at holding up a coach. But could one dance with you otherwise than upon wings?'

She tried to read what thoughts lay behind those eyes aglint in his mask and his sardonic mouth. By what miracle, she asked herself again, had he eluded the police and all the town believing he was under arrest? She gave a look in the direction of the loggia from where Lord Tregarth was watching them, beside him the Somershams, and she observed the former turn and say something to Sir Guy, who nodded and then gazed speculatively towards her and Nick.

Idly he followed her gaze. 'I advised you not to fear he would discover me.'

They were close together now in the

minuet and she found herself unable to dam up the torrent of impatience surging within her any longer. 'I must know what happened,' she whispered. 'Take me somewhere so you can tell me without any danger of eavesdroppers.'

'But your friends? You would not wish them to think you too closely acquainted with such a suspicious individual as myself.'

She glimpsed the humorous quirk at the corners of his mouth and she realized he was not entirely unaware of how much and often he must be vilified and stigmatized behind his back; and that he could smile his mocking, secret smile, all carelessly unconcerned, though such knowledge must sometimes taste not a little bitter and as of ashes in the mouth. 'I will speak to Lady Somersham,' she told him quickly, 'and make some excuse to explain my absence for an hour.'

'And an hour will be time enough for me to tell you all you want to hear?'

She caught her breath at his tone and it was as if the music soared to a celestial plane, all the colourful movement of the ballroom seemed suddenly to possess an extraordinarily magical quality. Transported, she took his hand, leading him through the dancers. 'Do you wait here, I will return as quickly as I can.'

She hurried to Lord Tregarth's loggia, where Lady Somersham came to her at once, her fan all aflutter. 'Where is he? Do not tell me you have deserted him? I could not bear to hear such news. And you have given him up so soon,' with a mischievous look towards her husband who, with Lord Tregarth, had joined the other guests attacking the oysters and champagne, 'I will find him for myself.'

'Do I look as if I have deserted him?' As the other eyed her sharply, Chagrin went on: 'He has to leave for an hour or so' — she astonished herself with the glibness of tongue with which she found herself improvising — 'some unexpected and urgent matter of business to transact — '

Lady Somersham burst out laughing. 'Can you not picture Guy's and Lord Tregarth's faces when they learn you have deserted them for your Mr. Rathburn, upon a matter of business?' she mimicked Chagrin. 'La, you are grown vastly different from when you were last in London.' Her manner grew more serious. 'Do you watch out, darling. Remember his is not the most enviable reputation in the town. I am not sure you are wise in embarking upon this escapade.'

'You have seen him tonight — do you imagine I can come to any possible danger with him?'

The other's eyebrows arched above her mask. 'It all depends upon what you mean by danger.'

'If it be that which I fancy you have in mind, then he is in as great a danger himself.'

Lady Somersham's pretty mouth opened. 'La,' she breathed, 'you *have* grown up!'

'Oh, my darling,' Chagrin grasped her hand tightly. 'He has overnight become my world.'

The pressure of her fingers was warmly returned. 'And you are happy is all that signifies. Do you not worry, I will make your excuses with Guy and the others.' Then, as Chagrin turned away with a grateful murmur, she added: 'Though you are grown up, darling, do not in your enthusiasm let yourself become too big a girl,' laughing delightedly at the shocked blush that appeared beneath Chagrin's mask.

She pushed her way through the laughing, chattering throng to where the tall, dark figure stood and, slipping her arm in his, Chagrin was led through the crowd in the direction of the vestibule. The feel of his arm, firm and strong, against the curve of her breast buoyed her up so they seemed to make their way with effortless ease. They had reached the vestibule when she experienced yet once again that dread grip about her heart. Behind her of a sudden sounded the meancing tones she had heard earlier. 'Watch your pockets, watch your pockets, I tell you.'

She swung round, gripping Nick's arm fearfully, as the rotund, pompous figure displaying his red waistcoat advanced towards them. But instead of tensing to effect a hasty departure he remained relaxed and nonchalant, giving the Bow

Street Runner a casual glance. Mr. Townsend drew nearer, she braced herself for disaster, her heart racing.

'Good evening to you, Mr. Rathburn,' and Nick inclining his head in acknowledgment of the other's greeting, 'do I see you about to take an early departure?'

'You do, Mr. Townsend, though we shall be returning later, when perhaps you would do us the honour to join us in a glass?'

'Delighted, Mr. Rathburn. I will keep as sharp a look-out for you as if you were any pickpocket,' and with a loud guffaw and an extravagant bow to Chagrin the tub-like man proceeded on his way towards the ballroom again, uttering his warning cry, Chagrin staring up at Nick utterly baffled.

'*Mais je ne comprends pas,*' she murmured helplessly. 'I was sure he must be dangerous to you.'

'Mr. Townsend is engaged only in nabbing pickpockets,' he told her mockingly, 'not the brazen rakehell you have so recklessly selected for your companion tonight.'

In the hackney which Nick had directed to convey them to the Rose Tavern in Russell Court by Covent Garden, she explained why she had become so fearful at the sight of Mr. Townsend: even had he outwitted his enemies, so they were, as seemed apparent, holding the wrong Captain Lash, Morande's body had been found and his death attributed to Nick. He reassured her that the Frenchman's reputation being so ugly, there were numerous individuals in the underworld whose deadly enmity he had incurred, of whom any one could have seized an opportunity to revenge themselves upon him. As for the police they would not trouble overmuch to seek his murderer out, being not entirely ungrateful to whoever had rid the world of so evil a villain.

Nick preferred to keep to himself the exact truth, which was that, acting forthwith upon the information he had laid before the Blind Beak, police officers had removed the corpse from the area behind Half Moon Alley, subjected the house to an intensive search for further evidence which would prove useful towards establishing the link between the French spy and his employer in Paris; and moreover that he himself had been instructed by Mr. Fielding to use his best talents to secure that precious paper the Comtesse de l'Isle had thought necessary to return and retrieve.

Chagrin was inquiring abstractedly whence they were going, and he replied non-committally to a well-known tavern of the town where they would be welcomed discreetly and where they could talk. They had discarded their masks, Nick slipping them both into his pocket, and by the street-lights' illumination and glow from shops and houses they passed they drank in each others' faces as if trying to imprint upon their memories for ever every feature, every plane and contour.

'You may observe me at the Rose in the environment to which I belong, appropriate enough for one of my status, though of doubtful suitability for the Comtesse de l'Isle,' he told her. 'Its atmosphere you will find a trifle different from your fine Paris *salons* or London's Society drawing-rooms.'

'And I am with you,' she replied, 'it matters little where we are.' She could feel herself blushing again beneath his scrutiny as she remembered Lady Somersham's last warning remark, and to cover her confusion she whispered: '*Alors*, do you recall this morning, you said how that we rode together for a brief moment in a carriage and then bade each other adieu.'

'*Alors*,' his teeth flashed at her, 'I always knew we should meet again.'

The carriage jolted through a deep puddle and as she clung to him his mind went back to that night five years since, and now as his arm round her waist held her close he found her even more yielding. Hungrily their mouths sought one another's.

'You are really you?' she asked him breathlessly. 'It is not your twin whose kisses burn me?'

'Why,' he queried, 'will not one Nick Rathburn suffice?'

'You must tell me,' she exclaimed, her

smooth brow marked by a frown of bewilderment. 'I am all impatience to know how, while the broadsheet-sellers cry your arrest and imprisonment, you are yet free — '

'Not free,' he corrected her. 'I am your prisoner. It is become not uncommon,' he explained, 'for miscreants like myself occasionally to operate masquerading as someone else in the same manner of business. A reprehensible practice, you may say, one rogue to perpetrate a crime in the name of another so the other risks being apprehended for it. But indeed is not Humanity for ever suffering for the evil others commit? This Captain Lash had several times presented his pistols at victims, declaring himself the notorious Nick Rathburn. But for the fortunate chance I was always able to prove an alibi I must have suffered innocently for the Captain's guilt.' Her fingers entwined themselves in his and her eyes were warm in the shadows of the carriage. 'Not unnaturally I grew a trifle impatient of his fondness for wearing my name and determined to pay him back when the occasion occurred, in his own coin. The occasion arose last night.'

'I never knew,' she murmured. 'I thought it was you.' He took her in his arms again. 'I did not think to tell you.' He shook his head at her gently. 'It is a price you must suffer for my acquaintance. Mine is an uneasy life, subject to sudden shocks and alarms, which is why no man counts me his friend.'

'And woman?'

He stared down at her for several moments without speaking, the rattle of the swaying carriage, the clopping of the horse's hooves, the crack of the coachman's whip and watchman calling the time of the night, the shouts of link-boys and sedan-chairmen and the noise of passing traffic seeming to isolate them in the silence of their own carriage and emphasize its intimacy. The hackney pulled up. 'It is the Rose,' Nick said. He handed back her mask. 'Best wear it again, or I shall spend my time repulsing blade after swaggering blade who will instantly leap to carry off so tempting a prize.'

She heard the sounds of singing and raucous hilarity within. Quickly she obeyed and clung to him tightly. The link-boy's torch flaring and hissing above them, Nick with gentle reassuring tenderness bent his mouth to hers — soft, warm — and she refusing to give up his kiss. All smirks and winks, the link-boy flung wide the tavern door and urged them into the yawning blaze of light and clamour, tobacco-smoky and heavy with the fumes of wine and gin, of beer and brandy. The clink of glasses and bang of drinking-mugs as some drunken songsters beat time to a ballad-singer, and locked still in their oblivious embrace, they were welcomed with a delighted roar of laughter, shouts of ribald encouragement and thunderous applause.

17

They were seated in a shadowed corner, the excited interest in their arrival at last dying down, though they continued long to be the object of admiring glances and knowing winks. The landlord himself, all rubicund affability and, with much bowing to Chagrin, came forward to attend to their wants, advising Nick in a conspiratorial whisper behind his hand of the excellent vintage of a recent supply of champagne to which might be added a dash of brandy of most celebrated bouquet. He then grew rhapsodical over a consignment of oysters freshly arrived that afternoon from the sea with brown bread-and-butter sliced thin as poppy-leaves; to be followed by some more substantial dish such as boiled chicken, duck roasted, boiled leg of mutton and capers, bullock's heart roasted, venison, beef steaks, chops and oxtails, roasted neck of pork, hashed fowl and beans, duck and eggs and potatoes, roast woodcock, hot rabbit or hare and cold ham and tongue, brawn, potted mackerel and prawns, trout potted and sturgeon.

They had oysters and champagne laced with brandy, followed by young chicken and celery and roast potatoes and fruits. The wine arriving at once, they drank to each other and then mine host. His arm tightly round her waist, Nick and Chagrin raised their glasses to the convivial company of the Rose, which brought forth such a roar of answering toasts the tavern rafters fairly rang and was the signal for a wall-eyed fiddler to strike up a tune, followed by the ballad-singer, a buxom doxy complexioned like a rustic wench and a shy, demure manner with her bawdy verses. Those of her audience with a fancy for it were quickly accompanying her.

So to the music and songs, the ribald roars and buffoonery about them, Nick and Chagrin, she suddenly finding herself most marvellously famished, savoured the oysters and champagne and brandy and other dishes that followed. Chagrin could not resist joining in the general laughter, for it was infectious, though her knowledge of English vernacular saved her from realizing most of the ballad-girl's innuendo and suggestiveness. Nick, explaining some of the meanings behind the so innocently sung words, sent a blush glowing beneath the mask she still wore.

The moment arrived at last when Nick must stake all on his next throw and, with characteristic nonchalance, he beckoned over a waiter and instructed him to serve a final goblet of brandy for them upstairs. 'You are very bold,' she whispered, 'so sure of yourself.' For a second he thought he had lost, that she had remembered she was the Comtesse de l'Isle and he but a no-account sharper and thief, and inwardly he reviled the fortune of birth and blood, a barrier between them which might not be surmounted even in the overwhelming transports of passion and yearning of the flesh. But, taking her hand, he found it trembling in his like an imprisoned bird and he knew then the game was his.

'How else should a gambler play,' he

asked, his voice low and husky, 'for such high stakes?' And confident now what her answer would be, he added: 'The dice, are they loaded too heavy against me?'

The upstairs room Nick had secured, all warm and bright with a blazing fire, needed no candlelight to add further illumination. It was low-ceilinged, with comfortable dark furniture and the four-poster bed wide and the sheets drawn back white and gleaming. The brandy decanter and glasses awaited them, catching the glint of the fire and the flames throwing shadows leaping on the walls. She made as if to take off her mask, but some quirk of humour bade him stop her.

'Not yet,' he said. 'Do you appear mysterious and intriguing, the far-off unattainable of my dreams.' The sweet scrape of the fiddle reached them, as the wall-eyed fiddler came stumbling up the stairs. He remained there in the darkness near their door long after Nick had thrown him several coins, his music in their ears as he tore off her mask.

When she fell asleep at last he lay

curiously wakeful, not closing his eyes while slowly the fire died until the room was in darkness. She stirred and gave a moan so that he gazed down at her face, pale and luminous in the darkness, her eyes still closed. He had watched her of a sudden lie quiet in his arms, experiencing a deep compassion and tenderness at exhaustion's final triumph over the fire ablaze within her which he had set aflame. She stirred again and flung one slim, white arm across him and moaned more loudly.

'Chagrin, darling . . . what is wrong?' But her dark-lashed eyelids were still closed: she was speaking in French in her sleep. He bent over her, listening, trying to catch the meaning of what she was saying. He wondered if she was dreaming of him, but the first name she uttered was not his.

'*Morande, Morande, ne me touchez pas avec les mains sales,*' she whispered, her face twisted with horror. '*Je suis voyagee de Paris,*' she went on. '*Je viens de la part de Madame Du Barry. Voici mes lettres de créance.*' Her voice rose.

'Non, non, Morande, ne me touchez pas. Lâachez moi donc. C'est pour l'honneur de la France qu'il nous faut collaborer, vous et moi. C'est pour ça que je viens vous voir.' She was speaking in low tones once more. 'C'est Madame Du Barry qui m'a envoyé. C'est a cause d'elle que je suis ici. C'est pour la France que nous aimons: C'est pour venger sa defait.'

Her voice trailed off and Nick's features were grim and sharp, eyes narrowed. How the heavy thoughts which had tormented him and kept him from sleep beside her crowded in upon him, rushed the defences his mind had thrown up against them and bent them down. Throughout the previous day, since her return to retrieve from the house in Half Moon Alley the document which betrayed her as a secret agent for the Du Barry, he had at the back of his mind pondered his next move.

She moved uneasily and at the sight of her locked in the helplessness of sleep, trapped in her dreams, the conflict which had raged within him during the past hours tore at his inner-most soul with renewed ferocity. That heartrending compassion and love she evoked in him struggled once more with the deadly, unyielding demands of his profession upon the trampled battlefield of his emotions. When the little tragi-comedy had played itself out, when he had made his report to Mr. Fielding, he would have washed his hands of her. She moved again and suddenly her eyes opened and his heart constricted as he saw the fear and bewilderment of her dreams disappear from her gaze.

'*Mon amour*,' and her arms reached up to him. The irony of the web of circumstance in which he was held, that the one woman he desired above all the world should have fallen in love with him, believing him to be a desperate rogue, simultaneously with his discovery she was herself a cheat, no devil in hell could have devised.

'I fell asleep,' she was saying. 'I could not help it.'

'I know.'

'And you? You slept also?'

'I slept too,' he lied.

'But you awoke before me.'

He nodded. 'It was you who woke me,' he lied again.

'*Je te demande pardon, chéri*,' and her arms twined round him more tightly. He felt them tense briefly as he said in her ear:

'You were talking in your sleep.' She lay back amongst the pillows, her eyes wide and shining in the gloom. He saw the change in their expression as he continued deliberately: 'You spoke in French.' As he anticipated, the guarded look faded.

'I must have something on my mind,' she whispered lightly.

Now was the moment. Tell her now he was aware it was Morande and the Du Barry she had on her mind. Then she would know he knew. Or, he wondered, was it not equally likely that she, unaware of his own secret, might not suspect him of having put two and two together? 'You spoke of Morande.' He decided to put this newly-arrived-at possibility to the test. Then after a pause: 'There was another name also.'

'Whose?' He could not mistake the

238

faint quiver of apprehension in her query.

'Madame Du Barry.' She did not answer and, affecting a shrug, he went on casually. 'Though why mix such an oddly assorted pair in your dreams, only you can say . . . ' Of a sudden she began trembling violently, crying out as heartrendingly as any utterance of her dreams. 'What is it, beloved?' Impulsively he held her to him as if she were a child. She was shivering in his arms like one assailed with the ague. He could hear her teeth chattering while he sought to comfort her with his kisses. After some minutes he stood beside the bed.

'Where are you going? Do not leave me.' Her voice was so piteous he knelt beside her again. 'Do not leave me.'

'Some brandy will warm you.' He moved quickly across the darkened room and half filled a glass from the decanter.

'I — I am all right,' she murmured, and he took the glass from her and she lay in his arms, her trembling subsiding. He began to feel the warmth stealing through her slender, rounded body.

'It was only a nightmare. It is finished

now. It will trouble you never again.'

'*Au contraire*. The nightmare is only just beginning.'

'Morande is dead.'

'*Il est mort*,' she said, 'but I am alive. I must go on in his place. Oh, Nick. Suddenly I feel so desperately alone.'

He clasped her more tightly to him. '*Au contraire*,' deliberately mimicking her to give her assurance. 'You are not alone. You have me.' She began talking wildly in French until he quietened her. 'Tell me what it is you so greatly fear. I will face it with you.' And a spate of words burst from her so fast in her own tongue and in English he had constantly to interrupt her in order to understand what she was saying. She told him how she had become involved in the scheming of those in France concerned with Britain's ruin. How, on this last journey to London, she had been entrusted by the Du Barry to take Boehemer's place. He listened, his brain divided into two, one half all keyed up grasping at the significance of her revelations, the other dragging back at the dread future lying in wait for her. He pretended he had difficulty in understanding the implication of her story, until at last he could not help but realize she was a secret agent for France.

'Do not despise me,' she implored him. 'Love me no less because of what I am.'

He gave not a damn in hell for politics or governments, he answered her; his whole preoccupation was with his private war against society; whatever quarrel France sought with Britain was not his concern. He was no soldier to be slaughtered upon some bloody field battled over for what cause no one, not even the generals and the kings urging their armies forward, could remember. She appeared convinced by the sentiments he expressed. 'I felt so alone, I had not realized before — before Morande's death what a dark road I had taken. Listening to Madame Du Barry it seemed a noble, worthwhile cause I was serving.' As if speaking her thoughts aloud, she said: 'You are fortunate in owing no one your allegiance.' His expression grew speculative as she continued. 'You are an adventurer, a soldier of fortune, wearing your loyalty on your sleeve.' What was she driving at? he conjectured, for there was no doubting the underlying significance of what she was saying. Her eyes were burning into his beseechingly. 'Fate threw us together again at an hour when of all men you were the one I needed most. Oh, Nick,' she moaned desperately, 'you will help me?'

Her words struck him with the same impact, the same revelational force as that lightning flash by whose illumination he had glimpsed her on Blackheath two nights since. Now, instead of the shock of recognition, he was probing for the first time into the workings of her mind in all their subtle cunning. Now his ice-cold brain was informing him she had plotted to lure him on to taking Morande's place ever since the latter's death. Had she not just now declared how he must appear in her estimation? An adventurer without allegiance, a desperate rascal who would sell his birthright without compunction, so the price were tempting enough.

A bitter fury possessed him, the realization driving deep, with all the piercing thrust of a dagger, into his vitals. How she had used her feminine guile to secure him for her traitorous cause. With cold-blooded calculation she had played her part, had even sold herself to him; bought, so she believed, with her body his complacent agreement to assume the badge of infamy she held forth. How could he have been so vain, so dazzled by her wiles, to credit that he could ever gain her proud aristocratic heart? Her body, yes, he had possessed that, she had debased herself to that low level out of her twisted sense of patriotism.

They were both impostors, he mused, and then with an inward wry smile: except that he had not required to counterfeit his love for her. Even as these thoughts filled their place in his reckoning, he was automatically responding to the instincts of his profession. 'The credentials you carried, which introduced you to Morande? In whose possession are they now?'

She regarded him mutely, her glance searching his face, and then she told him what he already knew: of her return to the house in Half Moon Alley to recover what might prove to be damning evidence of her hidden intent. While he was promising himself he would have no difficulty in transferring the precious paper to his own person and that soon, either surreptiously or upon some pretext, to be passed on for the attention of the Blind Beak, she whispered: 'France will reward you, I vow it, as England never will.'

'And I am rewarded in cash I will rest content,' he drawled, with a disinterested shrug. 'Think you not I would spy for your Du Barry on any other account.'

She stared up into his face and then with languorous grace her slender white arms reached for him. 'And I?' she asked him slowly. 'I too am part of the bargain.'

18

Nick took breakfast at the Piazza Coffee-house, Covent Garden, after leaving Chagrin, pale-featured and sleepy-eyed, safely at Beaumont's, arranging to meet her again that night. The gossip at the coffee-house tables, which could not fail occasionally to interrupt his deep and troubled cogitations regarding Chagrin, seemed concerned entirely with the political situation both in America and also nearer home across the Channel.

Since the staggering news of General Burgoyne's disastrous capitulation had reached London several days before, rumours had become rife; people everywhere found themselves suddenly confronted with the possibility the war with America might be turning against hitherto all-conquering British arms. It seemed certain Louis XVI, inspired by America's success at Saratoga, would recognize the latter's independence as a first step towards forming an alliance with her, preparatory to openly declaring war upon Britain.

Wrapped up as he was in the toils of an exigency which struck at the very foundations of his own future, Nick could give but little ear to the talk and argument, surmise and speculation. Yet even when later that morning he inquired at Bow Street he was informed by Mr. Bond that for once the Blind Beak was not in court. 'The news, Mr. Rathburn,' the clerk, his eyes darting at him over his spectacles, hastened to impart, 'is that the Earl of Chatham is coming out of his retirement to make his counsel heard once more in Britain's hour of crisis. Mr. Fielding has gone to the House of Lords to hear the great man.'

In the early afternoon Nick continued his usual rounds, calling at the clubs and gaming-houses, visiting his tailor to discuss the cut of a new waistcoat, encountering all manner of rumours upsurging wave upon wave, against which theme of suspicion and hatred, bellicose tempers and sword-rattling his preoccupation with Chagrin provided a counter-point. At a time when he should be alert, his blood coursing through his veins the swifter at the blaring challenge of outside events, England's enemies threatening to arise on every side to crush her, his energies instead were concentrated upon the woman from whom he had extracted her admission she was a spy.

When later he called once more at Bow Street there was no sign of Mr. Fielding, and Mr. Bond conducted him upstairs to the sitting room there to await the other's return, leaving Nick to pace up and down the familiar, untidy room. It was growing dark when he crossed to the window as, amidst the rattle of passing carriages and rumble of carts, the shouts and mutters of wayfarers, he distinguished the sound of wheels drawing up outside. Into the light cast by the street-lamp and a lantern held aloft by a police officer the massive figure, swathed in his voluminous cloak, stepped from his carriage. Some moments later footsteps ascended and the sitting room door was flung open by Mr. Bond, who followed the Blind Beak in.

'Would you had been with me, young

Nick,' Mr. Fielding exclaimed as he was helped off with his cloak. He sniffed loudly as, rubbing his pudgy hands together, he made for the fire. 'By the dust your footsteps have raised pacing the carpet you have been awaiting me with not a little impatience to hear my news.' He turned to his clerk who stood at the door preparatory to leaving. 'You also, Mr. Bond, should have been present to witness such an historic occasion.'

'He spoke, the great Pitt,' said the magistrate, slowly wagging his head from side to side, 'the last speech he will ever make. He rose from his bed of sickness, bounded by despair at the ruin of our hopes in America and horror at the threat of invasion by those damned French. For, Mr. Bond' — stabbing a finger in the latter's direction — 'if France's fleet should join against us, where is our navy to protect our coasts, scattered as it is all over the Atlantic?' Mr. Bond duly drawing a whistling breath through his teeth, the Blind Beak proceeded: 'Despite his age and enfeebled heath, Pitt could not let go by the Duke of Richmond's motion to the

House our troops be withdrawn from America, without raising his voice in protest.'

'How did he answer the Duke of Richmond's motion?'

'Do you not be as impatient as Nick here, and I will come to it. That was the question,' Mr. Fielding went on, 'everyone was asking. What would Pitt, who had saved North America from the French, who had always criticized our tyrannous notions towards the Americans, what would he say now to Richmond's demand we quit America for ever? You had to cup your hands to your ears to hear him when, struggling with his crutches, he got to his feet to speak. 'I am old and infirm,' he said. 'I have more than one foot in the grave. I have made an effort almost beyond my strength to come here this day to express indignation at an idea which has gone forth of yielding up America.' His voice had risen but now it grew weak again as he spoke about France. 'Shall we,' he said, 'who, fifteen years ago, were the terror of the world, now stoop so low as to tell our ancient, inveterate enemy to take all we have, only give us peace? Let us at least make an effort and, if we must fall, let us fall like men.' He tried to say more, but the words would not come, then he fell back and those around me could see death written on his face.'

Mr. Fielding sat down as Mr. Bond poured him some wine and, as he motioned the latter to fill his own and Nick's glasses, he said: 'Not a doubt of it, these damned Americans' success at Saratoga will result in our being encircled by bitter enemies. Against which threat we must close the ranks.'

The Blind Beak put down his glass and shifted his massive bulk in his chair so that his black-bandaged face was bent upon Nick. 'What brings you here tonight? Has your pretty little Comtesse given you some hint why Boehemer was not on the coach?'

'I have some news on that score,' Nick replied guardedly and received an anticipatory nod before the other turned to Mr. Bond with instructions regarding court business for the morrow. The clerk closed the door behind him and Nick, under the impression the Blind Beak had sensed he wanted to talk to him confidentially, was ready to plunge into the subject so crowding his mind. It became at once apparent to him, however, it was because Mr. Fielding, himself, wanted to confide in Nick that he had got rid of Mr. Bond. There was an air about him of suppressed excitement which Nick, obsessed with his own preoccupation, had failed to notice until now.

The Blind Beak leaned forward, his hand reaching for Nick's arm. 'I was at the House of Lords upon other business, seeking advice on how to achieve an ambition which has been nagging at my very soul these past several years.' He pinched his double chin between thumb and forefinger. 'As none is more aware of it than you, this activity in my office has procured me esteem, which acceptable advantage has at the same time rendered me, shall we say, obnoxious to sharpers and cheats, thieves and robbers, whose wicked designs have been my vigilance to defeat. Were, therefore, His Majesty to be graciously pleased to confer upon me the honour of a knighthood, it would greatly strengthen my power and add much to my' — he coughed and corrected himself — 'to the Bow Street Runners' influence.'

Before Nick, somewhat confounded by the import of the other's disclosure, together with the realization of what the Blind Beak's ambition would mean to the object of his visit tonight, could make suitable reply, from the street was indistinctly heard: 'Pitt . . . the old man has gone . . . The Earl of Chatham is dead.'

They sat there in silence, the magistrate shaking his head gently to himself. 'Now indeed the last dim lamp of England is out,' he muttered, 'now indeed darkness folds the straining ship, and the breakers roar.'

The voices below passed and faded and then: 'Frankly do I tell you my wish to be still more useful to the community is the true motive behind this honour I seek. In order to achieve that upon which I have set my heart,' he went on, 'I needs must have the attention of His Majesty directed to some outstanding achievement. A *coup* of such spectacular nature the tongues in every club and coffee-house in the town will be set wagging.' Then the Blind Beak leaned forward to prod Nick in the shoulder. 'This creature, the Du Barry, for instance? And I could furnish proof positive to the Government of her machinations against us, that would be the sort of feather in our cap I have in mind. If only we had nabbed Boehemer, and as a result unmasked her, so Louis could be confronted with evidence of that woman's activities.'

He broke off as Nick got to his feet and began pacing up and down once more. He had but to inform the other he had the very means by which the Du Barry could be brought to ruin and disgrace and he knew without any possibility of doubt what the Blind Beak's response would be.

'I had imagined you had been impatient for my return' — the words reached Nick from the massive figure in his chair to halt his agitated pacing — 'on account of some item of information you had to impart to me, some significant hint secured from this Comtesse de What's-her-name. But is your imitation of a caged beast of the jungle indicative, in fact, not of your eagerness to confront me with news but of your own harassed state of mind?'

Nick wheeled round, filled with the not unfamiliar sensation that the other possessed some uncanny facility for probing into his innermost thoughts. Oppressed as one whose soul would be for ever damned, he stood before the Blind Beak and began speaking with grim urgency.

19

Madame Du Barry sat before her mirror, her magnificent hair knotted on the nape of her neck, and began preparing herself for the day. As always at times like this, she was reminded of the days when she had been the king's mistress. Wistfully she recalled how, at the mirror of her bedroom in the royal palace itself at Versailles, surrounded by her women-servants, she would receive her dressmakers: Mesdames Sigly, Pagelle, and the celebrated Bertin, with their hoop petticoats, full-dress costumes, cloaks of velvet and gowns of cloth-of-gold. She had adored expressing her taste in dress, inspiring every ingenuity and imposing upon the mode every coquetry she could devise.

Now, she remembered with a sigh, as the morning went on the courtiers would gather round her beribboned dressing-table, profuse with their compliments and jokes, delighting in her pretty childish laughter, while Nekelle, her favourite hairdresser, bent all his artistic delicacy to the task of building her fair tresses into the most ingenious example of his art. Then would follow a whole procession of the royal jewellers, always with some novelty to offer her, most imaginatively and artistically conceived by the greatest craftsmen of the day. They knew her passionate fondness for jewellery and would show her pearls, brilliants and gems of all kinds with which she loved to adorn herself.

Her recollection of an account she had once paid the jeweller, Boehemer — a million livres — brought her mind back to the present. At any hour now she would be receiving news from the Comtesse de l'Isle. She was impatient not only for the secret intelligence she was counting upon her having obtained and which Franklin would now be even more eager to see, but for the Comtesse's account of how the news of Burgoyne's crushing defeat had struck London. All Paris was rife with rumours of what the king intended since the signal fire had flamed across the Atlantic. Daily her lover brought her fresh items depicting the king's indecisiveness in this inspiring hour, when he should have struck bravely against England.

A tap on the bedroom door, and her *femme-de-chambre*, answering it, returned to convey the message Monsieur le Duc wished to see her. Madame Du Barry glanced at the clock, which indicated it was approaching the hour of eleven, somewhat early for Louis-Hercule to call. No doubt but that he had news of some urgency. Throwing the robe which her woman held for her round her shoulders, she went out into her boudoir where Brissac was waiting. 'What is amiss?' She saw at once the tenseness in his handsome blond features.

'I fear my news will upset you,' he told her. She glanced out of the windows at the greyness of the morning, her mind involuntarily returning to those other days when the skies over Paris had always been blue, the sun always shining. 'I have just left Lenoir.' At his mention of the name of the dreaded *Cabinet Noir's* ruthless chief she gave a gasp of dismay. 'I have always held it an error to underestimate one's foes. When the enemy is the English, it is an even greater mistake not to regard them with the utmost seriousness. It would appear your choice of the Comtesse Chagrin de l'Isle was not altogether a happy one.'

'She could not have been more suitable,' she flashed at him. 'As devoted to the cause of France as was her father before her and all the De l'Isles. A clever, cold-hearted young woman who has many friends across the Channel whom she has known a long time. How was it likely she would be suspected?'

'Nevertheless,' he replied, 'there is a certain police official in London, a blind man whom they call the Blind Beak, whose suspicions she aroused.'

'The Blind Beak,' she breathed. 'Morande spoke of him — '

'Morande *est mort*,' he told her. 'Found with his neck broken.'

'And Chagrin de l'Isle?' she regained her voice to ask, as she recoiled at the shock of his disaster-charged words.

'On her way here.'

Omitting to catch the cryptic tone of his reply, she clasped her hands together with a little smile. 'She will be able to tell us everything.' He shook his head and her voice rose in alarm. 'What do you mean? What have they done to her?'

'Nothing, as yet.'

'You were saying you have just left Lenoir,' her tone sinking to a whisper, 'after Louis himself had sent for you?'

He put an arm about her consolingly. 'His Majesty knows everything.' She held her head with that high arrogance he knew so well. 'No more,' she flung at him, 'than that I am a true patriot. That all I have done has been out of my love for France. Just because he and his Austrian butterfly are ready to bow the knee to those *cochons* across the Channel — '

'No use reviling the king and queen,' he told her gently, she subsiding somewhat before the calming influence of his phlegmatic personality she had come to understand and cherish. 'Since he came to the throne Louis has made clear to us the nature of his foreign policy. Even though all France is surmising he is about to effect a change in that direction, to ally us with the Americans, officially we are neutral in the war between them and Britain.'

'What could have happened in London?' she interrupted him.

'It would appear for some time the British secret service have suspected Morande was a spy planted by you in London. Their government required only proof to demand of Louis your activities be considerably curtailed. Your Comtesse,' he went on, despite her indignant exclamation, 'was trapped into supplying just that proof. There were, I believe, credentials from you, introducing her to Morande, and a sum of money you were paying him for his services.'

'Credentials — money,' she burst out. 'There was nothing wrong in that. The Comtesse could have been meeting Morande upon some business matter.'

He shook his head. 'But for the fact that your communication was tested for secret writing.' She drew a short breath as if he had struck her in the face. He continued. 'Your hidden message urging

Morande to supply detailed information regarding the amount of arms being shipped to America was deciphered.' He gave a sudden jerk of his head towards the window and moved to it. As she joined him she heard the rattle of wheels in the courtyard. Looking down, she saw the carriage drawing up and recognized the coachman's uniforms, the coat-of-arms upon the doors. 'The Comtesse de l'Isle,' she exclaimed. 'You told me she had been arrested.'

'Do you see that figure there in the shadows?' The courtyard lay dark beneath the sullen sky, and emerging from below the overhanging balcony she saw a form she knew at once to be one of Lenoir's secret police. Even as she watched, another man approached, and then she caught a movement a little further along and two similarly sinister shapes advanced towards the carriage as it halted.

'This manœuvre,' Brissac's voice rasped in her ear, 'serves two purposes. It establishes the connection between you and the Comtesse, while at the same time serving you warning to meddle no further in matters of politics.' She ground her teeth with fury, as he went on in the same calm tones. 'Lenoir's opinion is that His Majesty has behaved with remarkable leniency towards you. In order satisfactorily to placate London's protests at France's un-neutral activities, he has had to find a scapegoat. How much more delighted the English would have been had Louis named you, instead of which . . .'

He let his words trail off while, sick with rage and apprehension, the Du Barry watched as the coachman jumped down to open the carriage door and assist the slim young figure to alight. She stood there for a moment, smiling. Then the watchers above saw her expression change first to surprise then to frozen fear. The dark forms had suddenly stepped forward, surrounding her, and Chagrin was being ordered back into the carriage. She made as if to move towards the house, whereupon one of the men caught her arm. The coachman nearest her lunged forward in her defence. There was an instant flash and a report which echoed and re-echoed round the court-yard, followed by a scream. As the smoke cleared the coachman was revealed sprawled on his face in the mud at Chagrin's feet. A wisp of grey smoke curled slowly upwards like a gentle exhalation of breath from the pistol in the police officer's hand.

With a convulsive sob the woman at his side turned her head and, as Brissac clasped her in his arms, she moaned: 'What will happen to her?'

'The Bastille,' was the low reply. Comfortingly, her lover held the shudder-ing Du Barry close until the rattle of the carriage-wheels receded from the court-yard and finally died away.

20

Nick made his way through the early December evening towards St. Martin's Lane. Despite the fog which was strengthening from a misty hint to patches of ghostly vapour, the streets were, as usual, noisy with hawkers, vendors of hot pies — the latter especially doing a prosperous trade with passers-by seeking to reinforce themselves against the chill air — wandering ballad-singers, milkmen and milkmaids, the sellers of fresh spring-water, pedlars of quack medicines and charms, the cries of the butcher, the baker and the grocer from their stalls and shops, together with the town-crier shouting his news to the accompaniment of his inevitable bell-ringing, the scavenger pushing his evil-smelling cart and everywhere other bells of variable jangling hideousness.

Nick had but several minutes since quitted Bow Street Police Court where he had witnessed the Blind Beak's return from Buckingham Palace, having received his coveted knighthood at the hands of his most gracious Majesty, King George III. It had been something of an occasion. Crowds had collected in Bow Street to acclaim the new knight, who, as his carriage drew to a halt, had stood on the step proudly acknowledging the cheers and applause.

Back at his lodgings, Nick flung himself into his chair before the fire to sink into such a profound reverie his pipe of tobacco grew cold and he did not notice it. Inevitably his thoughts revolved around the strange trick of Fate which had so inexorably thrown Chagrin and himself together, only with equal remorselessness to tear them apart, and he himself decreed to be the instrument that was to hack away the bonds that had bound them.

At first, when his sombre meditations were disturbed by the sound of tapping at his window from the street, he concluded it must be Ted Shadow. Doubtless the one-legged rascal, observing a gleam of light from behind the drawn curtains which suggested Nick was at home, had quickly bethought himself of some item of gossip to dispose of in return for the price of a bottle of wine. The tap-tap was repeated more insistently until at last and with a sigh he raised himself from his chair and went to open the street door. It was not Ted Shadow he found facing him in the foggy darkness but a woman. He perceived her waiting sedan-chair at the same time as he caught the fragrance of her perfume. For one breath-taking moment he imagined it might be Chagrin, and then she spoke.

'I am Lady Somersham. We were introduced by the Comtesse de l'Isle one evening at the Pantheon. I hope you do recollect the occasion.'

'I do recollect it very well, but since we were all masked on the occasion, I cannot honestly say I recognize you.'

'La, you take me for an impostor?'

'You are aware of my identity,' he answered with a frankness she found engaging. 'You must also know my reputation demands I should preserve caution at all times.'

A movement of her hand from within her muff and: 'Perhaps this message I bring will convince you of my *bona fides*. It is from someone with whom we are both well acquainted. I think you will hardly need to guess at her name.' He held the door wide for her and she preceded him into his sittingroom.

'She gave it me before she left for Paris. You were to receive it in the event of certain circumstances arising.' He eyed her sharply. There was no doubt as to the implication in her words, and he was seized with a sense of foreboding. He glanced down at the letter again and then at her. 'Chagrin spoke to me of you at some length,' she was saying. 'She came to bid me *au revoir* on her way to spend her last night in London with you.'

The letter crumpled in his hand convulsively; he was remembering only too well those last hours with Chagrin before the dawn light warned her it was time to return to Beaumont's, preparatory to taking her place in the coach for Dover. 'What news have you of her now?'

'When did you last have word from her?'

It flashed through his mind this woman might know more about his relations with Chagrin than he had supposed. It occurred to him Chagrin might even have confided in her, revealing the truth behind her visit to London. He dismissed the notion as being unfounded, for he could not believe she would have given herself away even to a close friend. Would she, in order to secure some end of which he was unaware, have betrayed him to Lady Somersham? Choosing his words, he replied: 'You spoke just now of certain circumstances arising under which you were to deliver this to me.' He tapped the letter. 'Since I am ignorant of the nature of these circumstances I should be obliged to you if you would choose to enlighten me.'

She gave him a long puzzled stare. 'You do not know what befell her on her arrival in Paris?' Still he remained silent and she drew a tremulous sigh. 'That she is now imprisoned in the Bastille?'

For a moment the room seemed to spin

round so that he gripped at the table with one hand. The Bastille? What dreadful nonsense had this woman got hold of? The Blind Beak had assured him the Comtesse de l'Isle would suffer no more than a severe reprimand and the warning she must not leave France without permission, for which permission she would have to wait a long time. That, together with the knowledge that she who had imagined she was duping him had herself been duped, was to complete her punishment. Since her departure, he had, as he had expected, heard nothing from her. Only the Blind Beak had passed on the news to him to the effect that all had gone as had been arranged between those concerned in London and Paris regarding the Comtesse de l'Isle. And now what was this woman telling him?

'It has come as much of a shock to you as to us. Neither my husband nor I can possibly imagine why she should have suffered this disaster, except that the times being what they are, with hatred and suspicion mounting between us and France.' She shook her head helplessly.

'Perhaps Chagrin gave way to some trifling indiscretion when she returned to Paris and brought down upon her head this cruel onslaught from the authorities. You may know her family have since Louis XV's death been out of favour with the present régime.' He nodded absently. She seemed to be fully convinced her information was correct. 'What puzzled me was that she should have anticipated some disaster might overtake her.'

'She must have given you an explanation,' he said.

'She spoke about it lightly. A precaution, she said, against the Channel packet being wrecked or her coach meeting with an accident.'

'It must appear obvious to you,' he said, 'all this has struck me like a bolt from the blue.' She nodded sympathetically, and he continued, his jutting brows drawn together: 'You seem so sure the intelligence you have received concerning Chagrin is true.'

'We have many mutual friends in France,' she explained. 'When at first I heard nothing from her I assumed she

270

was staying with someone outside Paris. Then her continued silence caused me to have inquiries made and at last I received the truth.'

'There is no possibility of a mistake?'

'Rest assured I should not be telling you this unless my source were irrefutable. Her disappearance fits in with what I know of the methods of the Paris police. Their *Cabinet Noir* strike suddenly and secretly. Believe me, we should be fortunate if we saw Chagrin for a long time, ever again even' — her voice sank momentarily — 'but that she has influential friends. They will move heaven and earth to secure her freedom.'

'I shall go to Paris myself,' he rapped out, but she shook her head.

'Could your presence avail her more than those already there who are intimately acquainted with every subtle twist and turn of authority, in a strange city amongst strange people, who, for all we be separated by a mere strip of water, employ means very different from those we should use in similar circumstances?' Even as he protested again he must try and rescue her, must exert his utmost in an attempt to atone for his betrayal of her, for he knew now without a doubt what the crumpled letter in his hand would tell him, he grasped the logic of Lady Somersham's reasoning. 'More than likely,' the other conjectured, 'the reason for her arrest is because it is known she has friends here. Your arrival could only stress this fact, thereby increasing her danger a hundredfold. It is because I foresaw what your impulse might be that I was prompted to bring her message personally. Now, I dare say, you would prefer to be alone.'

He stood with her at the street door. '*Là*, Mr. Rathburn, try not to imagine the worst. You may rest assured everything is being attempted and will continue to be attempted to ensure her safe release. I do not doubt but that in a very short while I shall be able to bring you good news. If indeed she herself will not have communicated with you.'

Returning to the sitting room he impatiently tore open the envelope. He read slowly and re-read every word. How utterly, how cruelly he had wronged her. Here in these closely written pages, from which arose a hint of her elusive perfume and which he crushed to his mouth again and again in his agony of remorse and longing for her, she made it clear to him she was no cheat luring him to her side, but had loved him with every beat of her heart, cherished him with every particle of her being.

A little while later found him ascending the stairs towards the sitting room over Bow Street. He had set out to confront Sir John with the accusation of his perfidious concealment of the truth regarding Chagrin's fate. The police officer, however, who had admitted him into the house greeted him with the information, which in his paroxysm of bitter anger towards the Blind Beak he had forgotten, that he was being entertained by his fellow magistrates and friends to celebrate his knighthood. Telling the man he had a written message which he would slip under the sitting room door, Nick had continued upstairs with the fixed determination to await the

Blind Beak's return.

The door was, as he had anticipated, locked, but withstood the thrust of his powerful shoulder only briefly before it burst open. The curtains were pulled back so the light from the street-lamp outside added to the illumination supplied by the fire glowing in the grate. Nick took in the familiar surroundings, the table littered with papers and documents, the worn carpet and comfortable armchairs, the bookshelves from which the magistrate was wont to instruct Mr. Bond to read him aloud on matters of law and judicial procedure. Then his gaze was held by a picture that was caught in a shaft of lamplight streaming through the window. It was an oil-painting of that fat, black-bandaged figure in his magistrate's robes and hat, the gold seal bearing the arms of the City of Westminster, his badge of office suspended round his neck by a wide ribbon. It had been painted some several months since by the famous Royal Academician, Sir Joshua Reynolds, and was a source of great pride to the Blind Beak.

As he stared at it, seemingly to Nick the bland, plump face was fixed on him in return. He moved away a little and the brooding features seemed to follow him. In his imagination, aflame with hatred towards himself for his Judas-like betrayal of Chagrin and keyed up to denounce his employer for having deceived him with such cruel cunning, the full mouth appeared to curve in an enigmatic, mocking smile. With a sudden curse, Nick drew his sword and the long, narrow blade flashed in the street-lamp beam at every thrust he made at the picture as if he were attacking a living creature. Again and again the blade slashed at the canvas until it hung in ribbons and then, his eyes narrowed into brilliantly glittering slits in his dark, envenomed face, Nick swept the documents and papers from the table to the floor with another savage lunge of his sword. Snarling and mouthing curses with insensate incoherence he suddenly flung the sword at the wine-decanter and glasses so that they were shattered at one resounding stroke, the wine dripping like blood into a pool on the carpet. His destructive rage mounted and, with wild strength and uttering demoniacal shouts rising above the noise of splintering wood and smashing glass, he began hurling everything he could lay his hands on about the room.

21

As the huge towers and the high massive walls of the Bastille rose forbiddingly before her on that dread March day Chagrin de l'Isle was convinced she was entering a tomb from which she was destined never to return. The fortress-prison's reputation was such, the sight of it must strike terror into the hearts of most beholders, so cruel and horrible the accounts that circulated Paris of infamies practised behind its walls, impregnably and for ever locking within their confines its grim secrets. The prison gates closing upon her, the turnkey led Chagrin to a room which, though cell-like in appearance, was to her gratified surprise yet airy and light, adequately furnished with bed, table and chairs, and a fire had been kindled in the corner fireplace.

While the atmosphere of the Bastille lay heavy upon her and she was haunted by the knowledge it held numerous wretches less fortunate than she, being awakened often in the night by the cry of some soul in torment, Chagrin quickly realized her term of imprisonment was being made as easy for her to bear and comfortable as was possible. Hints dropped her by the jailer who visited her daily made it evident the influence of the Duc de Brissac and Madame Du Barry was being exerted for her welfare and safety. '*Ne vous inquiétez pas*, Mademoiselle la Comtesse,' he would encourage her. 'You will be out from here in no time at all. And a few weeks' or months' stay in the Bastille is considered to be not so dishonourable. You would be surprised at the number of well-known personages who have kicked their heels awhile within these old walls.' Chagrin did recall hearing of members of several illustrious families who, proving not altogether amenable to parental control, had been sent to the notorious prison, there to cool down their impetuous spirits.

She was permitted to leave her cell every day and walk in the courtyard, and to receive correspondence, including that from Madame Du Barry, whose first item of intelligence disclosed to her how she was the victim of a plot devised by that cursed spy-chief, Fielding of Bow Street, how he had employed a certain Nick Rathburn as his secret agent to ensnare her.

The days stretched into weeks. She received no hint Nick had sought to discover what fate had befallen her. She could arrive at no conclusion other than that he had played her false, and, resolving to banish him for ever from her heart, she concentrated all her dreams and faith in the future upon the political news she received not only from Madame Du Barry, but from members of her family, together with the gossip her jailers passed on to her. Higher had ascended her hopes of release, for with the dramatic improvement in America's fortunes, the pressure brought to bear upon Louis to throw in his lot with the Americans against the British daily grew increasingly irresistible. When at last Louis had announced France would ally herself with the new independent nation over the

Atlantic against the old enemy across the Channel all France was set aflame with enthusiasm, which penetrated the thick walls of her prison, and Chagrin felt confident the moment for her release was at hand. Swift, however, as were the turn of events, she had been left to languish where she was, though continually in receipt of reassurances she would presently emerge freely pardoned. Eager as she was to play her part in the struggle, she must patiently count the days.

Her patient resolution was much sustained by the brusque sympathy of the turnkey, who, despite his sinister grin twisting up one side of his hatchet-face, had from her first day of imprisonment, encouraged her against giving way to despair. Then one evening towards the end of August on retiring for the night and drawing back her bedclothes from the pillow she saw revealed a piece of paper. On it was scrawled crudely in English: 'Do not blame N. R. Instead, forgive.'

She lay in bed trembling, the message crumpled in her hand, wondering at whose instigation it had been sent her. Someone who was aware of her association with Nick Rathburn, that seemed certain enough. Was it genuine or a subterfuge by which someone planned to trap her, test where the loyalty of her heart lay? Until the dawn began to edge the darkness from her cell, harassed by doubts and fears, over and over again her thoughts shuffled, searching for the hidden truth behind the message and she afire all the time with the hope it was a sign from he whose memory she knew she could never so long as she lived utterly efface from her secret dreams. Her mind had flown to the turnkey, that he had been responsible for smuggling into her cell that slip of paper. During the following day she sought for some hint from him, but never did he offer her the slightest inkling which could prompt her, however discreetly, to question him. Only that twisted grin and gruff manner.

Thrice during the summer did she receive similar mysterious and equally cryptic messages, each urging her to forgive 'N.R.' — that he was not to blame for her betrayal. Once the piece of paper bearing the crude charcoal scribble she found beside her candlestick when she awoke one morning, obviously placed there during the night; another time a few words had been pencilled in the margin of a volume of Villon's poems left in her cell while she was out walking in the courtyard; the next occasion a communication fell out of the fold of a handkerchief.

Always the scrawled words filled her with mingled wonder and misgiving, while at the same time a great wave of exhilaration would lift her up, poignantly recalling to her those too-swift hours she had spent with Nick Rathburn. If it were he, and still she could not be sure she was not the object of some machination directed against her, was he in Paris? Near by perhaps, waiting and watching for her? Her heart raced at the thought. Or was someone in the city acting on his behalf? Or was it neither, but some trick being perpetrated upon her for reasons she could but guess at by those in whose power she found herself, or even some cruel hoax?

One grey afternoon towards the end of that long dragging year of 1778 she received a visitor. A spruce middle-aged individual, his personality so toned in with the dullness of the day as if it suited itself to the colour of its surroundings, she could not afterwards recall one item of his appearance. It was the dreaded head of the *Cabinet Noir*, Lenoir himself. He explained the reason for his visit, which was that he had come from the Duc de Brissac and they had been discussing her imminent freedom.

'I do fear,' he admitted dryly, 'adjustment to our new foreign policy has not taken place in every direction as swiftly as you, for example, would have wished, and it has been thought so far indiscreet to remind His Majesty of the fact a certain scapegoat lay in the Bastille, committed there at his command.' Chagrin, aware the Du Barry had escaped imprisonment at her expense, and quite prepared to endure the sacrifice for the sake of one who was exerting a vital influence upon the destiny of France, gave him a non-committal smile. 'Of course, the honest Louis,' Lenoir was continuing, 'and all of his advisers are not of one mind.' Once again the pursed-lip smile. 'If they were, if every man shared his neighbour's views, how should I recruit my spies?' He tilted back in the chair in which he sat, placing the tips of his bony fingers together, his expression far away. 'The *Cabinet Noir* is accused of employing servants and hawkers, pawnbrokers and cheap journalists, even thieves themselves, who are allowed to go unmolested in repayment for their services. But, Mademoiselle la Comtesse, it is not only amongst such persons I find my agents! Do you not imagine that even in the most high-up circles there are those with something to hide?'

Suddenly there came a long drawn-out scream from somewhere in the Bastille's depths. After it had died away, leaving Chagrin's blood still running cold there was a stillness. Lenoir examined his carefully manicured finger-nails, then shifted his chair forward and brought his mild gaze to bear upon her.

Chagrin wondered if the somewhat

unsubtly vouchsafed information concerning spies and informers was aimed at her personally. Was it prompted also by the mysterious messages she had received? Could it be, she asked herself, he was addressing to her some sort of warning that beneath the surface of diplomacy and Court intrigue ran dark waters deep and menacing, and she having launched herself upon them there was now no drawing back for her?

'For one engaged in the activities I am considering,' he murmured, flicking a particle of dust from his coat-lapel with his handkerchief, 'it is important that an attractive woman, inspiring in men the most natural of emotions, should never fall into the trap of allowing herself to reciprocate these sentiments.'

A brief silence, then the sound of footsteps along the stone corridor outside and the jangle of a jailer's keys. Was he about to reveal himself as the instigator of the mysterious messages; was it not, she asked herself with inward dismay, Nick after all? She speculated upon how report of her brief association with him had reached the ears of those in Paris, with their interest in her visit to London. She had made little attempt to hide her feelings from the Somershams, for instance, though they would have been discreet. Of course, the gossips of London would have spread their tittle-tattle concerning her, Lord Tregarth for instance, she recalled, not being exactly averse to hearing the sound of his own voice.

'You must know,' Lenoir's voice jerked her back to her present circumstances, 'when it comes to dissimulation, the art of falsehood, the craft of deception, there is none better qualified than your Englishmen. And ruthlessness is the order, nor friendship nor love stands in his way. None so cold-hearted exist as that evil breed across the Channel. But as to that,' his words an insinuating purr, 'you have personal experience of having been treachery's victim.' He paused, waiting for her to make some reply.

'I believe I was betrayed,' she said, 'but by whom? One person I knew could have been a secret agent, though I thought him only a gamester.'

He gave a shrug of indifference. 'This Nick Rathburn, eh?' His eyes suddenly flat and fixed on her. 'He found himself meagrely rewarded for his pains. The betrayer betrayed, disowned and discredited by his employer,' and she giving no sign that what he was saying was a dagger piercing her, 'cast aside like a discarded glove.'

'He is dead?' her voice harsh, bereft of any emotion.

'They are shaping a noose for him even now. A spy who has served his turn, left to rot in London's gutters and stews.' Her finger-nails digging deep into her palms, it seemed she could no longer silently endure the impact of the other's words but must cry out her anguished longing to know more of Nick Rathburn's fate, and then footsteps sounded outside the cell, the rattle of the jailer's keys.

'Monsieur le Duc de Brissac.'

Lenoir rose to greet the newcomer and Chagrin caught the swift significant glance exchanged between them. Then Brissac had taken her hand. In his expression she read his reassurance she had emerged satisfactorily from her interview with the head of the *Cabinet Noir*. 'I fear I omitted to inform Mademoiselle la Comtesse you were to be expected,' the latter was apologizing with glib smoothness.

'I cannot hope to prove as entertaining a guest as you,' Brissac said, then to Chagrin: 'I bring you, however, greetings from Madame Du Barry and,' an almost imperceptible pause and a sidelong glance at Lenoir, 'her felicitations at the welcome news of your imminent return to surroundings less confined.'

'Since Monsieur le Duc doubtless has his carriage waiting,' Lenoir murmured unctuously, 'I am sure he would be only too glad to escort Mademoiselle la Comtesse to her home.' He paused at the cell-door, turning to them both, then his gaze fixed upon her. 'Unless, of course, you have any suggestion why your *adieu* should be delayed?' But while Brissac chuckled appropriately, she could only shake her head dumbly, her thankfulness at this out-of-the-blue prospect of her swift release confused by the unanswered questions that set her thoughts athrob; since, if his information regarding him were true, it was unlikely Nick was responsible for the secret communications she had received; had they been at Lenoir's design? If so, had his object been to discover her state of mind regarding the man he had pictured to her as a cast-off spy, disgraced and whose ignominious end was inevitable? Lenoir was speaking. 'I will, while you prepare yourself to take your departure, make the necessary arrangements with the officials. I shall return shortly and we may leave together.'

When he had gone, Brissac's blue eyes twinkled at her. 'You must have played your cards, dear Mademoiselle la Comtesse, with exceeding dexterity and discretion.' His handsome features clouded slightly as he threw a glance after Lenoir, as if reminded of something not altogether to his liking, then they brightened again. 'Madame Du Barry will be overjoyed to see you.'

'I have been, I am truly thankful to *le bon Dieu*, fortunate compared with many other prisoners of the Bastille.' She forced herself to concentrate her attention upon him. 'But being shut away from beloved Paris, for here one might be a million miles distant, is severe punishment.'

She observed a speculative expression flicker across his face. 'In which respect,' he began hesitantly, 'do you earn my sympathy, since you will be allowed to enjoy the delights of Paris but briefly.' She stared at him uncomprehendingly, only dread once again gripping her. 'You have been chosen for a mission abroad,' he said quietly, then, as footsteps and the jingle of keys drew near, added quickly: 'You are directed to set sail within the week.'

22

The face of the man who sat in a corner of the night-cellar beneath a crumbling old house of the Rookeries appeared leaner than ever, every feature sharpened against the whetstone of bitterness, the very bones and tautened flesh a mask chiselled from flint, the brows above the dark, glittering eyes jutting forward in an even more crag-like outline. About him arose the mutter of voices, the jingle of glasses punctuated now and again by the thud of a mug against a rough table in emphasis of some tipsy argument. He drew at his pipe, slowly expelling a spiral of smoke, and ran his fingers through the white streak, now a trifle more prominent in his dark hair, and then reached for his watch.

It was approaching midnight on this early April evening in the year 1780, some twice twelve-month after he had severed his association with the Blind Beak.

Returning the watch to his pocket, his eye carelessly took in his inevitable black velvet coat, the cuffs of which, however, looked distinctly threadbare about the edges, while his breeches of the same material showed somewhat shabby at the knees. Many and varied were the vicissitudes which had attended his career during the past two years. Seeking to drown the savage and despairing remembrances of his remorse and agony at his treachery towards the one creature in all the world he had ever loved, there was no lowest tavern which had not suffered from his drunken brawling, his virulence in a quarrel inflamed in a split-second to the challenging flash of his sword; no club or coffee-house whose gossip was not continually including reports of his reckless profligacy; hardly any gutter from Fleet Street to Berkeley Square which had not served him as a night's resting-place, except when he chose forgetfulness in this or that bagnio or whore-house.

At the onset Sir John Fielding had striven his utmost to divert him from the hopelessly violent, inevitably disastrous path he was treading. Returning that night accompanied by Mr. Bond to find his sitting room reduced to a shambles, and learning who had been responsible for the destruction and had rushed forcibly from the scene, the Blind Beak had called alone upon Nick the following morning. He had endured the curses and vituperative accusations hurled at him enigmatically. 'Do you deny you deliberately concealed from me the knowledge of what her fate would be?'

'I do not deny it,' was the impassive response.

Advancing upon him as if he would strike him to the ground, Nick had grated: 'Were you not the blinded old mass of fat you are I would beat you to pulp with my bare fists.'

'I should have imagined,' the other remonstrated mildly, 'your revenge was already gorged by the violence you have perpetrated upon my possessions.'

'Nothing can ever absolve you from the foul deception you practised on me. I had rather a thousand times you stabbed me in the back to the death than I should have been tricked into betraying her.'

'As to that, you were my agent,' the Blind Beak answered him levelly, 'in which secret employment there was no place for emotions of the heart, or tender dalliance with a creature activated by dark designs against England — '

'I could have saved her from causing a jot of harm.'

'Knowing you were enamoured of her, could I have trusted you not to be turned by this Frenchwoman's wiles from your rightful course? It is a ruthless business I am engaged in. My one obsession is service to my king to the best of my ability, and to that end, none — man, woman or child — shall bar my way.' His voice became remorseless in its tone. 'You were infatuated with this damned Du Barry's spy. My purpose could not be more manifest, which was to take advantage of your situation to encompass her destruction.'

'That you have destroyed me in the process,' Nick snarled, 'is of little consequence.'

'It is you who are destroying yourself. I am here now to beg you to draw back from the abyss.' His voice had assumed a gentler tone, his expression a less grim aspect.

'Save your pleadings with which to dupe some other spy,' Nick had sneered, turning his back on him. For several long, silent moments the Blind Beak remained, his sombre features bent in the direction of that rangy, implacably rigid figure vibrant with vengeful hatred towards him. Then with a heavy shrug and a drawn-out hissing sigh he had lumbered out of the house.

Her accusing ghost dogging him day and night, Nick had felt impelled to make an effort to reach Paris, boldly to attempt Chagrin's rescue, even at the cost of his own life. He was held back upon calmer reflection by the fear Lady Somersham's warning had stirred in him that such a venture on his part was not only foredoomed to failure, but must of a certainty heighten the danger in which Chagrin was already placed as the grim result of his treachery. Tortured by visions of the suffering she was enduring, hag-ridden by nightmares in which she denounced him for his fiendish betrayal of her trust, he flung himself into a round of dissipation in a desperate hope of ridding her from his heart and mind.

Against the background of alarms and shocks of the continuing war with America and France, who had at last come out into open alliance with the former in the spring two years before, and with Spain and the Dutch marauding the seas so that Britannia's trident was almost wrested from her grasp, Nick Rathburn plunged down the path of debauchery and excesses. While that renegade Scotsman, Captain Paul Jones, ravaged the Irish and North Sea under the new flag of America, Nick's old haunts continued to know him.

The coffee-houses and taverns hummed with reports of how Charleston lay at the mercy of British arms, Virgima swarmed with invincible English cavalry: London's *salons* and clubs buzzed with the news of how General Cornwallis and his redcoats were surging victoriously through Georgia, and French naval attacks against the

British at Newport and Savannah; while argument everywhere rose and discussion grew more heated at the prolongation of a war which was to have been brought to a brilliantly swift conclusion. And Nick frequented the brothels and gaming-hells, truculently savage when the luck ran against him and aggressively drunk when he celebrated good fortune, his hand ever ready at the sword-hilt, tongue sharp to challenge anyone critical of his conduct to back their words by their pistols.

Weariness with war increased; the argument extended Britain might be better employed battling with her problems at home, where unemployment, the starved and homeless, and disease and misery among the poor were rampant, instead of combating the new notions of liberty and equality which inspired the young nation across the Atlantic, or attempting to shut out similar ideas stirring France's more liberal thinkers and philosophers. And Nick Rathburn pursued his hell-bent way. Paradoxically, side by side with the emergence among more enlightened Englishmen of new understandings for the need of tolerance towards the struggling, blood in the streets of Glasgow and Edinburgh and the menacing tide of religious intolerance began sweeping in the direction of London. And Nick Rathburn encountered the increasing suspicion that, when his luck at the table ran out, he was not above swinging it in his favour with the manipulation of a card or spin of a dice.

One by one the doors of the gaming-houses closed against him. Thus debarred from obtaining the means by which he could continue his brawling, swaggering career, he perforce sought to turn his hand to the profession in which he had first become adept as a child of the Rookeries. Now the intelligence his underworld acquaintances such as Ted Shadow were able to furnish him he utilized to his own advantage.

Already he had suffered several narrow squeaks, already he had owed his escape from disaster to the lucky star under which, he convinced himself with characteristically sardonic fatalism, he had been born, and his mode of living, having sapped his alertness and blunted the quickness of his eye, so his operation of a *coup* had lost its boldness of execution, and in order to lessen the risks of discovery and capture, he engaged his attention more and more upon easier cribs to crack.

Tonight, for instance, he was awaiting the hour when he should take his leave of this den of thieves and third-rate scoundrels in the heart of the maze of narrow streets, twisted alleys and wretched ruins of St. Giles's, to keep a rendezvous with a certain Dr. Kelly. He went out into the street just as the chimes of St. Paul's were reverberating on the air, and, headed in the direction of St. Marylebone's Church, gliding like some solitary phantom through the dark, evil-smelling alleys and courts, padding along gloomy passages and down uninviting byways, where here and there sprawled a beggar in his rotting rags, a homeless waif huddled in hungry exhaustion, or lurked murderous thieves and footpads alert for the unwary.

Presently he was approaching the gates of the churchyard of St. Marylebone. Out of the darkness a voice greeted him in an undertone. 'Rathburn?' And to his muttered assent: 'All is quiet.' The cloaked figure with a slouch-hat pulled over his eyes looming up at him was Dr. Kelly, whom Nick had met by chance one afternoon off Wardour Street, the doctor bumping into him while escaping from a gang of bullies hard upon his heels. Dr. Kelly, a snub-nosed young man, had been visiting a poor, sick woman in the vicinity. Her drunken husband had accused him of trying to murder her, then, enlisting the aid of several cronies, set upon him. Nick had guided the dishevelled and breathless fellow expertly through nearby courts and alleys until the threatening shouts of the frustrated pursuers died away. Later, over a glass of wine, the doctor, observing him to be of a desperate character, withal possessed of undoubted resourcefulness, had made a proposition to Nick by which he might earn himself an odd guinea. Hence this meeting under the cover of night at St. Marylebone's Church.

'I have the carriage standing by in

readiness,' Dr. Kelly was whispering to him. 'The coachman is discreet enough.' Pushing one of the two spades he was carrying into Nick's grasp, they set off, the former leading the way. Now they were inside the churchyard. The doctor, having produced a darkened lantern whose cautious light showed them the path, they stopped beside the grave, the earth of which was but freshly turned. The air about them was dank and struck chill to their bones so that they both dragged their cloaks more closely to them. 'This is it,' Dr. Kelly muttered, and set down the lantern. They stood for a few moments, tensed, listening carefully. Only the eerie hoot of an owl within the church tower, no other sound to be heard, and each began digging. It was as they were unwrapping the shrouded shape their efforts had disinterred that they heard the voice of a nightwatchman.

'Who is it, there in the churchyard?' Dr. Kelly cursed under his breath and quickly extinguished the pale beam from the lantern. They stood like two statues, attempting to subdue their heavy breathing. 'Someone there, so there is.' The watchman's Irish brogue reached them again and now they could see him advancing, his lantern casting shadows jigging along the path between the gravestones.

'We had better run for it,' the doctor whispered.

Nick dissuaded him with a hand on his arm. 'He will only raise a shout,' he muttered through his teeth, 'and I am in no mind for being chased by the mob. Besides, it means our night's work for nothing.'

'I also do loathe the thought of leaving the corpse behind,' Dr. Kelly agreed.

'Do you leave this to me.' Nick was unarmed, having had in mind the nature of his work that night, apart from the spade he held, and he did not relish the prospect of having no other means of protection with which to fight a way through the angrily demonstrative inhabitants in the vicinity, brought from their beds eager to wreak their fury upon the pair of them. The watchman was now but a few yards away. Nick could observe his eyes bulging suspiciously and his mouth open ready to shout the alarm. Then he whispered to him hoarsely: 'Is it you, Paddy, from Dublin itself?' And giving the doctor a sharp nudge in his ribs that brought forth a gasp: 'Speak to him in the blarney,' he urged in low tones, 'tell him it is Dr. Kelly you are, from Dublin.'

The watchman's expression as he reached them grew less suspicious. 'My name is not Paddy, so it is, though to be true I come from Dublin,' his Irish accent becoming even more pronounced. 'But who is that do you say now?'

'Dr. Kelly' — the doctor, quickly following Nick's advice, his accent suddenly thick enough to be cut with a scalpel — 'and I am thinking you are my old friend, Paddy Moran, no less, who I cured of the fever last summer.'

'Indeed I was with the fever in the summer, though I do mind no doctor easing it,' emitting an impressively hacking cough in support of his claim.

'It is a rough chest you have there. Next time I am this way I bring you a potion to soothe it. Meanwhile, buy yourself a warming glass of liquor.' There was a clinking of coins changing hands.

'It is grateful to you I am, Doctor. Would there be after anything I can do to help you this minute, now?'

'And you do look the other way for a few minutes. A poor soul, a patient of mine she was, buried this afternoon and her mother never seeing her to say good-bye, I have vowed to take her back.'

The other gave a grunt of approval, then, with a solemn warning to them to exercise the greatest care not to be seen, continued on his way through the churchyard, leaving Nick and Dr. Kelly to proceed with their task. After much nervous fuming and sweating on the latter's part they managed to convey their burden into the waiting hackney, and they set off, the third macabre passenger sat between them upon the carriage-floor. 'A gentlewoman in distressed circumstances,' Dr. Kelly explained to Nick, mopping his face with a handkerchief. 'Died of puerperal fever yesterday. But I fancied she was noteworthy for a lateral curvature of the spine and bowing of the great long bones. Just the type of malformation that will interest John Hunter, of whom, doubtless, you will have heard.'

A little later found them at Mr. Hunter's house in Golden Square. The famous surgeon was in his dissecting theatre, a red-haired, rugged-face man who greeted them in a strong Scottish accent. 'This is the woman I mentioned to you, Mr. Hunter.' Dr. Kelly indicated the cadaver which lay incongruously on the floor. Nick was glancing round with idle curiosity at the array of glass jars containing grisly specimens and portions of human anatomy, and a huge skeleton hanging from one wall.

Mr. Hunter knocked aside one of the numerous open volumes strewn on his desk and scattered about the floor, and, assisted by Dr. Kelly, began to unwrap the shroud. 'Are you certain she is dead?' he queried, and at the other's assurance, glanced up at Nick with a wink. 'An impudent resurrection-man the other night sold me his brother as a subject for dissection. One of my pupils happened to receive him, stripped the fellow and laid him on my table ready for me. When I arrived I discovered he was not dead, but dead drunk. I quickly restored him to consciousness, but on regaining his wits, the rascal took such fright at his surroundings he ran out minus hat, coat and shoes.' He indicated the heap of clothing in the corner of the room. 'Nor has he returned for them.'

He turned to Dr. Kelly, who had launched into a flow of technicalities concerning the woman's peculiarities, interposing a grunt of satisfaction as he listened. As the other concluded, Mr. Hunter observed: 'The poor woman will serve excellently for the purpose of my studies.' He flung the shroud over the corpse again. The door opened and the manservant appeared, staggering under the weight of a huge supper-tray crowded with a repast of roast duck and chicken, a large meat pie, some brawn, together with a pudding, jellies and tarts, which he set down amongst the books, surgical instruments and specimen-jars, going out again, quickly to return with bottles of Madeira and glasses. Nick partook only of a glass of wine, pocketed his fee and, while Dr. Kelly and the surgeon busied themselves over the supper-tray, the latter waving his fork at the corpse, declaring he must get to work on it at once, he took his departure.

Through stinking, ill-lit alleys and dark sinister courts, presently he paused at the door of a house half in ruins, within which he found several young women seated round a table in the light of a single, flickering tallow-candle flame. Some were playing cards desultorily with narrow-eyed men, sharpers, thieves or the girls' bullies, while a coarse-featured hag, a glass of liquor at her elbow, lolled before the smoking grate. A rope was slung over the fireplace from which hung stockings and petticoats; nails in the walls held a good assortment of bonnets, befeathered hats, cloaks and tawdry gowns.

As he leaned against the doorway he attracted no more attention than quick, shifty glances. Only a young woman, in a green jacket and striped petticoat with a

crinoline, her hair netted and ornamented, turned to smile at him, pouting
as Nick's gaze passed to a dark-haired girl
near the fire with her skirts and petticoats
drawn over her firm, rounded thighs,
busily engaged paring her finger-nails
with a penknife. He crossed to her and
with a sudden movement caught her
roughly by the chin and pulled her face
up to him. Her gypsy, slanting eyes met
his with an insolent stare, and without a
word exchanged between them, she led
the way out of the room and up the
rickety stairs, a rat squeaking from under
their feet.

23

The clanging of a bell and a stentorian voice brought him out of his sleep with such a dread-filled violence he was soaked in a cold sweat. In the dim light that found its way through the ragged curtains and filth-encrusted windows, he perceived the gypsy-eyed girl stood over him. He clasped his hands about his ears to keep out the clanging bell and raucous chant. 'It is the bellman of St. Sepulchre's,' she said. 'There are some condemned to be taken from Newgate presently.'

Something in her attitude caused him of a sudden to reach into the pocket of his threadbare, black breeches and, hearing no answering clink of coins, he grasped the doxy's wrist. Exerting a vice-like pressure, he forced her to release the money she had attempted to filch from him. He pushed his way roughly through the press of wretches gathered in the doorway and stumbled into the street.

The air all about him was filled with the clangour of the bell accompanying the solemn exhortations. 'All good people pray heartily to God for these poor sinners now going to their death.' Already the streets leading to the Stone Jug were aswarm with people, meat-pie vendors, the drinking-booths, street-pedlars and broadsheet-sellers doing a roaring trade. Caught in the chattering, yelling stream, swollen by those drunkenly singing and blaspheming who, like himself, had emerged from dens and cellars along the way, on whose doors was chalked the familiar sign: 'Drunk for a penny, dead drunk for twopence, clean straw each morning,' he was borne towards the prison.

As he reached Newgate the booming of churches all around struck the hour of eight o'clock, and a deafening roar from the crowd heralded the arrival of the hang-man's cart rumbling over the cobbles, to draw up outside Execution Gate. All about him the mob was yelling, joking and laugh-ing as they waited for the condemned felons' appearance. 'One of them is a 'prentice who robbed his master of threepence,' someone cried in his ear, while another spectator volunteered the information there were four felons altogether for whom the Tyburn Tree was waiting. The boy, a bargeman taken in smuggling, a lunatic, caught trying to burn down the home of a Catholic in Hoxton, and a burglar. The voice of Nick's informant was drowned in another shout as the doomed quarter suddenly appeared; the poor bedraggled waif, the burglar, whom Nick knew well by sight and reputation, the bargeman, a hulking, sullen-looking fellow, and the incendiary, a poor Tom o' Bedlam dancing as well as he could in his chains and laughing with pleasure at the reception accorded him by the densely packed cheering throng.

Nick watched them hustled into the cart and driven upon their last journey. The three of them, enveloped in fear, oblivious of their lunatic companion still dancing up and down, waving his arms and chuckling. Nick presently found himself able to extricate himself from the thinning stream of humanity and made his way to the nearest grog-shop, where he sought to drown the black premonition overwhelming him.

It was about this time that Mr. Bond was knocking on Sir John Fielding's sitting room door to announce the visitor who was expected. The clerk eyed the latter over his spectacles, closed the door upon the Blind Beak and descended the stairs thoughtfully. Mr. Bond was still unable to comprehend Sir John's vindictiveness towards Nick Rathburn, becoming month by month more venomous. Since his former secret agent had returned to the dark way he had once known, Sir John seemed implacably determined to encompass Nick Rathburn's destruction.

Mr. Bond could only attribute this frame of mind to the evident deterioration in the Blind Beak's state of health. His arduous activities in his police court, where he daily spent hour after hour in the foulest atmosphere to be encountered in London, were at last sapping even his prodigious vitality. Still shaking his head, the clerk, with a glance over his shoulder in the direction of the sitting room, continued downstairs to his own office.

Early that afternoon Nick raised his head from his arms spread upon the grog-shop table to snarl a curse at whoever had possessed the temerity to prod him awake. Again the sharp prod in his ribs, and, reaching out instinctively, his hand gripped a wooden stump and he drifted up out of the alcoholic depths bemusing him, opened one eye to meet that toothless grin.

'You makes a handsome sight, Mr. Rathburn. As handsome a picture of an afternoon after the morning afore as ever I set eyes on.' Ted Shadow glanced over his shoulder at the motley collection of rascals round the wretched boozing-den, hunched over their drinks, making sure he could not be overheard.

'Have you done?' Nick muttered. 'Then adieu and rot you for waking me.'

The other, pulling a chair close, his wooden stump sticking straight out before him, on which he hung his hat, bent his mouth close to Nick's ear. 'Wake your sodden senses, Mr. Rathburn. I have an item of news will earn you a handful of guineas.' Painfully Nick opened an eye again. 'A matter of employment for you and not so trifling neither. A crib to be cracked and no one better than you could do the cracking.' Nick would have turned away once more had not the other's hands gripped him, forcing him to listen. 'And no risk at all, Mr. Rathburn, to your life or liberty.'

'When?' evincing a faint show of interest.

'Tonight.' Nick, groaning as if the tiny spark that had been fanned alive had died again, Shadow threw another cautious glance around the half-empty, sleazy den, then turned once more to his ear. 'Just to fall through a window into a house where are pieces of jewellery to be took for the taking.'

'Play the house-breaker? Is it that you have to tell me?'

'Pox on your boozy wits,' the other exclaimed, exasperated. 'Would Ted Shadow take all this trouble running you to earth in this rat-hole unless to put in your way an operation of a particular sort?'

'What sort, and you so sure I do not

hold my neck in hazard?'

'A certain gentleman in the town,' whispering hoarsely again, 'has in the past bestowed rich jewels upon a Covent Garden actress who became his doxy, you understand. This lecher now quarrels with the bitch, seeks to recover the gifts he made her. I learn he is casting about for someone to undertake this operation with cunning, not to say discretion, so who do my thoughts fly to?'

'Who,' Nick replied, 'but a besotted gull who would pay you over-well for your information?'

The other drew back and permitted himself the luxury of a stream of curses. 'Of all the ingratitude, Mr. Rathburn,' he exclaimed in hurt tones. 'Would Ted Shadow, who has served you faithful this long since, try to wheedle out of you a price for an item and it not worth it?'

'Yes,' muttered Nick unequivocally, forcing himself upright, groaning the while and clasping his head in his hands at the agony the movement caused him. 'What does this tight-fist lover offer as a price for the return of his knick-knacks?'

'Twenty guineas.' Nick jerked up his head. 'I thought such a price would penetrate your skull.'

'How much do you take?'

'Five for myself, the rest all yours.'

'And the danger all mine too,' Nick grumbled, brushing the back of a hand across his bleared eyes.

The other shook his head vehemently. 'No danger in it at all. Do you not understand, Mr. Rathburn, this is to be a faked performance?'

'Did you mention his name?'

'A certain Lord Tregarth,' Ted answered.

Nick eyed him unblinkingly, his mind filled with the picture of the last time he had met Lord Tregarth. Cursing under his breath, his head sank once more in his hands, while the other observed with surprise the swift change in his mood. 'What is it about his lordship twenty clinking guineas will not put right?'

'We have met before,' Nick said.

'And if you have?' the other grimaced impatiently. 'Why, it should make it all that easier for you. You might squeeze an extra guinea or two out of him since you are acquainted. Come, Mr. Rathburn,' placing an encouraging hand on his shoulder, 'it is an easy crib as I have told you and you could make good use of the money.' Idly he wondered what lay behind Nick Rathburn's swift descent from the position he had once occupied, what twist of Fate had reduced him to circumstances no better than those of a wandering beggar without a roof over his head, his only shelter being the lowest brothels of St. Giles's. Some wench, he hazarded the guess, was responsible. Shaking his head, he set about persuading Nick fifteen guineas so easily earned and not a jot risk to himself — he need barely stay sober even — was not to be sniffed at.

Reminded of the lightness of his pocket Nick presently began to listen. According to Shadow, there was no time to be lost. Lord Tregarth was anxious for the return of his gifts of jewellery before his discarded light-o'-love disposed of them for cash, and was ready to discuss the operation with whoever would undertake it promptly, so it could be brought off that very night. 'You can inform him I will present myself at his house at four o'clock and receive his instructions.' Nick rasped his fingers over his unshaven chin. 'By which time I will have visited the barber and the Turkish bath to put myself in the necessary frame of mind.' Shadow nodded approvingly and recommended they should meet again at a coffee-house on the morrow, when Nick would hand over the other's share of the money.

After he had gone, Nick remained staring unseeingly before him. Then, gulping off a glass of brandy in an attempt to steady his nerves, he presently made his way to a bath-house in St. James's Street, where, after being shaved, he found himself lying back in a tiled hot-steam room. Following a vigorous massage he was wrapped in a robe and, reclining on a couch, sipped hot black coffee and finally fell asleep.

And while he lay lost in his dreams Ted Shadow, who had made his way not to Lord Tregarth's address, but to Bow Street, was reporting the success of his interview to the Blind Beak.

24

Lord Tregarth had appeared not to recognize Nick, who recalled they were masked on the occasion of their meeting at the Pantheon that night two years ago. Some quirk of humour impelling him to disclose himself: 'Indeed, and I know not what to say,' the other had mumbled, with a glance at Nick's shabby coat and threadbare breeches, darned black stockings and well-worn shoes, albeit they had been newly polished. 'How is it the same person to whom I was once introduced by the Comtesse de l'Isle should now be offering me his services in a somewhat disreputable enterprise?'

'Do you distress yourself not unduly,' Nick replied casually. 'A man of my circumstances inclines to pursue a somewhat erratic career. At the moment my fortune lies at that low ebb I am obliged to accept commissions about which I might otherwise possess certain scruples.'

'It distresses me to learn you presently find yourself in desperate straits' — Lord Tregarth extended his gold snuff-box to Nick, who shook his head — 'yet I must confess I find it more comfortable to take such as yourself into my confidence than some common thief I originally thought to engage.'

Nick gave a sardonic lift to an eyebrow in acknowledgment of the compliment. They faced each other in the other's library overlooking Grosvenor Square, the rich oak-panelled room lined with books, whose heavy leather bindings caught the late afternoon light that streamed through the tall windows. Lord Tregarth was attired in an elegant plum-coloured jacket in the latest fashion with an embroidered waistcoat and his cravat of gleaming whiteness edged with frothy lace of silver.

'No doubt you will have witnessed Mrs. Devenish's performances at the Haymarket Theatre,' Lord Tregarth was continuing. 'She had attained some position as a player, being especially successful in breeches roles.' Nick had several times admired curly-haired Peg

Devenish enacting dashing young men in a roguish, somewhat strident style which showed off her lithe, boyish figure to excellent advantage. He had also been aware she was not averse to gaining the protection of whatever man-about-town was prepared to contribute most financially to the style of living she favoured, but which her playhouse-earnings proved inadequate to provide. 'It is irrelevant to relate how the charming creature and I first became acquainted, sufficient that I became passionately devoted towards her and she appeared to return my affection, though I counted myself fortunate a person so young should reciprocate the love of one old enough to be her father.' Nick revealed by no movement of a muscle what he was thinking, but retained a suitably grave expression. 'I installed her in an elegant villa overlooking Marylebone Fields,' the other went on, 'where I visited her as frequently as I could to pass the time in her society. She set up her own carriage and a suitable retinue of servants, and also retired from the boards.'

Lord Tregarth produced his snuff-box again and, Nick still not availing himself of a pinch, took a sniff to cover his evident embarrassment occasioned by his narrative. 'My munificence towards her did not decrease by the lapse of time. Mrs. Devenish frequently received presents of jewellery from me, which marks of attention were constant as they were various.' He sighed involuntarily, gazing pensively out at Grosvenor Square, beginning to grow hazy at the approach of an April twilight. 'Then I encountered a young blade in her box at the theatre whom she introduced as her cousin. This arousing my suspicions, I decided to watch her more closely, bribing her servants to inform against her. The night before last, when she had excused herself from a supper-party in my company on the pretext she was feeling unwell, I received information acting upon which caused me to surprise her with her so-called cousin in circumstances placing doubt beyond question.'

Lord Tregarth gave a delicate cough. 'I have already acquainted myself of her young paramour's circumstances which are such that, knowing Mrs. Devenish as I do, convince me she will be persuaded to dispose of her possessions in order to retain his affections. I find it a galling thought that the magnificent jewellery I gave her will be auctioned off to assure the continuation of her association with a young puppy who has supplanted me.' His eyes flashed and his features suffused apoplectically, the veins at his temples standing out like wriggling snakes. 'In brief — '

'I am to retrieve as much of the jewellery as I may,' Nick concluded for him, 'and return it to you?'

The other nodded, touching his high-bridged nose with his handkerchief, and shortly afterwards Nick, having obtained several guineas on account of his fee for the successfully completed operation, was making his way from Grosvenor Square, idly turning over in his mind his instructions for gaining admittance to the villa by Marylebone Fields. And he had glanced back he might have perceived Lord Tregarth from behind the library-window curtains watching his departure with a speculative eye.

There was a pale crescent of moon in the sky, obscured now and again by drifting clouds, and a light mist from a pond in Marylebone Fields across the way lent an eerie air to the scene. Standing in the shadows of some trees overhanging the garden of the villa, which lay back from the road, Nick glanced about him. He had made his way on foot after fortifying himself against the night's adventure ahead of him with a beefsteak at Dolly's Steakhouse in Paternoster Row and a couple of bottles of wine topped off with a good measure of cognac. The spring night was reasonably mild so it had been unnecessary to wear a hat or cloak which would have hampered his task. A carriage clattered past, by the light of whose lamps he glimpsed a woman attired in her elegant finery, no doubt proceeding to some fashionable gathering. His mind went back to his association with Casanova, the many grand assemblies at Madame Corneleys's and that vividly remembered if brief appearance at Lady Harrington's on the occasion of his first meeting with Chagrin.

A bitter smile flickered across his lean, saturnine features as his thoughts clung to the past — so near and yet so far away it might have been a different world he had known. A sense of oppression descended upon him. Had he not just about reached the end of his tether? He asked himself, as he stood there in the darkness, the grey mists creeping about him like mocking wraiths, what was to be gained by going on? What instinct of survival beat so forcibly within him he could not even now give up hope that somehow lay a way which, if only he could strike it, would lead him upwards out of the hopeless abyss into which he had descended? With a tremendous effort of will he shook off the wave of depression threatening to drown his spirit, and emerged from the shadows.

The villa was half hidden from the road by the trees, their branches rustling above him as they caught an occasional capful of wind. The tall railing either side of the gate joined a high wall at right angles, each of which enclosed the house and, as Nick knew from Lord Tregarth's description, met an equally insurmountable wall at the back. A door was let in one side of the wall, securely bolted and barred, however. The windows were dark. Again Lord Tregarth's information was that Mrs. Devenish would be at a supper-party, no doubt accompanied by her new lover, and was unlikely to return before the early hours of the morning. The servants would have retired to bed except for the personal maid, who would be dozing in her own room awaiting her employer's return.

The procedure Nick was to adopt in order to earn the remainder of his twenty guineas, less five to Ted Shadow, was straightforward enough. The gate uttered a slight complaining squeak. Closing it carefully behind him, he moved swiftly across the narrow lawn, and gained the protective shadow of the high wall on his right. His footsteps noiseless on the turf, he reached the side door in the wall, whose heavy bolts he could discern. Opposite him a few paces away was the villa's kitchen door. He scanned a window above, opening, as he had been informed, on to the first-floor landing, where was situated Mrs. Devenish's bedroom. Beneath this window ascended some rustic woodwork entwined in wisteria and a relatively simple matter, as Nick gauged at once, to climb, thereby effecting an entrance.

He smiled thinly to himself. Lord Tregarth had not misinformed him so far as the means of access into the house were concerned and, pausing to listen to make sure no one within was stirring, he started to climb. In a few minutes he knelt on the window-ledge. Dexterously working the blade of a claspknife between the window-frame and the inside-catch, he was soon rewarded by the sharp noise of the latch snapping back. Quickly and silently he opened the window and swung himself inside, to drop lightly on to the landing. No sound of any movement in the house and he ascended the few stairs to the passage outside the bedroom which was his objective.

A small candelabrum stood on a table

next to the bedroom door, and behind him, beyond a narrow flight of stairs, another light glowed, presumably in the room where the maidservant was dozing. Nick, turning the door-handle quietly, went into the bedroom, leaving the door open behind him so the light from the landing would supply sufficient illumination by which to work. Expertly he rummaged through the ornate dressing-table backing on to the thick velvet curtains, which were closed, and, first taking out a pistol and black mask, placing them within easy reach, filled both side-pockets of his jacket with rings, bracelets, brooches, necklaces, earrings, everything of value upon which he could lay his hands. 'Every gem she possesses,' Lord Tregarth had told him, 'is a gift from me.'

His attention was of a sudden attracted by a noise, and cautiously drawing back the edge of a curtain he glanced out. The moon was shining brilliantly, unobscured by any cloud, so that the garden was clearly illuminated. That bleak smile touched the corners of his mouth as he recalled Lord Tregarth's advice regarding the conclusion of the operation. 'So long as you leave no doubt behind it is an outside *coup* perpetrated by some housebreaker.' He was to exit the way he had come.

He remained deep in thought, then picked up his pistol and mask and, selecting a comfortable chair, leaned back, nonchalantly crossing his legs, to await Mrs. Devenish's return. He must have dozed off; at any rate he was suddenly awake, with no idea how long he had been sitting there. He was moving to the curtains again, as the sounds of the carriage-wheels outside stopped and there came the snuffling of a horse. Now the moon was hidden by a bank of cloud, but he could discern beyond the railings the carriage drawn up and in the glimmer of the lamps a shadowy figure entering the gates. A few moments later he heard the front-door bolts being drawn back, the door closed, and voices which he took to be those of Mrs. Devenish and her maidservant drew nearer, tones raised petulantly about the chilliness of the night and would a warming bowl of negus be prepared. He heard the commiserating reply as the other hurried off. He returned to the chair which was out of line with the door, waiting with pistol cocked. A hummed snatch of tune approached, the light outside moved and she stood in the doorway holding the candelabrum in her hand, failing to see him in the darkness and dazzled by the candlelight. Crossing to the dressing-table she saw him reflected in the mirror.

'Do you cry out, it is the last syllable you will utter.' His pistol covered her menacingly as she raised a hand to her mouth to stifle a scream. 'Close the door.' Her wide eyes were fixed upon him for a moment, then she moved quickly to obey him. 'You will tell your maid you wish to remain undisturbed.'

'What do you want?' she asked him, low-voiced; facing him again, the door closed behind her. He grinned at her, rising nonchalantly to his feet. She threw a look at her dressing-table, some of the drawers of which gaped open, and as she framed the question he tapped his pocket.

Some of the courage which had drained from her at the sight of him now began to return and her eyes flashed. 'Caught red-handed.'

'Not exactly, I have been here some time. I did not require all that long to lift your jewels.' Her expression became puzzled and then she turned at the maidservant's voice outside the room. 'Remember,' Nick rapped under his breath, 'what you are to tell her.'

She eyed his pistol for a moment. 'Do not disturb me yet. I will call when I require you.' A puzzled silence, a muttered grumble and then receding footsteps. Mrs. Devenish returned her perplexed glance to Nick. 'You mean you deliberately awaited my return?'

'I fancied what I have to tell you might be of interest.' She hesitated irresolutely and then reached for a chair and sat down. 'Forgive me if finding me here came as something of a shock,' he went on smoothly. 'What I have to say may also occasion you some slight surprise.' She merely gazed at him blankly. 'It was Lord Tregarth engaged me,' Nick continued, and she gave a start, 'to rob you. His motive — he resents the prospect of your disposing of the gifts he has made you, in order to obtain money with which to support your new lover.'

She rose to her feet with a gasp. 'What monstrous lies are you saying? He could have told you no such thing.'

'I would have no object in informing you of this unless I thought it to be true.'

'A lie,' she cried. 'I have no new lover, only Lord Tregarth. It is no secret,' she flung at him. She began to wring her hands in bewilderment. 'I am at a loss to understand what all this means. You would not seem to be an ordinary thief.' He gave her a sardonic bow and she went on. 'And you tell me this fantastic tale.'

'Lord Tregarth was lying, then, when he informed me of the motive for his plot to recover the jewels he gave you?'

'Why should he tell you all this?' — giving him an up-and-down glance of disbelief — 'an individual like you, a stranger — '

'We had met before.' But, catching his reflection in the mirror, shabby and haggard, pistol glinting in the candle-light, he could not blame her for doubting him. He began emptying his pockets, placing the contents on her dressing-table. She watched him with calculating eyes as if mentally checking off each item. 'Shall we say,' he suggested, 'a practical joke where I was to be the victim, you but his unsuspecting accomplice. But for a fortunate chance, earlier' — he threw a glance at the window — 'I might have been snared by his jest. As for these they would have been safely returned to you.' He was mentally upbraiding himself, allowing his drink-sodden wits to overlook the extraordinary coinci-dence, which at any other time must have aroused his immediate suspicions, of Lord Tregarth acquainting himself with a rogue like Shadow who, in turn, had put him in touch with, of all people, Nick Rathburn.

And he had not perceived those two Bow Street Runners skulking in the shadows of the garden he would by now have been caught in the trap so cunningly laid for him. He regarded Mrs. Devenish speculatively. Her white shoulders gleamed in the soft candlelight, which cast a provocative shadow between the rounded boldness of her *décolleté*. 'Since my frankness has saved you any harm from this ill-devised comedy, perhaps you would reciprocate by accommodating me with your carriage for my return to my lodgings?' Her look was quizzical. 'It is late for walking,' he explained and with a raised eyebrow in the direction of the windows, 'unsavoury characters are abroad.'

She hesitated and then gave a shrug. 'You are quite the most extraordinary thief. But it is right you should be conveyed safely home. I will see the carriage is ready for you at once.'

A little later, a cloak thrown about her against the misty night air, Mrs. Devenish at his request accompanied Nick to the gate. Chatting lightly they proceeded along the path, and he could imagine the baffled expression on the faces of the watchers in the shadows awaiting him, expecting he would quit the villa as instructed by the wily Lord Tregarth. That glimpse of them from the bedroom window had warned him he had been lured into yet another trap set by the Blind Beak.

The revelation of Shadow's treachery came as no surprise. He knew the wooden-legged rascal's philosophy to be even more cynical than his own, and capable of cold-bloodedly betraying a friend with never a qualm, so long as the price be high enough. Offering a fervent prayer of gratitude to his lucky star which continued still to shine over him, a sense of exhilaration bore him up at having once more triumphed over his ruthless adversary at Bow Street. The measure of that inexorable determination to destroy him was indicated by the lengths to which, even enrolling Lord Tregarth as an ally, the Blind Beak had gone.

Opening the gate he experienced the added uneasy sensation Mrs. Devenish herself might be a willing party to the machinations directed against him. He thanked her for facilitating his departure, while her smile in the light of the carriage-lamps was seemingly innocent.

'Do you believe,' she murmured, 'I shall speak to his lordship most sharply concerning his manner of amusing himself at my expense.' He made an appropriate reply, almost convinced of her sincerity, and stepping into the carriage directed to be driven to the Blood Bowl Cellar, off Fleet Street where, dipping into the guineas jingling in his pocket, he planned to celebrate his luck.

Barely half an hour later he was lounging casually over his drink and chewing reflectively upon a clay pipe-stem, far away in his mind from the noisy scene about him, for it was a rendezvous notorious for flash coves, thieves and their doxies, together with shifty-eyed fences on the look-out for any with stolen property to dispose of, when his attention snapped back to the present at the entrance of a familiar tub-like figure attended by two sturdy individuals who also sported the unmistakable red waist-coat. A sudden quiet had fallen as, with a faint smile, Nick wondered who might be the object of the newcomers' unwelcome concern. Even when they approached him he remained unconcerned, raising his glass nonchalantly at the foremost of the trio.

'Good evening, Mr. Rathburn.' Mr. Townsend pulled out a chair for himself and, elbows on the table, faced Nick, a sly smirk upon his rubicund face.

'And what, Mr. Townsend, have I the pleasure of buying you in the form of refreshment?'

'Nothing, Mr. Rathburn, thank you all the same, since I should not have time in which to drink your health.'

'What duty, Mr. Townsend, requires your vigilance so urgently as leaves no leisure for a convivial glass?'

'The duty I now pursue,' came the ponderous reply, 'which is to require your company to Bow Street.'

Nick grinned at him disarmingly. 'Your invitation bears a pressing tone, and yet I do not fancy accepting it.'

'Fancy or otherwise, you will do well not to refuse,' and Mr. Townsend threw sidelong glances at his two grim-visaged companions.

A faint premonitory tremor rippled under Nick's scalp as he involuntarily harked back to the means whereby he had a short while since outwitted his foes, searching for any flaw, any contingency he had failed to foresee. 'A Mrs. Devenish,' the other was continuing relentlessly, 'on returning home tonight to her villa by Marylebone Fields surprised an unexpected visitor. This person escaped, and with some jewellery, but not before his description had been noted, which suits you in every detail.'

'I cannot be but flattered by the delectable Mrs. Devenish's interest in my physical appearance.'

'You do not deny being discovered by her tonight?'

Nick shrugged airily. 'Since we had a private matter for discussion between us my presence there should be not entirely incomprehensible, but that at the conclusion of our meeting I took my leave with so much as a single item of her property adhering to my fingers is as absurd an accusation as it is unjustifiable.'

'Which being the case, according to the

words of your mouth, you raise no objection to being searched.'

Mr. Townsend, rising to his feet, that smirk upon his face, leaned towards him. The other two individuals had moved round to him with alacrity, and again that crawling sensation seeming to cause each separate hair above the nape of his neck to rise on end. He stood up with lazy grace, his veiled glance flickered with slow, studied insolence over the others' faces. There came a sudden movement from the Bow Street Runner on his left and a hand plunged into his coat-pocket, reappearing to the accompaniment of the man's triumphant grunt, and from whose thick, horny palm, a flat, diamond-encrusted brooch, glittering and winking, met Nick's momentarily transfixed gaze.

Simultaneously with the realization he had been tricked at the last, his reflexes urged him into immediate action. With a bitter curse, ramming the table into Mr. Townsend's protuberant stomach so that he collapsed with an agonized groan, knocking the other police officer off-balance, in the same movement he smashed his clenched fist savagely into the face of the fellow clutching the brooch Mrs. Devenish must have contrived slyly to plant in his pocket. The cellar was in an uproar, everybody on their feet with yells of encouragement, some leaping upon the tables to roar their admiration, and anyone in his path giving way before his desperate rush, he reached a narrow door in a corner of the cellar and vanished from sight.

He was speedily followed by both of Mr. Townsend's officers — the former still lay breathless the table atop of him and not a soul showing any concern — wrenching the door open after their quarry. Having stumbled about in a winding passage, shortly the pursuers found themselves back where they were, with frustrated expression and uttering baffled oaths, Nick having taken a secret stairway known to but few *habitués* of the Blood Bowl, and, closing its cunningly concealed entrance behind him, he ascended to the darkness of Fleet Street and was lost in the labyrinth of alleys and lanes that lay beyond.

25

Throughout the rest of that night and next day Nick remained hidden in a deserted hovel of rags and sticks in an encampment huddled about a deserted copse near Melancholy Walk, St. George's Fields lying across the river, which sheltered straggling vagrants. Listening to the rain beating against the leaky roof, for a thunderstorm had burst just after dawn, he felt grateful towards the elements, which were as discouraging to the Bow Street Runners out searching for him.

Darkness fell again, bringing with it a cessation of the downpour, and Nick decided to venture forth and find somewhere to eat. No morsel of food or a sip of drink, other than rain-water cupped in his hands, had he tasted since his escape from the Blood Bowl. And so, a slouch hat purchased on his way to shade his face, he ate ravenously that evening of roast veal in the dim corners of a low eating-house in the Tottenham Court Road, hidden behind a daily newspaper which reported his escape from Townsend. On the same page he read one of Sir John Fielding's advertisements: 'Nick Rathburn did evade arrest by the Bow Street Runners last night. He is wanted for housebreaking and is a notorious criminal, aged about thirty, five foot ten inches in height, very slender, of pale debauched countenance and dark eyes and hair, the latter being marked by a white streak. He did wear a shabby attire. Whoever will discover or apprehend him so that he be brought to justice shall have one hundred guineas reward to be paid by Sir John Fielding at Bow Street Police Court. If any person knowingly conceal him from justice it is a felony and they will be prosecuted for the same.'

Even as, with a twisted smile, he concluded reading, a shadow fell across his corner and a piece of paper slapped on the table. 'A proclamation,' a pockmarked individual growled as Nick glanced quickly up at him, 'from the Blind Beak. And you can lay this Nick

Rathburn by the heels there is a hundred guineas for your trouble.' Nick thanked the fellow for his advice and the other moved away distributing more copies of the proclamation. The story of his escape was now all over the town, as he discovered for himself later, drifting from ale-house to tavern and gin-shop to night-cellar, everywhere receiving fresh evidence of his notoriety. No one but seemed to be discussing him. Suddenly, it seemed, he had become the most-talked-of personage in all London.

By the early hours of the morning he had contrived to remain unchallenged, though there had been instances when, coming under the shrewd eye of a stranger, he had decided discretion was the better part of valour and faded swiftly into the safety of the dark street. He was reaching the conclusion if he were to continue to evade capture he must obtain for himself both new clothing and more money. He recalled mention by some passing flash-house acquaintance of a pawnbroker in Drury Lane, offering not only a selection of fashionable attire, obtained mostly from impoverished players disposing of their wardrobes, but a large quantity of jewellery, not forgetting any takings on the premises not safely stowed.

He set out for the pawnbroker's shop and on reaching it discovered there was a side-entrance along a narrow, dark alley. He encountered little difficulty in forcing the lock and entering. Quickly he selected from the dim mustiness of the overflowing shelves and crowded counter a black velvet jacket with breeches to match, a ruffled shirt, elegant black hose, diamond buckled shoes and all finished off by a top-hat *à la mode*. He had discarded his seedy attire for the magnificence of this new wardrobe and was buckling round his waist a silver-hilted sword he had taken a fancy for when voices from upstairs, apparently those of the pawnbroker and his wife talking to each other in frightened tones, reached his ear. Nick raised his voice. 'Do you shoot dead,' he called, as if addressing a band of confederates, 'the first person who dare show their face.' Promptly the tremulous murmuring above ceased. His bluff having thus succeeded in gaining him a little more time, Nick added to his booty a gold watch, a diamond ring, grabbed a handful of money, both gold and silver, and betook himself off.

The following morning he had taken lodgings off Cheapside for himself and his latest charmer, Moll Frisky, she of the volatile charms and soft pointed fingers that could be at once caressing and grasping, lovingly teasing and greedily covetous. It was all one to him, for back of his mind lay the knowledge his time was running short, the remaining hours of freedom few. This must be the case, however he skulked in the darkest corner of the Rookeries, or hid in the most wretched thieves' kitchen. Always some creeping rogue, mouth watering at the prospect of that hundred guineas reward, would be on the alert for his appearance, ready to betray him.

Now he knew that, while he possessed the wherewithal to attempt it, now, while the going was good, should he quit the town, shake the dust of London off his feet for a long time, if not for ever. And he wished he was free yet to seek fresh fields: Bath or Bristol, York or Chester, or across the Border, Edinburgh. There were a score of cities where the Bow Street Runners would find it next to impossible to trace him and where he might still find easy cribs to crack and pursue his reckless course with less danger to his skin. But like some player in a piece whose every scene he must enact and every line he must speak is already written for him and he must not deviate from his role, so Nick was impelled to play his part to the final curtainfall, London his stage and audience. The echo of the hated Blind Beak's words would haunt him, ringing with unerringly true perception back of his mind: '*It is you who are destroying yourself.*' And still he found himself drawn, like the needle to the magnet, to the abyss-edge. It was as if he longed to taste the vault-cold breath of doom in his throat and, while on one hand elude death's inimical embrace, on the other seek it out as if it were a gladly welcome friend.

Enjoy life then, as boldly as he may, and so he strutted in his new magnificent attire, enlivening tavern and boozing-den with his rakehell carousing, Moll on his arm; even on one occasion, still more daring and following a riotous dinner, he drove with his doxy in a hackney-carriage past the Stone Jug itself. His fabulous luck held for two days and nights. The third evening he was sat drinking alone in a St. James's bagnio, Moll having deserted him, his pocket now considerably lightened, pondering where next he could strike to augment his depleted funds. Presently he informed one of the girls he was leaving and a hackney be fetched for him. The sultry-eyed harlot threw him a long glance, but no premonition of imminent disaster disturbed his equanimity as a few minutes later he paused unsteadily at the street door, top-hat tilted rakishly over one eye. Boldly he stepped into the waiting carriage, and met a brace of pistols prodding him in his stomach, while two pairs of hands grasped each arm and he was forced back into the seat by a Bow

Street Runner on either side. Above the pistols loomed the familiar rubicund features of Townsend.

'Now, Mr. Rathburn, do you sit quiet. You are going with us for a little ride.' Nick fought savagely, behind him the voices of those who, rushing from the bagnio, crowded the pavement.

'Murder,' he shouted. 'Help, for God's sake. I am attacked by rogues. I am murdered. Help me, for Christ's sake.' But no one moved, only the shrill peals of mocking laughter from the bagnio's whores answered his cries, the handcuffs snapped over his wrists and, followed by a shout from the mob, the hackney drove off towards Bow Street.

A little later he found himself stood in the same spot from where, in company with Casanova, he had the last time faced that massive black-bandaged figure. Mr. Bond, shooting a look at him over his spectacles, was reading out the charge. Sir John Fielding's double chin was sunk upon his cravat while he sat there quiescent, for all the world as if he had never heard mention of the prisoner's name before. Townsend, himself giving evidence, described how Mrs. Devenish had raised the alarm upon returning to her Marylebone Fields villa, to discover she had been victim of a robbery.

Nick, his teeth bared in a cynical grin, glanced about him occasionally to observe the spectators; rabble off the streets with no better home to go to jostling with the blades and rakes of the *beau monde*, together with journalists waiting to pick up a tid-bit of news, the fetid air made less noisesome by the perfumes of several fashionable darlings and the scented powders and pomades of those *beaux* to whose arms they clung, come to feast their fascinated gaze upon the scene. Nick, befettered now about his legs as well as at the wrists, yawned with simulated boredom to express his utter lack of interest in the proceedings as they took their customary course.

'The night-watch being advised of what had happened,' Townsend was saying, 'who, in turn, communicated the news to a Bow Street Runner, I made my way to Marylebone Fields and received a description from the victim of the crime herself, which agreed in every particular with the prisoner known as Nick Rathburn, a person of notorious reputation — '

'Notorious?' Nick interrupted him with a snarl. 'As what? A common housebreaker? Or for being a spy once in Bow Street's pay, until sickened with his employment?' His words produced a stir of excited interest in the court, the journalists' heads came up with a jerk and then their pencils moved the swifter over their writing-paper. Mr. Bond stood up.

'You will hold your tongue' — shaking his head reprovingly at Nick as if to say he should know better than to behave in so unseemly a manner. Then he turned with a cough. 'He says, Sir John, he was employed by the Bow Street Runners as an informer.'

'Indeed? Are we to understand he expects anyone in their right senses to believe I descend to such practices?'

'He has twice before been brought before you' — the clerk seemed to be explaining how such a scandalous accusation could come to be voiced — 'and doubtless would brazen his way out of this present charge.'

'You have no need to tell him,' Nick jeered. 'His hearing is unaffected. He knows my voice well enough.'

It occurred to him the Blind Beak, despite his ample appearance, seemed to have sagged physically and, though the powerful force of his personality still dominated the proceedings as of old, yet it taxed even his mighty resources; the grey skin glistened unhealthily in the flickering light. For a fleeting moment a spasm of pity moved in the depths of Nick's heart, to be crushed with a bitterly muttered imprecation as Mr. Bond turned on him warningly. 'If the prisoner does not show his respect for the court, he will straightway be sent to Newgate.'

'I will be sent there anyway,' Nick retorted, which caused the other, just about to sit down again, to dash his quill on his document-littered table with violent exasperation and bob up again crying for order.

Nick allowed his attention to wander as Mr. Townsend continued giving his evidence. That flash of intuition he had experienced as he was bidding Mrs. Devenish adieu at her villa had been amply justified. She had either been a party to the plot from the beginning or had realized the nature of the trap prepared for him, and that he was wary of it. In order to keep in favour with her protector she had cunningly slipped the brooch into Nick's pocket on the way to her carriage, then had advised the police officers on the scene she had been robbed. He realized there could be only one outcome, unless he was extremely fortunate, resulting from tonight's proceedings. He yielded to no sense of despair, only a kind of stoic lethargy, the conviction the game had gone on long enough, that it was time for him to throw in his hand.

'How does the prisoner answer to the charge?' The voice of the Blind Beak brought him back to his present surroundings.

Nick eyed him for several moments with an air of casual indifference. 'And it would have the slightest effect,' he drawled, 'I would speak my mind and tell you what you already know: that the charge is one trumped up at your own instigation.' Another ripple of murmurings and whisperings, nudges and grimaces, the journalists' pens moving agitatedly again. 'Revengeful devil that you are,' Nick added, 'and may your fat carcass rot in hell.'

Yet again Mr. Bond made to jump to his feet, but those suave, sibilant tones restrained him. 'The prisoner is remanded,' Sir John said, his demeanour unmoved, 'and will be taken to Newgate to await his trial.' That bleak smile flitted once more across Nick's saturnine features as he recalled the time long ago when he had last heard the other direct he should be conveyed to the Stone Jug. He had fought back then, stridently cursed the blind figure who had pronounced those doom-laden words upon him. This time he merely shrugged with a studied air of insolent nonchalance.

Presently the coach bearing him and two police officers drew up outside the prison entrance to Newgate Street. Nick passed into that foul, fetid air, laden with disease, and so poisonous, only recently the judge, in the Old Bailey adjoining, together with sixty persons — witnesses, court attendants, and jurymen — had died of typhus. Even the accused had been carried off with the fever ere the hempen collar claimed him. As he passed through the iron-studded gates, turnkeys and jailers hung about him like so many carrion-crows at a gibbet-corpse, their rapacious claws ready for bribes.

'Two shillings and sixpence,' a burly individual, reeking of gin, demanded, 'and you do not wish to repose in there straightway.' He jerked a grimy thumb at the Condemned Hold on the other side of the entrance-lodge, from which sounded raucous shouts and drunken quarrelling.

Nick produced from his pocket the requisite fee which would save him temporarily from the grimmest lodging in the prison.

'You will find yourself there soon enough,' observed one of the officers who had escorted him from Bow Street.

Nick shrugged. 'And the Blind Beak, pox on him, has his way, you may well be right.'

'Do you confess,' was the reply, 'you

asked for the worst side of his tongue. It serves his reputation little good, a rogue such as you boasting you were once a police-spy.'

'As if you do not know he is out to send me to Tyburn no matter what I do or do not say.' Then the turnkey was conducting him through another door. He was anxious to conserve the few guineas he still possessed concealed upon him against the time when he might need them more desperately than even his present grievous situation required. And so he was led down slippery steps to a dark and dismal dungeon where no light penetrated, whose very stones and mortar were encrusted with filth, and which was crowded with miserable wretches, cursing and yelling obscenities as the door opened quickly and then clanged shut, and, trampling on the lice under his feet so that they crackled like sea-shells strewn upon a garden-path, he slumped down, his back against the slimy wall, and rested himself as best as his fetters would allow him while the echoes of his jailer's footsteps outside died away.

26

His trial at the Old Bailey drew the gaping sightseers to the court. Despite the abominably stinking atmosphere, damp streaming down the walls and the fetid air hazing the windows, the gallery was crammed with members of the *beau monde*, the fops snapping their snuff-boxes, the feminine fluttering fans, pointing fingers, giggling and whispering, chattering like starlings in the roof, and, gathered outside the Old Bailey, a vast multitude vainly sought to gain admittance into court.

As the facts of the case against him — supported by his past record of conviction, imprisonment in Newgate, escape, his being charged again in Casanova's company, much being made of Sir John Fielding's clemency on this occasion — were set out, Nick realized the proceedings were merely perfunctory. The dull, pious old judge, the bunch of herbs before him with the object of warding off gaol-fever, was all impatience for the black cap to be placed on his wig. He held no hope the verdict would be anything else but guilty; and after it was presently pronounced and he, yawning ostentatiously during the long mumbling and discursive harangue which followed, Nick heard himself finally sentenced to be hanged by the neck at Tyburn upon Wednesday, June the 7th, in two weeks' time.

In the Condemned Hold, elaborate precautions were taken to prevent a repetition of his former escape. He was handcuffed, doubly manacled about both legs, chained to the stone floor and a good watch kept on him. Those felons sentenced to death before his trial having already taken their departure upon their last journey, he found on his arrival he was the cell's solitary tenant, for which circumstance he was duly grateful — the air would be that much freer to breathe. Visitors began flocking to Newgate, pinching their noses against the vile stench of foul human beings, to obtain a view of that notorious criminal, Nick Rathburn, and the keepers were busily reaping a rich harvest of admission fees. Among his visitors was Dr. Kelly, and Nick good-humouredly asked him had he come to register a claim on his corpse.

'I had thought,' was the reply, made in all seriousness, 'to have a hearse waiting near the Tyburn Tree in which to carry you off to Surgeons' Hall. They are much in need of cadavers for their dissecting-tables.' He frowned reflectively and added: 'I should have to watch out, for the mob if they knew my intent would tear me apart to prevent my plan.'

'Since I am most likely to have little interest in what transpires,' Nick replied, 'you can hardly expect me to share your concern with your problem.'

An unexpected visitor was none other than Jem Morgan, who brought some bottles of wine, announcing he had recently become mine host of the Nag's Head Tavern in Oxford Street, where he planned to preside between his prize-ring engagements. He had remembered Nick from the Blackheath encounter. 'You were bold enough then,' he said, 'but now you look to have suffered a knock-out blow. Jem Morgan was never a man to strike another when he be down, so I thought to cheer your sorrow a trifle.' And he sat listening engrossed as he persuaded Nick to recount how he had contrived to effect his sensational escape from Newgate years before. 'To think so much could be done by the aid of an old nail,' he marvelled, eyeing the gyves around Nick's wrists and shaking his cropped head. As he took his leave he was declaring he would have such a tale with which to entertain the frequenters of his hostelry they would stop to listen for hours. Then one day who should stump in most sorrowfully but Ted Shadow.

'Had I but guessed, Mr. Rathburn,' he snivelled, 'my thoughtless act would bring you to this.'

Followed a rigmarole of explanation, how he had been misinformed and misled by the Blind Beak, who had cunningly bamboozled him into believing he was serving a just cause in denouncing his erstwhile employer, and further protestations of his grief. Nick heard him with a sardonically raised eyebrow, then Shadow lowered his voice and, casting glances round in his characteristic manner to reassure himself he was not being overheard: 'I know some friends who have cut a body down from the gallows before now and restored it to life. Why should you not be served likewise? A carriage waiting at the Tree and, soon as we can, we will get hold on you and off to a surgeon.'

'I am aware,' Nick smiled bleakly, 'a highwayman or two in the past have been resuscitated, but it is said for the rest of their careers they suffered an intolerable crick in the neck. Think not I am ungrateful to you, but I do doubt but my neck would for ever after be too crooked for my cravat to be worn *à la mode*.' He gave a touch to the fine snowy whiteness at his throat which he still contrived to keep neat and clean. Presently the other departed, promising to return as often as he might and do all he could to make amends for the hurtful wrong he had committed.

To the prison chaplain and other

reverend gentlemen who would frequently call to see him Nick remained on banteringly good terms. 'You are all of you gingerbread fellows,' he mocked the chaplain once, 'who visit me more out of curiosity than charity and to form broadsheets and ballads on my demeanour.'

One religious man of somewhat decrepit appearance, who intoned prayers continuously until the cell reverberated with his mournful chant, intrigued Nick a trifle on account of the fact that he invariably arrived unaccompanied, though the turnkeys who conducted him to the cell accorded him the greatest reverence and respect. There was about him an air of purposefulness, a sudden penetration in his glance, Nick fancied, a curious watchfulness somehow inconsistent with his sanctimonious aspect.

'I fondly believe,' he told his visitor one afternoon, 'you are some spy, sent to ferret out if I have a file or saw secreted upon me with which I might effect my escape. This do I take most to heart, for, you must know, to me one file is worth all the Bibles in Christendom.' To his barely concealed amusement, the response to his

361

thrust was a fish-like sagging of the jaw. The other seemed about to say something, thought better of it and shuffled away. He continued to call, however, and his prayers rang out with undiminished fervour, though Nick decided his gaze, when now he caught it resting upon him, was even sharper than before.

On the last May morning of the year, and so far as he could foresee the last he would ever know, Nick was surprised by the arrival of Sir Joshua Reynolds, who introduced himself as inspired with the idea of adding to his long list of portraits of celebrities and distinguished personages the most-talked-of rake-hell of the hour. 'And when you have transposed my likeness to your canvas,' Nick advised him sardonically, 'I know who you will find as a purchaser for it. Sir John Fielding — he has space on his sitting room wall.'

'And my work is good enough,' Sir Joshua observed as he set-to with his paints and brushes, 'it will of a certainty claim its place in the Royal Academy.'

'You would have me hang twice,' Nick answered, 'once at Tyburn and again at

Burlington House,' to be informed his portrait would become familiar to a wider public than that of art-lovers alone, since Sir Joshua intended to see to it mezzotints of his painting would be engraved for circulation to all the popular print-shops. All that day, by the light of sputtering candles, Sir Joshua painted. Nick sat beneath a barred window, his black suit carefully brushed as usual, the cravat fastidiously tied about his throat, only the handcuffs about his wrists, which his lace ruffles could not altogether hide, marring his raffish elegance.

Further evidence of the spread of his renown appeared next day when Shadow hurried in waving a newspaper at him wherein he read:

'Rathburn is now secured at last:
Reynolds has fixed the felon fast.
Oft though he loosed himself before,
The slippery rogue escapes no more.
Reynolds, 'tis time to gild with fame
Th' obscure, and raise the humble name;
To make the form elude the grave,
Tho' Life in vain the rogue implores

An exile on the farthest shores,
Thy paint-brush brings a kind reprieve
And bids the dying robber live.'

By now the Condemned Hold had filled with more visitors: journalists seeking tid-bits of gossip for their newspapers and Grub Stret hacks intent upon securing material with which to write up Nick's life. To them he gave full play to his mordant sense of humour, concocting for their benefit variously embroidered version of escapades and scandalous exploits in which he was reputed to have participated. Then the blades of the town would arrive, some who sought his company on their way to the houses of high society, there to dine on stories of their meeting with New-gate's most notorious scallawag, or to boast next morning round the coffee-houses and taverns of having shaken hands with none other than that rakehell, Nick Rathburn.

Among those frequenting his cell were gamesters and sharpers, *habitués* of thieves' kitchens and night-cellars and other members of London's criminal fraternity, who brought with them their condolences, impossible schemes for effecting his escape, together with bottles of wine or sustaining liquors, rich food-stuffs and an occasional gift of money, with which to pay the doxies of the town who brought him freshly laundered shirts for his person and sheets for his bed.

So the time passed; rarely would he be dragged up like a hooked pike, out of the black terror of a dream and in a cold lather of sweat, to choke and claw at the rope that had been tightened round his neck, to sleep again, at last lulled by his doxy's kisses. Only fleetingly did he allow his thoughts to drift into reveries of his early days in the Rookeries; of Doll Tawdry; sudden pictures recaptured on his mind of that triumphant escape from the Stone Jug; recollections of his life with Dr. Zodiac and Queen Mab; Casanova and at the house in Spring Gardens, remembrances of the fashionable *salons*, Vauxhall, Drury Lane and London's gay assemblies.

Inevitably he would recall his first meeting with Chagrin and he would have to fight off the memory of her with fierce desperation. And then would rise unbidden to the surface of his eddying thoughts the brooding figure of the Blind Beak. Gritting his teeth, Nick would shake off the grip of memories, fasten his attention on to the bawdy anecdote with which a wench would be regaling him over a glass of wine, or some item of intelligence Ted Shadow, for ever commiserating with him on his situation and swearing his steadfast devotion, brought him.

As well as his news and other gossip, most of which revolved round the clash of armies in America and accounts of French naval attacks on British forces along the American coast and in the West Indies, reports were reaching Newgate of the anti-Catholic riots spreading London-wards from the North where raged a ferment of religious intolerance. Persecution, with blatant attacks against the houses and shops, churches and chapels and upon their persons, of those of Catholic religion, grew daily more rife round about the Metropolis itself. Protestant organizations and clubs were being formed, their avowed intention to root out Papism from the land, striking terror into the hearts of harmless men and women whose only crime was that they professed the Catholic faith.

A member of the House of Commons, one fiery-tempered reckless-natured young Scotsman, Lord George Gordon, whose anti-Popery speeches were as incoherent as they were ridiculous, had been adopted as leader of their cause by the Protestant agitators and, for an emblem of their blood-thirsty ambitions, a blue cockade, with, as a battle-cry: 'No Popery.'

On the night of June 2nd, the Stone Jug hummed with the news that a crowd sixty-thousand strong had followed Lord George Gordon to the House of Commons, where Parliament was in session, he to demand in their name the law against the Catholics be reverted to its original repressive and prejudicial measures. The Government refusing to take precipitate action, which decision so aroused the ever-growing multitude's wrath, they attempted to storm the doors and the military were sent for. By the time troops had arrived, however, the crowds, tired out with the day's excitement, had begun to disperse — not all to return peacefully to their homes, large numbers forming themselves into separate mobs intent upon deeds of violence.

For the next two or three days reports filtered into the prison that Catholic chapels, the houses of priests and any suspected of being sympathetic to the religion of Rome, were attacked and burned, pulpits and benches, pews and even altars were thrown into the street and burned. Soon Nick was not dependent upon rumour or hearsay, first-hand information reaching him from those rioters who had been arrested and cast shouting and cursing into Newgate, there to cool their anti-Papist passions. He heard them claiming all London was fast falling under mob rule and indeed the shout of roving riotous throngs penetrated the prison walls. When he received intelligence that the rioters, growing satiated with their attacks upon the defenceless Catholics, were intent upon attacking Newgate itself, to release those of their fellow-rioters, Nick for the first time began to speculate upon the possibility of making his escape.

On the Sunday afternoon prior to the fatal Wednesday, Nick, sweating in the summer heat in which the gaol festered and reeked of the stench of rotting human beings, received a visit from Ted Shadow, his hat decorated with a huge, blue cockade, toothless grin spread from ear to ear.

'We will have you out, Mr. Rathburn, before you are much older,' he enthused in his usual conspiratorial tones. 'And you will not be taking no poxy road to Tyburn neither,' thrusting a blue cockade which he had produced from his pocket into Nick's hand. 'It may prove your passport to freedom.' He bubbled over with stories of the excesses perpetrated by the mob. 'They will set half London alight before they finish. Half-crazed and boozed up to the gills they be.'

It seemed the authorities were completely at a loss; though troops and cavalry had been called out, more houses and chapels had gone up in smoke. Even Lord Mansfield, the Lord Chief Justice, who had recently acquitted a Catholic priest wrongfully accused, was a victim; his great house in Bloomsbury Square, full of priceless pictures and rare books and manuscripts and his vast library of legal volumes and documents, was completely gutted by the torches of the mob.

That night Nick lay awake, grinning thinly to himself with visions of eluding after all the fate to which he had philosophically resigned himself and had been prepared to meet with his characteristic stoicism.

He awoke of a sudden with a rough shaking at his shoulder and a figure bending over him, his shadow on the dank wall distorted evilly by the dim light of his lantern. 'Wake the dreams out of your eyes. You are going to enjoy your little treat earlier than you expected.'

Struggling out of his sleep it was borne upon Nick by the jailer that, scared by the threat of the rioters' attack upon the Stone Jug, Mr. Ackerman, the governor, had determined there should be no risk of rakehell Nick Rathburn being rescued from the Condemned Hold. He would make the journey to Tyburn that very Monday morn, when Holborn and Oxford Street would be less crowded and Tyburn more sparsely attended.

'It will not be such a fine procession for you,' the turnkey commiserated with him. 'But you will dance just as nimbly at the end.'

27

Half-past seven, the prison-bell tolling mournfully as Nick was conducted to the gate-house where his arms were pinioned at the elbows — his shirt open at the neck, wearing breeches, spruce flowered waistcoat, his hair neatly combed, chin freshly shaved, which privileges he had obtained by his last few coins to the turnkey. Nonchalant and debonair as ever, while the fetters about his ankles were knocked off by the morose-featured individual waiting with his block and hammer, he drank off the glass of brandy given him and waited coolly for his handcuffs to be removed. But no move was made to free his wrists and he gave an impatient curse. 'Do you think I should want to wear this jewellery?' It was indeed customary for the prisoner's handcuffs to be removed after his arms had been bound.

'You forget your reputation,' the fellow

with the hammer answered him. 'It be feared you might not reach Tyburn safe without the iron on your wrists.'

To the surprise of those about him, expecting him to answer with some characteristic quip, instead Nick's face darkened. As the hangman approached to loop round his neck the rope he spat at him: 'Keep off, knight of the halter, until these damned things to be removed.' The other hesitated and glanced at Mr. Ackerman himself, who had stood in the background and whose gaze suddenly narrowed with suspicion. With a nod to the turnkeys, ordering them to hold Nick securely, he came forward and began to search him. Suddenly he jumped back with a muttered oath, blood dripping from his fingers which had encountered inside the lining of Nick's waistcoat the sharp-edged blade of a clasp-knife. There followed a desperate struggle until at last the knife was wrested from him.

When he realized his last throw of the dice had failed, that his lucky star no longer shone above, Nick smoothed his ruffled hair as best he could with his manacled hands, joking with Mr. Ackerman. 'A present from a friend, and but for your insistence upon my wearing these poxy brancelets I would have escaped you at the last.'

He passed through Execution Gate and ascended into the cart awaiting him. Leaning casually against his coffin resting athwart the cart which was to accompany him on his two-mile journey, he called an airy time of day to the driver. A length of heavy chain secured his manacled wrists to the cart-floor. The bright June air was suddenly filled with the chimes of the neighbouring clocks striking the hour of eight. The cavalcade set off, led by prison officials, some on horseback, others in a coach, Nick accompanied by the prison chaplain of mournful aspect and in rusty black, the cart flanked on either side by mounted troops and peace officers and behind them another company of troops. Since they were conveying only one malefactor to Tyburn the procession was a short one.

At the junction of Giltspur Street and Newgate Street and the Old Bailey, they halted by the porch of St. Sepulchre's Church, where the deep-toned bell boomed out above a scattered crowd, most of whom, Nick observed, sported the blue cockade in their hats or displayed it in their coats. On the church steps stood the sexton clanging his own hand-bell rhythmically while he delivered his solemn exhortation.

'All good people pray heartily unto God for this poor sinner who is now going to his death and for whom the great bell doth toll. You who are condemned to die repent with lamentable tears. Ask mercy of the Lord for the salvation of your soul through the merits of the death and passion of Jesus Christ who now sits on the right hand of God to make intercession for you if you penitently return to Him. The Lord have mercy on you. Christ have mercy upon you. Christ have mercy upon you.'

Nick, his expression indifferent and lip curled contemptuously at the sexton's platitudinous mumbling, heard groans of sympathy from the onlookers and caught admiring glances from several ogling wenches who threw him kisses as the cavalcade proceeded down the deep slopes of Snow Hill. Reflecting idly upon Ted Shadow's mortification upon learning how the Blind Beak had made certain his lust for vengeance would not be denied, Nick was borne up Holborn Hill. The street being broad and more blue-cockaded crowds being encountered, the soldiers, apprehensive of any attempt to rescue its doomed occupant, enclosed the cart more tightly.

Despite Mr. Ackerman's precautions, news of Nick Rathburn's execution date having been put forward had begun to spread about the town. Excited and curious throngs were inceasing to such an extent that the steps of St. Andrew's Church they were now approaching were, Nick could see, crowded with spectators. As the procession slowed down he searched on either side of him with a seemingly casual air, but alert for a sight of Shadow's face.

Nowhere could he perceive in the thickening crowd anyone he knew. His only source of hope was the predominance everywhere of the blue cockade.

There reached his ears murmurs and shouts against his escort. Many raised their fists, so the chaplain by his side, gabbling prayers in his ear, was throwing anxious glances at the mob. Scowling, Nick glanced down at the irons about his wrists. Had they been free, had the knife smuggled into him by one of the strumpets not been discovered, he would surely have severed the rope about his elbows.

Unshackled and unpinioned he could have plunged into the crowd whom he felt certain would have aided him. 'Jump for it,' urged a fellow in a butcher's apron all bloodied. 'We will see they do not get you back.' At which others in the mob raised a cheer, followed inconsequently by cries of: 'No Popery, no Popery.'

Nick held up his manacled wrists to show the heavy chain which dragged at them, to evoke loud cries of sympathy for him and howls of execration against his captors. Suddenly noticing a coach that had appeared among the crowd some hundred yards behind, his hopes leapt. Had Shadow somehow learned of what had happened? Nick recalled how the other had spoken of a coach he would have ready at hand as near as possible to the gallows with hot blankets in which to wrap his body after he had been turned off, and a surgeon waiting to bleed him copiously and apply friction to stimulate circulation.

A hanged man might be resuscitated, so long as he could be speedily cut down, the soldiers and officials eluded, and conveyed to safety, and Nick kept his eye on the coach, striving to discern whether it was drawing any nearer through the impeding throng. Then he saw it turn aside to make its way down another street and he realized it could not have been Shadow after all.

The procession was now reaching the beginning of Oxford Street and his wry smile widened a trifle as a rough voice hailed him. It was Jem Morgan at the first-floor window of the Nag's Head and holding aloft a tankard which gleamed in the sunlight. 'You may pay for it on your way back, Nick Rathburn.'

The cart halted directly under the

tavern window so the brimming tankard could reach Nick over the heads of the drolls calling out their jokes, wishing him good health. Raising the drink by his manacled hands, Nick fancied he detected a glint in the prize-fighter's eye over the tankard-rim, as if the other was endeavouring to convey some sort of signal to him.

Even as the thought occurred to him, Morgan called: 'That should help nail your thirst,' and above the hubbub about him Nick caught a sharp sound inside the tankard, which sent his mind back to his conversation with the prize-fighter at New-gate. Draining the quenching wine he heard something again and, keeping his mouth open wide, felt the cause of it against his tongue. He jerked his head forward, choking, and spat into his hand held close to his mouth. Grinning at some wit who shouted: 'Do not choke yourself now, Nick, and spoil the hangman his fun,' Nick threw back the tankard, which was deftly caught and the cavalcade proceeded on its way.

The walls of Hyde Park came into sight and the wide space before it which led into Edgware Road. Here the huge grandstand was filling with spectators and then Nick beheld the Tree, a great wood triangular structure from whose three cross-bars could hang a score or more of malefactors. The crowd already assembled and sweating beneath the sun loosed a great roar as the procession made its slow progress towards the gallows, and above the clamour Nick could hear repeated again and again the battle-cry: 'No Popery, no Popery.'

The cart drew to a halt underneath one of the cross-bars and Nick, standing taut and tensed, knew in a few more minutes all would be over. His mouth was dry, his heart pounded at his ear-drums as if they must burst, his brain was afire, a spinning chaos behind the nonchalant mask he wore. Eyebrow raised in sardonic amusement, he glanced about him as the chaplain began offering up a final benediction preparatory to clambering down from the cart, and the hangman fixed the rope to the cross-bar overhead.

The rough hempen collar coiled cold round his warm neck. Nick heard the intonations in his ear and observed the hangman from the corner of his eye, at the same time noting the increasingly apprehensive glances the soldiers and officials gave the sea of threatening fists and all around shouts of abuse.

The blue cockades seemed to reflect the hot blue June sky itself . . . now the clenched fists rose and fell in time to the mob's fever-pitch roar . . . the horse in front of him gave a whinny of terror. It was, Nick knew, now or never. There were shouts for him to make his farewell speech, mingled with the confused babel in his ears like the pounding of a mighty torrent breaking over his head.

A voice kept jabbering over and over: 'God help me . . . Christ save me . . . God save me . . . Christ help me . . . Christ help me,' and he barely realized it was his own voice, or that the flecks of froth floating before his vision were from his twitching lips. Then, a sudden jangle of chains at his feet and with a great cry of exultation, his long dark eyes aglitter, he raised both hands, those broad-palmed, oddly tapering hands of steely strength, to be met with a tremendous howl. Held between a thumb and forefinger was the twisted rusty nail Jem Morgan had slipped into his tankard; then he plunged it into his breeches-pocket to draw forth his blue cockade which he waved high.

Another terrific roar greeted him and, as the hangman closed in, Nick caught him a back-handed blow that knocked him clean out of the cart. Slipping his head from the noose and leaping on to the coffin, Nick, still waving the blue cockade, rasped: 'No Popery, no Popery.' His hoarse cry was taken up by thousands of voices in another deafening yell, the mob threw itself upon the soldiers and police officers, and he dived into the struggling mass.

28

Early evening found him in the forefront of a band of rioters advancing along the Strand towards Temple Bar. He had emerged from the battling mass round the Tree, the spectators eager to help him escape from the scene, one stripping off his cravat to give him, in order he would look less conspicuous by its presence. 'Not of the finest lace, but more comfortable than the one you wore.' Another, saying the day had grown too warm to wear it, threw him his jacket, somewhat threadbare but accepted gratefully to help add to his change of appearance. Another passed him his slouch hat to cover up the distinctive white streak in his dark hair, while several dipped into their pockets to give him money. All about him congratulations and enthusiastic praises for his audacity; so he tingled with exhilaration and laughed aloud in excited triumph.

Less conspicuous in his borrowed plumes, he had disarmed suspicion as to his identity by crying out to those on every side: 'Nick Rathburn has escaped the hangman. He is somewhere in the crowd.' Presently, half-way along Oxford Street, he ceased to employ this subterfuge, since the interest of the stream of people bearing him irresistibly along was centred less upon Tyburn than upon anti-Catholic violence. Sporting his blue cockade in the hat he had acquired, not a person could he see without a similar emblem. From the windows of houses on either side hung blue streamers; improvised flags of the same hue had appeared, at street-corners and from balconies shouting men and shrieking women harangued the dusty crowd: 'No Popery, no Popery. Down with all Catholics. Kill, burn, destroy.'

Any hopes he might have entertained of getting free of the crowd had been dashed at every attempt. Twice turning down a side-street he was each time swept back by another mob emerging to join the rioters into the main human river. In any case what would he have achieved by escaping from the protective anonymity of the crowd? Reports of his escape would have flashed round London, and alone in the taverns or dens of St. Giles's he ran the risk of being seen and betrayed by some rogue, while to seek the quieter suburbs or outlying villages would be even more hazardous. The tentacles of the envenomed Blind Beak would reach out and grasp him most easily in those parts where he must appear more conspicuous.

So, conceiving of nothing more expedient to his safety than to be borne with the great throng wherever it flowed, he had made a virtue of necessity by remaining in the circumstances events had cast him, to decide later upon a course of action.

The hours passed beneath the sweltering sun. The vast multitude, spreading slowly and haphazardly in the direction of Fleet Street, had begun to break up into separate bands ranging from a score to a hundred or more persons, some to wreak their fury upon any house that did not display the blue cockade, or a blue flag or had not chalked upon its door: 'No

Popery', pillaging, burning and terrorizing any occupants. Others halted for food and refreshments at taverns, grog-shops and coffee-houses *en route*. Many whose thirst required slaking so continuously were rendered unable to proceed any further, but lay insensible in drinking-establishment corners or sprawled in the gutters.

Nick had found himself attached to a mob numbering fifty bloodthirsty men and women. The force of his vibrant personality gained him a sort of leadership, shared with a Pig Street shoemaker name Babylon, squat, barrel-chested, brutal-visaged and foul-mouthed, who carried a pitchfork with which to goad any rioter he suspected of lacking in enthusiasm; and a sloe-eyed buxom wench named Rose. 'Rambling Rose,' she had ogled Nick, 'that is me, but I would cling to you when my ramble is done.' She was a serving-wench, she asserted, from a fine house in Berkeley Square, adding her shrieks of encouragement to the shoemaker's stentorian bellow, waving a blue silk curtain stolen from her employers.

The rabble was armed in every conceivable manner: some brandished rusty swords or pikes, others carried pickaxes and sledge-hammers, staves and cudgels, several bore old muskets or pistols which, though they lacked the necessary ammunition, made a desperate show and could be used club-wise. Nick himself had been presented with a barrel-stave, from one end of which protruded two ugly nails.

During the afternoon, news had circulated amongst the rioters that every soldier in London and its outskirts had been called to duty, regular troops and the militia assembling at their barracks being directed to strategic positions in the streets, which intelligence was greeted with challenging boasts.

Nick, the shoemaker and Rose and their supporters had found themselves at the door of a house in a side-street upon which the chalked 'No Popery' was absent. The house-owner, whose terrified family were hiding upstairs, protested he was no Papist whereupon Babylon demanded the other's Bible, to see if it were the Protestant version or not. Upon it being produced forthwith, Nick had observed with amusement the shoemaker holding the Bible upside-down pretending to read. 'It is the right religion,' he had declared. 'It is Lord George's religion, by God.'

And so, caught in the swirling eddies of the crowds, Nick and his companions had been deflected through Lincoln's Inn Fields until now they were proceeding along the Strand, Temple Bar ahead and Fleet Street beyond. 'Where are we going?' Rambling Rose was screaming, 'to plunder the Bank?' An answering shout of laughter and then suddenly above the guffaws Babylon's roar.

'That is it. We are for the Bank and all its gold.'

Whereupon Rose shrieked with delight, flung her arms first round the shoemaker's bull-like neck then hung upon Nick, screaming: 'To the Bank. The Bank and all its lovely gold.'

As they neared Temple Bar, sudden and sinister sounds — the rattle of musketry — momentarily quietened the exultant shouting. Now occurred a tumult above which arose the screams and groans of those wounded by that first volley. As the mob recoiled from this first sign of authority to be encountered, Nick saw the line of soldiers drawn up across the street. A servingman carrying a plate of oysters scuttled across and with a pained glance at the smoking muskets disappeared through a tavern door. An ensign bawled to the crowd to turn back or they would receive another volley. The rioters, shouting imprecations and shaking fists, hesitated, then Babylon leapt forward brandishing his pitchfork. 'To Newgate, then. The Bank will come later.'

'To Newgate,' and, shouting and huzzaing, the mob swung into the side-streets, streaming back into Lincoln's Inn Fields. Nick paused with Rose and one or two others to help the less badly hurt to scramble to their feet; those seriously wounded, together with several dead men and women, one of the latter with a moaning babe at her breast, were left for the soldiers to attend to.

Nick was of little mind to find himself

once more in the vicinity of the grim walls he had not long since quitted, but there was nothing for it; free from the Stone Jug and the noose, he found himself a prisoner of the mob, from which he dare not, even if he might succeed in the attempt, turn aside, for fear of exciting suspicion concerning his identity or that he was some Papist sympathizer.

Through the streets between Fetter Lane and Gough Square he, the shoe-maker and the girl with their followers swarmed and proceeded apace until they emerged at Holborn Hill. There they encountered more rioters engaged in destroying the Old Black Swan distillery. Already furniture had been dragged out of the place, heaped into bonfires and set ablaze, while casks of unrectified spirits and liquor from the vaults were being broached by yelling men and women. In a moment great sheets of flame and clouds of smoke ascended as the gushing liquor caught fire. Men and women, children and mothers with babes in their arms, emerging from the noisome courts and surrounding blind-alleys, found themselves suddenly caught in the inferno, while others, recklessly hurling more and more furniture from neighbouring houses, added fuel to the flames.

Some completely berserk creatures were wallowing in the pools of spirits, lapping it up from the gutters and then shrieking insensately, reeling and staggering into the flames, to be roasted alive in blazing rum and gin. Nick observed a man leaning from one of the windows of a nearby coffee-house from which hung blue streamers, bellowing: 'No Popery. Burn the Catholics,' and throwing coins to encourage those scrambling for them in their orgy of destruction. Black flakes from the inferno floated in a vast cloud above, then there was a sudden tremendous roar and great flames spouted heavenwards from the heart of the conflagration in columns of fire which must have been seen for miles around.

Rose, who had been clutching Nick's arm, fascinated by the ghastly spectacles, screamed aloud at this new devastation. 'The vats have caught fire,' Nick told her grimly. At that moment he caught sight of two fire-engines which had been brought with the purpose of protecting neighbouring property. He saw the firemen working their engines and the flames shoot up more fiercely than before. 'The wells be full more of spirit than water,' he shouted, to halt the firemen from adding fuel to the flames. Then, Rose clinging to him and accompanied by Babylon, he was swept onwards to the direction of Snow Hill.

Passing a tavern-yard, he perceived a sturdy fellow whom he had noticed by the fire-engines now pumping away at a pump which was producing not water but gin from the distillery cellars, doling the stuff out at a penny a mugful, or as much as could be carried in a hat to the miscreants quickly gathering round him. Then the shoemaker was guffawing with delight, Rose uttering shrill peals, and Nick could not forbear a thin smile of amusement as they passed a reverend gentleman pushed against a house by a trio of footpads, coolly relieving him of his gold watch and purse.

Passing a French silk-merchant's house in the hands of despoilers, Rose rushed forward to snatch a cage of canaries, about to be added to the bonfire of furniture already blazing, from a virago with matted hair and gin-bleared eyes. 'They are Popish birds and should burn with the rest of this Popish house.' The harridan would have cast the cage into the flames had not Nick wrenched it free, presently handing the prize over to a woman companion to decorate it with a blue cockade.

Now Newgate, looming up beyond the house of a Mr. Rainsforth, the king's tallow-chandler, came in sight, from which flames and smoke belched and the roadway aglisten with melted tallow. Nick and the rest edged their way past, holding their noses against the choking fumes, to push their way through the great concourse assembled outside the prison, its grim walls silhouetted black against the night sky clouded with banks of smoke from the numerous fires dotted about London, lit up at intervals by the reflection of the flames.

Nick, together with Rose and Babylon, found himself urged by their followers, who themselves were pressed forward by other crowds converging upon the scene, into the threatening gathering outside the prison-gates howling for the release of the rioters. 'Deliver us our friends,' demanded some. 'You are holding good Protestant prisoners.'

Presently Nick observed a side-door in the prison-gate open and Mr. Ackerman, pompous of bearing as ever, faced the sarcastic huzzas and yells, at length contriving to make himself heard.

'Get you back to your homes,' he replied imperiously. 'Your fellows will be justly dealt with.' He had barely finished speaking and his obduracy greeted with howling execrations when from within the prison itself arose an echoing:

'No Popery, no Popery.'

Inflamed by the voices of the prisoners, their friends without grew more threatening. 'Hand them over,' they roared, 'or we will come and get them ourselves.'

For a moment Nick believed Mr. Ackerman would stand his ground, then a hail of stones smashed about the gate, some missing him narrowly, and he turned and dodged through the sidedoor, which slammed behind him. Stones smashed the prison windows, pickaxes and sledge-hammers beat against the gates, ladders appeared as if from nowhere, up which the rioters scaled the great walls.

Within a few moments a window of Mr. Ackerman's private dwelling was completely shattered from inside, the head of a triumphantly grinning rioter appeared, shouting encouragements to his followers below. There ensued the usual spectacle of furniture and household goods being hurled from every window and set alight in a heap against the prison-gates, which in turn caught fire.

Mr. Ackerman reappeared, surrounded by a group of officials who began forcing a way through the mob, belaying any in their path with their cudgels. The last sight Nick had of Mr. Ackerman was as the encircling crowd turned upon his escort, snatching their cudgels to bela-bour them until they, and he himself, sank beneath the waves of beating fists and infuriated shouts.

At this moment occurred a diversion. To the accompaniment of wild cheering a coach, dragged by some fifty crazed-looking fellows, came in view, atop which sat a young man looking more agitated than pleased by the frenzied scene. Nick realized this must be Lord George Gordon himself, the impetuous leader of the anti-Papists, who, as the coach made its way through the multitude, was making efforts to speak, at last obtaining some sort of silence. 'For God's sake, go home. While you behave in this unpeace-able way, nothing can come of our cause. The Government will never listen — '

He was howled down by his followers' battle-cry; even his appeal went unheeded. In any case few of the vast multitude could have heard his exhortation; to the rest the uproar of those near their leader led them to imagine the latter was encour-aging their destructive lust, and they renewed their attack upon the gaol with increased ferocity.

Not a stick of Mr. Ackerman's

furniture had not been heaped upon the bonfire, and, the prison-gates already ablaze, firebrands and flaming pieces of tow were hurled over the massive walls and through smashed windows, while wines and liquor of all kinds were being carried in pails, jugs and hats from the governor's cellars, to be drunk in great glee.

Nick was among the first inside the prison. Pandemonium reigned, the women especially screaming in fear of being roasted alive in the fires flaring up, while others clamoured to be released. One such imploring voice came from the Condemned Hold itself where, as Nick learned of several overjoyed men and women dashing past him to freedom, four wretches had been thrown that day after he had taken his leave.

Nick led the rush to the cell and, seizing a sledge-hammer from a drunken rioter, battered at the door, aided in his efforts by a score of axes and crowbars. In a few moments four dazed-looking creatures, one a pitiful old crone, another a thin boy of no more than fifteen summers, his ribs showing through his rags like a washerwoman's basket, were lugged out triumphantly.

'A clear way, a clear run,' Nick shouted at the boy, whose teeth were chattering with fear and bewilderment mingled, 'to the sweetest music in the world, the clank of broken fetters.' The other flew off, swift as an arrow from a Tartar's bow.

By now, parts of the gaol walls were red-hot, so those rushing out through clouds of black smoke and gushing flames would scream with agony as they encountered the searing stone. To Nick the wild forms careering past had the appearance of demons capering madly about some unearthly inferno; above, smoke clouded the sky, luridly tinged by the fork-tongued flames licking the disintegrating walls.

Sickened by the sight of the mob's unabated destructiveness Nick, with Babylon and Rose, whose clothes had been ripped off to the waist, her round breasts smudged black and half her hair singed away, joined a stream of the crowd which was dispersing at the news that a detachment of Light Dragoons, together with both foot and horseguards, had been despatched to the gaol, while other reports were to the effect that cannon were being brought up to reinforce the military.

Some were off to see the lunatics from Bedlam released, to gibber and prance through the streets, other bold spirits were for hunting lions rumoured to have been freed from the Tower. Then arose from several desperados, their eyebrows burned off, smoke-begrimed, the cry, 'On to Bow Street,' which new battlefront was taken up on either side:

'To the Police Court, Bow Street ahoy,' was shouted now. 'Burn it down,' a ruffian yelled in Nick's ear, then, more ominously: 'The Blind Beak, death to him,' from some other drunken throat and echoed by a bloodthirsty roar. 'Death to the Blind Beak. On to Bow Street. Kill. Burn. Destroy.'

29

They swung into Drury lane, Nick, Rambling Rose and Babylon in the van of the mob. The girl, stumbling along the street, littered with the scorched remains of a burned-out house, fell over a sprawled, blackened shape in the gutter. At first she took it to be some bedding — broken and blazing furniture lay strewn in all directions — when Nick, helping her to her feet, found himself staring into what was left of a once-familiar face. His glance shifted, the wooden stump had been burnt off.

A half-tipsy individual lurching from the doorway of the plundered house vouchsafed: 'Would have called the soldiers, he would, to save the police office from burning down. Papist traitor,' spurning the thing in the gutter with a drunken kick, 'was for rescuing the Blind Beak.' He described how the frenzied crowd, suspecting Shadow's purpose, had caught him, set fire to his wooden leg; then someone emptying a bucket of spirits over him, he had gone up in a sheet of flame.

'And so should all spies be served,' Babylon grunted. 'Burn, pox on you, burn,' and speared the charred corpse upon his pitchfork with a gruesome, crackling sound and hurled it into a nearby bonfire. Rose uttered a horrified shriek which broke off as Nick, sick to the stomach, struck the shoemaker in the face.

The squat figure teetered on his heels, blood pouring from his mouth, then collapsed with a moan of pain, his pitchfork clattering to the ground. Shrieking abuse at him, Rose lunged to attack Nick, who thrust her brutally aside so that she fell where Shadow had lain. At once the rest of the mob growled he was no true anti-Papist, then a shout brought everyone's head round. 'Bow Street is burning. The police court is afire.'

At the bestial roar that greeted the news Nick, of a sudden, experienced a tremendous release of hidden springs of action, instinctively he knew he must irrevocably free himself from the bonds of his past, or be for ever doomed. '*It is you who are destroying yourself.*' The words came back to him, ringing in his brain like a clarion-call above the tumult around him. Now, amidst this night of insensate destruction, of crazed terror, his innermost soul was illumined with the knowledge that of a certainty no longer could he remain prisoner of the dim half-world whence he had, like Lucifer to hell, returned. It must be freedom of his spirit now: to exist and yet be damned was no longer tolerable. He who had cracked the Stone Jug, had trod the tight-rope of deadly danger, who had escaped the noose about his very neck, beheld in a blinding flash of truth that escape in death were better than life on the abyss-edge.

For the second time in his strange history every nerve and fibre of his being, the very warp and woof of his character, the complex fabric of his philosophy underwent a shattering metamorphosis: involuntarily there passed before his mind's eye that moment past seven years since when he had stood in his dishonour and degradation beside Casanova at Bow Street and had encountered Chagrin's gaze. Then had he suddenly felt a sickening to his soul. Then had he known himself for what he truly was, the depths to which he must inevitably sink.

Once more he was faced with the knowledge he had come to a nadir of his career and vicissitude. And in a thunder-bolt shock of self-revelation he was transformed by the upsurging unconquer-able will to lift himself out of the mire and foul rottenness that had near dragged him under. Lift himself up by his own bootstraps, he would, and once more he experienced that tremendous elevation of the spirit as he grappled with the decision.

His thoughts sped to the Blind Beak in his extremity, galvanizing him to attempt, at whatever the cost, if it be his own skin, to wrest from the dread fate the rioters intended for him, that fat sightless hulk who, whatever else he may have thought best done in the line of his duty as he saw it, had given him his first chance to enlist himself in a future of service not without merit.

Animated by a grim determination, his narrowed eyes gleaming jets of resolution, he swung away from the menace of those before him and sped through a gap that had opened out in the throng. Presently, he saw the police court, from which smoke was already rising, accompanied by the smashing of windows and the chanting of: 'Down with Bow Street. Death to the Blind Beak. Burn. Kill. Destroy.'

He fought his way nearer and witnessed several police officers emerge, overpowered and cuffed and belaboured. Among them was Mr. Bond, spectacles caught on one ear, and all dishevelled, his expression distraught. 'Where are the soldiers?' he cried. 'Sir John will be burned to death.' Jostled and buffeted, the clerk passed within arm's length of Nick. 'Save Sir John. The soldiers? Sir John Fielding will perish,' his cries lost in a storm of jeers as he and his companions were roughly jostled out of sight.

Nick glanced up as a window of Sir John Fielding's sitting room shattered and a chair hurtled to the pavement. The window next it suffered similarly, a table crashing down, and from the splintered glass and wood demoniacal faces grinned. More furniture, a mass of documents and papers, books and ornaments, pictures, even the curtains wrenched away and cast to the flames below. A wild-looking creature leaned out, oblivious of the jagged glass, shouting: 'The Blind Beak himself be here. Do we throw him out, too?'

There was a roar of assent, and then another desperate individual appeared above, alongside the first. 'Throw him out?' he bellowed, 'or let him burn?'

Nick had gained the police court doorway, his blood running cold as all about him took up the challenge, some shouting for Sir John to be thrown to them, others urging he be left to burn. Keeping to the wall he fought his way along the crowded, smokefilled passage towards the stairs to the Blind Beak's sitting room. 'Let him burn,' came the shouts predominating now. 'Leave the Blind Beak to burn.'

Sparks flew from torches held by yelling rioters and, choking, Nick doggedly continued his way. He could hear more crashing of glass from above and then a mighty rending of wood as the sitting room door was torn from its hinges, to be hurled into the street. Of a sudden behind him arose screams and shouts of alarm. One side of the passage had caught alight and escape from the stairs was being cut off. A concerted rush from the building, a blazing torch falling in the mad dash to get out, and the staircase-foot burst into flames. Several remaining with him half-way up the stairs, plunging wildly downwards, Nick was left alone.

He reached the sitting room and from the doorway took in the scene of devastation, his gaze immediately fastening on the huge figure sprawled in an armchair, curtain-cords knotted round him, chin sunk on his chest, his black bandage awry. About him reeled three men still seeking any object on which to lay their hands, while two of their companions sagged helplessly in a corner, drunk on the wine from the smashed bottles and decanters scattered round the room. One of the trio still on their feet was attacking the wall-panelling with a crowbar, the other pair tackling a heavy table, one hacking at it with an axe while the other wrenched at one of the legs with bare hands.

Glancing over his shoulder at the red glow advancing from below, Nick drew the rioters' glowering attention as he moved forward purposefully; then the one with the axe let fly at him. He dodged and the other, wielding the crowbar, jumped to the attack. Nick stepped aside, thrust him backwards by the throat, so that he came up against the wall with a jolt.

The man who had thrown the axe now tried to close in, but Nick pushed him off with his left hand, and, as he came at him again, struck him a terrific blow under the jaw and, caught off-balance, he staggered helplessly up against the smashed window, balancing precariously for a moment, then, clawing at the air, toppled over and, screaming, disappeared from sight.

Struggling with the unarmed adversary who had leaped on him from behind, Nick, as they threshed the floor, managed to fasten his grip round the other's windpipe. At the same moment the man wielding the crowbar came at him again; mistiming his blow, his foot caught in a broken chair and he sprawled to his knees. Hanging on to his first opponent's throat Nick had reduced him to insensibility and, leaving him an inert heap, he got to his feet to carry on the fight to the man who was reaching for the crowbar. Nick picked up a heavy broken chairleg, bringing it down with all his force. There was a horrible crack and the other man dropped on his face, his neck broken.

Half choked with the smoke which was filling the room, Nick got to the slumped, helpless figure in the armchair, his toe stubbing against the crowbar and sending it clattering along the floor. He was untying the Blind Beak when a movement in the doorway brought his head up with a jerk. Crouched there was Babylon, his hair and clothes singed and smoking, blood still running from his mouth. In some miraculous fashion the shoemaker had managed to fight his way up the burning staircase. In his hand he gripped his pitchfork.

'Papist spy!' Babylon lumbered into the room, and simultaneously the pitchfork flew from his hand. Swiftly as Nick moved, one prong ripped a gash in his left shoulder, inflicting a grazing wound before it embedded itself in the wall behind him. With a thwarted grunt the ape-like figure came on, head sunk in his hunched shoulders, his arms swinging. Nick dived for the crowbar he had scuffed along the floor, in the same movement picking it up to hurl it at the shoemaker. The pointed end struck him full in the chest, stuck there like an arrow for a moment, while Babylon, mouthing a stream of curses, wrenched at it.

Nick spun round, wrested the pitchfork from the wall where it quivered and as Babylon, raising the crowbar he had pulled free, came staggering forward, the twin prongs buried themselves in the pit of his stomach. Nick turned away, not waiting to see Babylon sink to his knees dragging unavailingly at the grotesquely protruding shaft and roll over on his side, his legs kicking convulsively. Quickly Nick tore away the last bond that held the Blind Beak and, exerting every ounce of his strength, contrived to hoist the massive figure on to his back.

The dense billowing smoke halted him momentarily at the doorway and the heat from the blazing stairs burned into his aching lungs. The Blind Beak slung sack-like between the wall and him; he edged his way towards the head of the staircase beyond which the landing continued past the door of a room next the sitting room and stairs ascending overhead. Past the stairhead he gained the comparative safety beyond. As he did so the stairs behind him suddenly collapsed with a tremendous roar, and with it that part of the landing along which he had just passed with Sir John. Now the walls and the rest of the landing were afire. Up to the next floor, every bone in his body creaking under the weight of his burden, every nerve and sinew complaining agonizingly.

At the top of the stairs he was forced to halt, leaning against the wall, still with the Blind Beak on his shoulders, doubting if once he put him down he would have strength to lift him up again. The other's stertorous breathing indicated he was still alive. There came a resounding crash which shook the entire building as the sitting room floor caved in, accompanied by triumphant shouts of the mob outside. A tongue of flame licked hungrily at the foot of the stairs beneath him and, gritting his teeth against the agony tearing at every muscle of his body, Nick stumbled somehow to the third floor.

Now the heat was less intense, the air somewhat clearer of the clouds of black smoke. But the menacing roar of flames and the crash of falling wood and masonry as the house began to collapse under the fiery onslaught impelled him still upwards to the roof. He loosened the Blind Beak's cravat and made sure his heart still beat, though feebly.

Sir John muttered incoherently but

411

Nick never paused; another crash below and a burst of sparks followed by a plume of black smoke urged him upwards. Sweating and gasping he gained the fourth floor, kicked a door open, found himself in an attic opening on to the roof. He laid Sir John on the floor and, shutting the door behind him against the smoke, forced his trembling, exhausted limbs to the gable-roofed window. Opening it and dragging great gasps of air deep into his lungs that seemed to be afire, he clambered out to find himself looking over the back of Bow Street. All about him the sky was filled with the flickering glare of flames, billowing clouds of smoke.

The only course was to make for a house three or four rooftops away. Therein he and Sir John might shelter and escape the fury of the mob who would still be seeking them. Nick returned to the attic to find the Blind Beak struggling painfully to sit upright.

'Do you be easy,' said Nick, helping him rest against the wall. At the sound of his voice he observed the strange expression showing through the other's smoke-begrimed features, then the inscrutable smile lifted the corners of the full-lipped mouth.

'After all, am I in your debt again?' the Blind Beak croaked painfully, shaking his head.

Nick did not wait to puzzle out the meaning of this cryptic utterance. 'Our way lies over the roof-tops,' and the other mumbled in agreement. 'I dare not try to carry you now, for one slip and we should crash to the street.'

'I can stand on my own two feet.' To prove his words Sir John, with Nick aiding him, hoisted himself, grunting and groaning, upright. 'Do you guide me, I will follow close.'

Nick was out of the window and, leaning back, helped the Blind Beak climb up beside him. 'Keep yourself hid best you can, lest we are seen from below and the hue and cry raised after us.'

Turning to stretch out a steadying hand, he led the hazardous way across the roof-tops. Presently he had neatly forced an attic-window, and Sir John followed, puffing and wheezing and gasping out fervently in thankfulness for his safe arrival, into the empty room. The house they had entered turned out to be vacated, its occupants doubtless having fled the rioters. Taking a surreptitious glance outside, Nick saw 'No Popery' chalked upon the door prominently enough.

Feeling reasonably reassured they were safe from the mob's further attentions, he got the Blind Beak to bed in one of the upper rooms, obtaining water and sponging the begrimed face and hands and divesting him of his scorched clothes. All this time Sir John was hoarsely trying to impart to him whatever it was lay so uneasy on his mind but was persuaded by Nick to save his strength. Presently he fell into an exhausted sleep.

Standing before a mirror Nick peeled off his burnt coat, gingerly removed his shirt, all bloodstained from the flesh-wound he had received from the pitchfork. He could not refrain from a sardonic grin at his reflection: half his hair singed off, his eyebrows vanished and his face smirched with sweat and smoke and blistered from flying sparks. The back of one hand was scarred with a great weal, a leg singed from knee to ankle. After tending his shoulder-wound and burns as best he could, he finally dozed in a chair in the room where Sir John lay, the sounds of the rioters still in his ears, punctuated by the rattle of musket-fire, a woman's scream, the crash of falling masonry. He was awakened with a start by a hoarse whisper. 'Is all well, Nick? The street sounds quiet.'

Stretching his cramped limbs he went to the window. It was daylight although a black cloud sagged still over Bow Street. Cautiously glancing out he saw a party of soldiers removing several bodies huddled in the gutters. Sir John's voice reached him again from the bed. 'There is something you have to know' — the tones grew stronger — 'which must influence our future together, yours and mine.' Nick turned with a quizzical expression. 'I was bent upon encompassing not your ruin, but your salvation . . . '

Nick remained silent, his saturnine face shadowed against the window through which, resolutely piercing the overhanging darkness, stole the hope and promise of the new day. 'But my subtle designs, that in the end would reward you and me,' Sir John was continuing, 'and I do not deny I aimed to strike two birds with one stone, my calculated plot, do you hear me, Nick, had at the last to founder,' drawing an anguished shuddering sigh, 'upon the shoals of an unforeseen circumstance.'

And the sardonic lift at the corners of his craggy brows softening with a hidden gentleness, and as of old finding himself experiencing the extraordinary sensation the other was all the time observing him from behind his black bandage, Nick heard the Blind Beak unfold how Fate chose to step in to tangle his bizarre machinations and twist them all awry.

30

Nine o'clock of an evening some six weeks since London had quaked under the terror of Lord George Gordon's rioters, the tall, dark figure on the quarter-deck of H.M.S. *Swiftsure*, tugging gently at her moorings, idly contemplated the masts of fishing-boats and sailing barges, the ships' tenders proceeding to and fro against the warehouses and buildings of the waterfront as the July dusk deepened over Portsmouth Harbour.

He had but lately been conveyed from the busy quayside in the captain's barge, and come aboard the sturdy man-o'-war due presently to slip out on the evening tide, his baggage for the voyage stowed away in his cabin and now was taking a turn above decks. All about him the bustling activity of last-minute preparations for getting under way; sailors swarmed up aloft and harsh-voiced commands echoed across the water; the canvas creaked and bellied in the salt-laden breeze from off Portsea Island, sea-birds dipped and curved, uttering their poignant cries, the lap-lap against the ship's sides, in his nostrils the pungent smells of tar and bilge-water and all the time his thoughts and fancies far ashore in London.

Immediately following his rescue of and reconciliation with Sir John Fielding the latter had arranged for him quietly to slip away and, adopting a pseudonym, lie low in a deserted, rustic place, there to await the ship wherein he was to embark upon the secret journey the Blind Beak had ready planned for him. His only contact with London — despatches from Bow Street dictated to the ever-faithful Mr. Bond, recovering now from his sufferings at the hands of the mob — and newspapers to provide him with the current political news necessary to his own immediate prospects.

He had been duly amused to read the reports as well of his sensational escape from Tyburn the even more graphic accounts of the discovery in a Long Acre stews of his battered, bludgeoned corpse, the journalists giving full play to their colourful imagination and sententious moralizing in their versions of how that notorious scoundrel, Nick Rathburn, though eluding justice at the rope's-end, had yet met a deserved retribution in some drunken quarrel with his fellow criminals. Which device had been Nick's, suggested by his having witnessed, from the house wherein he and Sir John had found refuge, the corpses being collected in the grey morning light from Bow Street's gutters.

The Blind Beak was drawing to a close his narration of his elaborate scheme, aimed with characteristic persistence at reclaiming Nick for his service, and which had so nearly ended in disaster. 'Since I had failed to persuade you from obstinately pursuing your own violent road to ruin,' he had elucidated, 'to let you continue then, was my next best plan, to precipitate that perdition you so eagerly sought, since the sooner you reached it the sooner must you, like any wandering black sheep, return to the fold. Thuswise would I let necessity serve upon virtue.'

It was, however, vital to the outcome of his scheme that the world should believe Nick Rathburn had been ruthlessly hounded down, hence, as much as he twisted and turned, eluding a thousand cunning snares, his capture, as he himself had foreseen and anticipated with his fatalistic fortitude, was inevitable. 'But two persons shared my secret,' Sir John concluded, 'Shadow — no, not Lord Tregarth, never the real inkling had he of what was in my mind — and a certain clergyman visiting the Condemned Hold, whom, you may recall, incurred your suspicious disfavour, and was in fact an actor recruited through my good friend, Mr. Garrick. Expert in such matters, his role, at the appropriate time — and that two days before you were doomed to hang — was to make-up your features as if you were afflicted by typhus. Pronounced dead and with an excellent coffin ready prepared for your accommodation, the prison officials would have been only too anxious for your speedy removal from the premises.'

Sir John had sighed with disappointment that the circumstances of the riots, together with the determination of Mr. Ackerman, not being party to the plot, that Nick Rathburn should not be rescued by the mob, had forestalled him from putting into practice his ingenious if a trifle macabre stratagem. 'Poor Shadow, his death another of Fate's tragical twists, kept me in touch with your situation while you lay in Newgate, but was prevented from advising me of Ackerman's plan, of which of course I remained in ignorance, or would you have been saved your horrible ordeal at Tyburn.'

Nick's own account of his escape from the noose had excited the other's enthusiasm. 'You possess a boldness and unique resource; I could never rest until I had enlisted you again under my badge. Then, when you must go and blab out aloud in public — no, I know you were unaware of my contriving — you had been in my employ, though I had to deny it, yet my hand was forced further, for I was compelled to take the most elaborate pains that all suspicion should be allayed.

Only your presumed death would for ever end any conjecture.'

Nick had answered all was not lost, Sir John might still attain the aim he had so painstakingly and with such cunning plotted, and indicated how the world could be convinced his career had met its appropriately rakehell finish. The other approving enthusiastically and the deception being put into operation, the newspapers carrying the cleverly concocted fiction in due course, Nick Rathburn accordingly took his departure from the scene with, for an epitaph, that he had met his end where he had found his beginning, in a London gutter.

Now the canvas above creaked and cracked more loudly as the sails swelled to the breeze, the decks resounded to the clamour of running men going about their tasks, the rattle of winches and more urgent shouts of command; the brass of the cannon glinted, the pipe-clayed ropes glimmered white in the descending shadows, and the *Swiftsure's* timbers, moaning as if loathe to stir from her sheltered moorings, she weighed anchor and her proud bows nosed forward.

Nick watched the fading twilight more and more separate the vessel from the waterfront until presently it was a dark blur pierced by twinkling eyes of light. Now did he find himself engaged upon yet one more mission, bound to meet unknown hazards in the service of the ever-intriguing Blind Beak, obsessed with his ambitious schemes for creating an espionage system whose tentacles should spread half across the world to combat and defeat England's foes.

Nick had duly noted that the newspapers included among the despatches he had received, reporting the aftermath of the riots: how the troops had tardily assumed control over the situation; that Lord George Gordon had been conveyed to the Tower on a charge of High Treason and that one hundred and thirty-five rioters had also been arrested, twenty-one of whom were duly hanged at points near the scene of the crimes they had committed, had made much of French and American secret agents lurking behind the destructive upheavals.

One of Sir John's despatches headed: 'Secret Information', read: 'I have intelligence that none other than a certain American named Bailston, a leader of the Boston mob who destroyed the tea, had been in London in touch with Gordon, with what purpose in view it is not difficult to imagine.' Followed a list of others suspected of acting as secret agents for the American, Franklin, and the despatch had concluded: 'The execrable scheming of our deadly enemies abroad is to be found responsible for fomenting the riots.'

Smiling at the other's full-blooded, exuberant zeal, transparently seeking to condition him for the secret mission which lay ahead of him, Nick was reminded of those past days when the Blind Beak had first enrolled him as his underworld spy. Then had he been possessed of subtly winding schemes and wily plots for the attainment of his driving ambition to outwit and out-master his adversaries.

A few hours before he had embarked, Nick received a fare-well message from Bow Street. 'Would I might be present to clasp your hand in Godspeed, my dear Nick, but business, as usual, prevents my leaving London, nor does my health overmuch favour journeying to Portsmouth. But you will not require me to communicate to you the profound gratification I feel that you are once more in my service, which is dedicated to England's cause. The past mistakes of which we have both been guilty are done with, it is to the future we bend our minds, you and I, in mutual trust and confidence. This assignment you are undertaking promises much for you, more shining reward perhaps than at this moment of reading you can appreciate, but that you will learn something of from your sealed orders, which you will not open till safe cast-off from England's shores. What time you are outward bound I shall be thinking of you and wondering what is in your heart.'

The heavily sealed parchment crackled in the inside-pocket of his black full-skirted velvet coat as the breeze sprang more strongly from the English Channel and he turned away from watching the disappearing glimmer of Portsmouth

Town to tear open the envelope beneath the light of a swinging lamp.

'Now shall you have the secret of your mission when you reach America,' he read, 'and of my design to recompense you on the one hand for the hurt I once caused you, on the other hand to serve my own purpose. You must know then your Comtesse Chagrin de l'Isle' — Nick caught his breath as he read that magical name, and suddenly it was as if the Blind Beak stood beside him, his soft sibilant voice in his ear — 'was released from the Bastille and is herself in America, there to exercise her talents and beauty spying for General Lafayette behind the British lines. Your objective, therefore will straight-way be apparent to you. Win her over to our side (and you are not the resolute Nick Rathburn I know if you cannot). For your encouragement, during her sojourn in the Bastille I made it my business to ensure she was the recipient of intelligence that you were not solely blameworthy for her situation. I am blind enough but, thanks be to He who is all-seeing, not without foresight. Long had I visualized the advantage of securing the allegiance of one placed at the core of the enemy's camp. Such would be your Comtesse. The sure way of prevailing upon her to shift her loyalty would be through you. So you see, Nick, the power of the Blind Beak (as I am led to understand I am sometimes dubbed) is employed not invariably to destroy in hate and enmity.'

At the conclusion followed a postscript from Mr. Bond, wherein confidentially he expressed his growing concern for Sir John's health. Sir John had taken no rest despite his experiences during the riots, and he wished he could be persuaded to pause from his daily toil awhile, but on no account would he. But every particle of Nick's attention could not help but be concentrated for the moment and to the exclusion of all else upon the words that danced before his eyes in letters of flame. Shaken to the depths of his soul, the blood racing through his veins he read and re-read: ' . . . *Chagrin . . . is herself in America . . .* '

It could not be, it could not be, and yet

here it was writ down for him to read and trust in, and as his imagination hung upon the memory of that exquisite wraith from the past who was, of a sudden, part of his future, once more he could now look back and grasp how consummately had the Blind Beak fitted this final piece of the tortuous puzzle into place. How he must have relished, Nick thought, hugging to himself the secret he planned to spring upon him, and back there in Bow Street he would be thinking of him now, as he had promised he would be, when he was outward bound, those plump, bland enigmatic features transformed by a gentle mysterious smile . . . '*and this time your orders are: win her over to your side* . . .'

Slowly he folded the letter and could not entirely control the trembling of his fingers, returning it to his pocket, the Blind Beak's words rocking his brain: '. . . *is herself in America* . . . .' A score of questions milled around in his thoughts. How had she been assured he alone was not blameworthy for her tribulation? How had Sir John got into communication with her behind the Bastille's forbidding ramparts? But he cared not now what the answers might be, all that concerned him was the innermost knowledge that he would search the entire Americas for her, to win her for himself and for Sir John's cause. As his heart, exulting at the new splendid vision ahead, which he had thought for ever lost and put behind him, and every voice within him crying out he could make the dream come true, the strains of a sea-shanty were borne to his ear upon the freshening breeze:

'Hurrah, we be outward bound:
To Portsmouth Town we bid adieu,
To Sal, and Sue and Kitty too,
The anchor weigh'd, the sail
   unfurl'd,
All for across the wat'ry world:
Hurrah, we be outward bound . . . '

The sky was a smoky amber streaked with long, thin fingers of pale scarlet reaching up from the dark, silvery horizon, growing dusky purple as it merged into the sea whose waters spread towards the ship smooth and green from deepest olive to lightest emerald and everywhere reflecting the everchanging colours of the sky, the gulls wheeling and plunging at the gentle swell in silvery splashes and crying as they rose to wheel and circle and plunge downwards once more. Behind him Portsmouth lay dark and no single glimmer of light appeared. Then, above the great white spreading sails and where the larboard light glowed like a goblet of red wine, he saw the solitary star, brilliant and diamond-glittering, that had of a sudden made its appearance as if cast up and magically held against the vivid curtain now descending upon the day that was over.

'Oh, star, my lucky star, watch over and keep her for me. You shall guide us together once more in enduring love and enchantment.' And his heart was lifted up with a boundless rejoicing in the surety of knowing that, wherever she may be, however distant he must journey, he would find her and cherish her always. And the *Swiftsure* sailed on into the enfolding shadows, while that tall, black-garbed figure, the white streak in his dark hair ruffled by the salt sea-spray, remained on deck, until the ship swung into the English Channel, the Isle of Wight curled low to starboard, and set her course westwards, the sailors chanting:

‘ . . . All for across the wat'ry world;
Hurrah, we be outward bound . . . ’

THE BLIND BEAK
IN REAL LIFE

Sir John Fielding was born in London, 1721, and after assisting his half-brother, Henry Fielding, novelist and magistrate, himself became a magistrate at Bow Street in 1751, which office he held until his death. Like the French chiefs of police, the Bow Street justices not only arrested, but examined, the criminal, and Fielding, a shrewd detective and police officer, carried out these duties, and more. 'Quick notice and sudden pursuit' was his famous slogan, and, under his dynamic direction and powerful personality, his police, the Bow Street Runners, forbears of today's Scotland Yard, were fashioned. All this despite being stone-blind — which earned him the nickname, fearsome to the eighteenth-century underworld, of the Blind Beak — his conquest of his affliction surely rating as one of the most extraordinary triumphs of its kind.

The records do not in fact mention Nick Rathburn by name, but Sir John Fielding certainly used agents and under-cover operators to assist him in the bitter fight he waged, not only against criminals of every degree, but against French and American spies during the hazardous times of the American War of Independence and Britain's war with France. The events described in the foregoing pages have a basis in fact, certainly so far as the Blind Beak's character is concerned, while the adventures involving him and Nick Rathburn could have happened.

Sir John Fielding was author of several volumes on police-work, including *A Plan for Preventing Robberies within Twenty Miles of London* and *A Charge to the Grand Jury*. He also founded the *Weekly Hue and Cry*, today known as the *Police Gazette*, Scotland Yard's official newspaper. In 1780, a few months after this novel based on his life and times, and which his brooding presence dominates, ends, he died: 'Sir John Fielding, Knt., one of His Majesty's Justices of the Peace for the counties of Middlesex, Essex, Herts, Kent, Surrey and the City and Liberty of Middlesex, whose abilities as a magistrate could only be equalled by his humanity as a man, and whose loss will be most severely felt by the public, but none so much as the poor, to whom he was a warm and unalterable friend.'

He left behind him a London which he had never seen, but served so well, and for whose protection he had laid the foundations of a crime-fighting force which today is the envy of the world's greatest cities.

We do hope that you have enjoyed reading this large print book.

Did you know that all of our titles are available for purchase?

We publish a wide range of high quality large print books including:
Romances, Mysteries, Classics
General Fiction
Non Fiction and Westerns

Special interest titles available in large print are:
The Little Oxford Dictionary
Music Book, Song Book
Hymn Book, Service Book

Also available from us courtesy of Oxford University Press:
Young Readers' Dictionary
(large print edition)
Young Readers' Thesaurus
(large print edition)

For further information or a free brochure, please contact us at:
Ulverscroft Large Print Books Ltd.,
The Green, Bradgate Road, Anstey,
Leicester, LE7 7FU, England.
Tel: (00 44) **0116 236 4325**
Fax: (00 44) **0116 234 0205**

DEATH OF A COLLECTOR

John Hall

It's the 1920s. Freddie Darnborough, popular man about town, is invited to a weekend at Devorne Manor. But the host, Sir Jason, is robbed and murdered hours after Freddie's arrival. However, one of the guests is a Detective Chief Inspector. An odd coincidence? The policeman soon arrests a suspicious character lurking in the shrubbery. But Freddie alone believes the man to be innocent. And so, to save an innocent man from the gallows, Freddie himself must find the real murderer.

SHERLOCK HOLMES AND THE GIANT'S HAND

Matthew Book

Three of the great detective's most singular cases, mentioned tantalisingly briefly in the original narratives, are now presented here in full. The curious disappearance of Mr Stanislaus Addleton leads Holmes and Watson ultimately to the mysterious 'Giant's Hand'. What peculiar brand of madness drives Colonel Warburton to repeatedly attack an amiable village vicar? Then there is the murderous tragedy of the Abernetty family, the solving of which hinges on the depth to which the parsley had sunk into the butter on a hot day . . .

EXCEPT FOR ONE THING

John Russell Fearn

Many criminals have often believed that they'd committed the 'Perfect Crime', and blundered. Chief Inspector Garth of Scotland Yard is convinced that modern science gives the perfect crime even less chance of success. However, Garth's friend, scientist Richard Harvey, believes he can rid himself of an unwanted fiancée without anyone discovering what became of the corpse. Yet though he lays a master-plan and uses modern scientific methods to bring it to fruition, he makes not one but several mistakes . . .

TIDE OF DEATH

E. C. Tubb

England was starving when cheap power could have saved her . . . power that would have been available if the League of Peace had not forbidden atomic research . . . But two scientists ignore the ban and launch an experiment. However, the experiment succeeds too well: it gets out of hand, spreading a tide of black death across the country, and threatens the whole planet. Neil Hammond, a secret agent for the League of Peace, is sent to investigate, and uncovers a terrifying secret . . .